CRITICAL PRAISE
FOR SHARON GILLENWATER

"Sharon Gillenwater…draws readers in
and causes their hearts and imaginations to soar."
—*Romantic Times*

"For a romantic, uplifting experience,
pick up *Twice Blessed* today."
—*Romance Reviews Today*

"Gillenwater's sweet love story details the
inspiring discovery of grace and forgiveness."
—*Romantic Times* on *Twice Blessed*

"Gillenwater's latest is highly agreeable, with
intriguing…characters, a light Christian message,
and heavy doses of adventure and intrigue."
—*Library Journal* on *Highland Call*

"Sharon Gillenwater sweeps her readers up
in a powerful mix of characters and settings
and never fails to deliver a heart-touching tale
of love and faith."
—Annie Jones, bestselling author
of *Mom Over Miami*

D0190320

Sharon
Gillenwater

Standing
Tall

Steeple
Hill®

Published by Steeple Hill Books™

STEEPLE HILL BOOKS

Steeple Hill®

ISBN 0-373-81126-8

STANDING TALL

Copyright © 2005 by Sharon Gillenwater

Special thanks and acknowledgment are given to Sharon Gillenwater for her contribution to the LOVE INSPIRED COLLECTION.

www.SteepleHill.com

Printed in U.S.A.

For my husband's great-grandfather, Ransom Starr. In 1877, Ransom and his wife, Jessie, both twenty years old, traveled in a covered wagon from Benton County, Oregon, to homestead in the Palouse country of eastern Washington. Perhaps I should have waited and written their story someday. But since "someday" doesn't always come, I borrowed his name for my Texas hero. From what I've been told about Great-Grandpa Starr, I don't think he would mind.

Chapter One

West Texas
March, 1885

Sheriff Ransom Starr made the rounds of Willow Grove one final time for the night. Things were quiet for a Saturday in the often rowdy red-light district outside of town. Strolling back down Main Street, Ransom stifled a yawn. Everything was shut up nice and tight, with all the saloons downtown closing by two o'clock. Lanterns hung outside the entrance to a couple of hotels; otherwise the street was dark, with only a half moon lighting his way back to the office.

Times like this, when he had enjoyed about all the peace and quiet he could stand, he considered going back to work as a detective or maybe even opening his own agency. It wasn't a notion he dwelled on, but he tossed the idea around now and then.

Contemplating a catnap, he caught a glimpse of something moving on the second floor veranda of the Barton Hotel. He stopped, hiding in the shadows and watched, wondering if his tired eyes were playing tricks on him. There it was again—a dark silhouette, crouched low, moving soundlessly along the balcony that ran completely around the building. The man reached an open window and slipped inside.

Ransom ran quietly across the street, drawing his Colt .45 Peacemaker. He carefully made his way up the outside stairway to the veranda, tiptoeing half the length of the building until he was a few feet from where the man had entered the hotel. Edging along the wall to reach the window, he peered into the room. The hotel guest snored loudly, obligingly covering up any noise the intruder made as he rifled through the man's saddlebags.

Deciding it was safer to confront the thief after he left the room, Ransom stayed close to the wall, about a yard back from the window, and hid in the darkness of the building. A few minutes later, the intruder climbed out the window onto the balcony.

As he straightened, Ransom stepped forward, the moonlight glinting off his revolver. "Stop right there and put your hands up where I can see them."

The man obeyed, palms open, both hands empty. Ransom barely could see his face. They were still too much in the shadows to distinguish any particular features. "Step to the left, against the railing." That would put him in the moonlight. The thief hesitated and took a step backward. It occurred to Ransom that the man might not realize who had a gun on him, so he moved into the light himself, knowing the star on his vest would be clearly visible.

He heard a little gasp. "I'm the—"

Someone hit him from behind, a hard full-body blow that sent him crashing against the balcony railing. The wood snapped with a loud crack, and he flew through the air as the railing gave way. A pistol shot rang in his ears. Instinctively, he dropped the revolver, bracing for the impact with the dirt street.

Though he tried to turn so he'd land on his side, his body was twisted when he hit the ground. A hot poker stabbed his low back, excruciating pain shooting down his leg. A split second later, his forehead bounced against the hard packed clay, pain exploding inside his skull.

Boots thundered along the boardwalk. "The sheriff's been shot! Get a doctor."

"Anyone see who did it?"

Not shot. He could barely breath, couldn't get the words out.

"Looks like he fell off the balcony."

"There's nobody up there now." A man bent over him and turned him over onto his back.

Ransom hollered in agony. Darkness encompassed him and sweet oblivion took him away from the pain.

"He's coming around."

Recognizing the voice, Ransom frowned. Mrs. Franklin, his landlady. What was she doing in his room? He felt as if he'd been stomped on and tossed

every which way by a Longhorn bull. He'd had concussions before. Didn't need a doctor to diagnose this
one. In the past, he'd wrenched his back a couple of
times and hobbled around bent over for a few days, but
he'd never experienced such throbbing, intense pain.
Wanting to move but afraid to, he started to take a deep
breath, then stopped halfway because his chest hurt. He
wondered if his back was broken, and how he'd hurt it.

He slowly opened his eyes, but his vision was
blurred and the ceiling spun around like a carousel,
making his stomach lurch. Breaking out in a sweat, he
closed his eyes again. "Mrs. Franklin?"

"Yes?"

He felt her take his hand. Such a gentle touch for
hands that worked so hard cooking and cleaning for a
houseful of boarders. Too bad she wasn't twenty years
younger. "Did I insult you?"

"No." She carefully wiped his face with a cool cloth.

"Why'd you hit me with the frying pan?"

She made an odd choking sound. A second later, she
cleared her throat. "I didn't hit you, but somebody did."

"Knocked you clear off the veranda of the Barton."

He recognized that voice, too. Doc Wilson. He remembered falling. And a gunshot. "Did I shoot myself?"

"No." The doctor chuckled. "Folks heard a gun go
off, so they thought you'd been shot. That and the noise
you made busting through the railing woke up everyone in the hotel."

Somebody turned up the lamp. Even with his eyes
closed, Ransom could tell the room was brighter. "Did
it hit anybody else?"

"If it did, they haven't mentioned it," said the doctor. "Can you open your eyes?"

"If you'll tie down the room."

"You've got a concussion."

"Figured as much."

"Had 'em before, have you?"

"Yeah. Couple of times. How long have I been out?"

"About half an hour. Not bad considering how far you fell." The doctor pried open one eyelid, peering into it. He let Ransom close that one, then checked the other. "What else hurts?"

"Everything. Mostly my back and right leg." Somebody had stripped him down to his drawers and undershirt. He vaguely hoped it had been the doctor and not Mrs. Franklin. Then decided it didn't matter. He was just glad he hadn't been awake for the ordeal.

"Can you move your fingers?"

Ransom obliged, wiggling them.

"Hands and arms?"

He moved his hands, then raised them, lifting his arms in the air. His back cramped, the hot pain shooting across his lower back and down his leg. He gritted his teeth, burying his fingers in the bedding, wadding it up in his fists.

"Muscle spasm?" asked the doctor.

"Yes," whispered Ransom, surprised he was able to make a sound. Even the time he'd been shot, he hadn't been in this much agony.

"Mrs. Franklin, I need some hot, damp cloths."

Ransom heard her leave the room. "Did I break my back?"

"I don't think so, but I can't be certain. I checked

your spinal column when we removed your clothes. Couldn't see or feel anything that looked out of the ordinary. There could be a break, and the bones just haven't moved enough to detect it. They usually don't."

Ransom opened his eyes again, wanting to see the doctor's expression. He could tell more from a man's face than from what came out of his mouth. Thankfully, the room didn't spin as much as it had before. He forced his fingers to release the sheet and tried to take a deep breath.

"Try to relax and tell me about the pain." Doc Wilson watched him closely.

"Throbbing ache in low back, down my leg." He held his breath against another jolt. "Now, sharp pain down my leg. Like fire."

"Your sciatic nerve has been compromised. Possibly the spinal cord as well. The hotel clerk said your body was twisted at an odd angle when he reached you." Frowning, the doctor shook his head. "Even if you didn't actually break a bone, there may be severe damage to your back, Sheriff Starr."

Fear sent a chill through him. "How severe?"

"Only time will tell. I'm going to roll you over on your side. That may give you some relief, and it will make it easier to apply the hot packs. Those should help the spasm."

When the physician shifted him to his side, Ransom couldn't hold back a cry of agony. Panting, he tried to relax, reminding himself that he'd been hurt plenty of times over the years and had always recovered.

"Bend your knees to a comfortable position. That should help."

Ransom bent his left knee, drawing his leg upward on the mattress. But when he attempted to do the same with the right one, it didn't cooperate very well. The pain was excruciating. Swallowing hard, he refused to give in to panic. "Can't move the right one much."

Without a word, the doctor threw back the sheet and lifted his leg for him, stuffing a pillow between his knees. "Better?"

"Yes. It's easing a little."

Mrs. Franklin bustled into the room carrying a metal basin filled with steaming cloths. She had two pieces of rubberized sheeting tucked under her arm. Setting the pan on the beside table, she carefully laid one waterproof cloth on the bed and gently tucked it beneath him. "Where should these hot packs go, Doctor?"

"From mid-back down to his low back." He ran his fingers along the muscles in Ransom's back. "All across here. It's as hard as a rock." They worked together applying the hot packs, then spread the second strip of rubber sheeting over it. "I don't want to give you any laudanum until your head is better."

"Don't want it. Brain's already muddled." Though the night's events had come back to him. Pity he felt too lousy to study them.

"If you change your mind in a few days, let me know." The doctor picked up his bag. "The best thing for you now is rest. Mrs. Franklin, make sure he drinks plenty of water and eats light but nourishing meals. A good beef or chicken broth with a few vegetables will do for a while. Today, you'll need to check on him every few hours, wake him up and make him drink some water."

"I can do that. You rest now, Sheriff. I'll be in the kitchen. Just holler if you need anything."

"Thanks." Ransom barely heard the rustle of her skirts as she left the room.

"I'll be back to check on you later in the morning," said the doctor. He stifled a yawn. "Think I'll go catch a couple of hours sleep myself."

"Good idea," Ransom mumbled, already half asleep. Though still in a lot of pain, the hot packs and different position had taken the edge off. He couldn't remember a time when he'd been more exhausted.

"Deputy Webb said to tell you he'd be over later. He's scouring the town, looking for the man who did this. We're assuming someone had to knock you off that balcony. Can't imagine the railing simply giving way."

"Two men."

Doc Wilson retraced his steps back to the bed. "Did you say two men?"

Ransom nodded, then wished for all the world that he hadn't. He also realized that no one else knew what happened.

"By the time folks got outside, there wasn't any sign of them," said the doctor.

"Need to see Quint." He wondered if there was any way he could reach the washbasin if his stomach didn't settle down.

"I'll stop by your office on my way home. If he's not there, I'll track him down."

"Thanks." Ransom peeked up at the doctor. "Did she leave the basin?"

"Yes. But I had her bring in a bucket earlier, in case you needed it. Feelin' sick?"

"Yeah."

"Nausea often accompanies concussions, but you probably already knew that. The bucket is there on the floor beside the bed."

Ransom breathed a sigh of relief. "Good."

The doctor laid a towel across the side of the bed.

"Thanks. Get me well, Doc." *Need to shoot some hombres.*

Chapter Two

"What if he throws me in jail?" Sixteen-year-old Matt Chastain watched the front door of the Franklin Boarding House, fear and worry etched on his face. "What if he doesn't believe I didn't mean to hurt him?"

His sister, Lily, slipped her arm around his waist, giving him a hug. Though she was four years older, he towered head and shoulders above her.

She didn't blame him for being afraid. She was worried about it, too. That's why it had taken her until Wednesday to work up the courage to see the sheriff. "We have to own up to what we did. From the things I've heard about Sheriff Starr, he's a fair man." A lump formed in her throat. "You know Papa would want us to try to make amends somehow."

"I know." Matt took a deep breath. When he spoke, his voice was thick, too. "Take responsibility." He sniffed and swiped at his nose. "We gotta make the sheriff understand. Those men have to pay for what they did."

Lily's resolve hardened, and she cleared her throat. "They'll pay. Especially the one who did the shooting. I don't care how long it takes to find him." She released her brother and started toward the boarding house. "Then I'll put a bullet through his black heart."

Matt caught up to her with one step. "Papa wouldn't want us killing anybody."

"They killed him, didn't they?"

"But, Lil, that doesn't make it right."

"I don't care." She stopped abruptly, fighting against the rage and grief that threatened to overwhelm her. "I want to see that murderer in his grave."

Sighing, Matt put his arm around her shoulders and nudged her forward. "Let's get it over with. After we talk to the sheriff, we may not have a chance for revenge."

Lily struggled to compose herself. To her way of thinking, when it came to her father's death, revenge and justice were one and the same. They walked up the steps of the yellow house, and she knocked on the front door.

A slightly plump woman with a tight bun of salt-and-pepper hair opened the door and studied them curiously. A red-and-yellow striped apron, lightly dusted with flour, covered her simple gray everyday dress.

"Mrs. Franklin?" asked Lily.

"Yes. Sorry, I don't have any available rooms."

"We're not looking for a room. We'd like to speak with Sheriff Starr, please."

The woman frowned. "Are you friends of his?"

"No, ma'am." Lily paused, not wanting to tell her too much. "We have a debt to pay. It's important that we see him."

"He's had too much company already this morning. But I'll ask him if he wants to see you. What's your name?"

"Lily Chastain. This is my brother, Matt." The woman left the door open and disappeared down the hall. Neither of them spoke while they waited on the wide porch. Lily wondered if Matt felt as much like racing back down the street as she did.

Mrs. Franklin returned, motioning for them to enter. "He said to come on in. But don't stay long. He's in a lot of pain. Needs rest, not half the town coming by to see him. His room is the second door on the right."

"Yes, ma'am." Lily nodded her thanks and went inside, glancing back at Matt to make sure he followed. A quick check in the hall tree mirror confirmed that she looked presentable. Her dark blond curls were still pinned up, all the buttons on her cream-colored blouse were fastened, and it was tucked neatly into her brown skirt.

When she reached the sheriff's room, the door was ajar. She knocked lightly and said a quick, silent prayer for God's mercy. Then wondered if there really was such a thing. There hadn't been for her father.

"Come in."

Lily took a deep breath and pushed open the door. During the time they'd spent in town, she had heard plenty about the sheriff. How he'd been a Texas Ranger and single-handedly captured several notorious desperadoes. Then, while working as a detective, he'd saved the judge and everyone else in the courtroom the day a murderer had pulled a gun on them. Folks were proud that he didn't tolerate any nonsense from rowdy cowboys or anyone else who decided to cause trouble anywhere in the county.

She'd also heard that he was tall, dark-haired and handsome as sin, with a smile that might make even a happily married woman daydream a little. Not that he fooled around with any of them, mind you. But he did have a way of making the ladies' hearts flutter when he walked down the street. He seemed a little larger than life, the kind of man who could stop a raging mob by himself or catch a band of outlaws.

She wasn't expecting the pale, haggard man sitting in a rocker, a cane propped against the window sill and his dark blue eyes dull with pain. *What have we done?* She barely stifled a cry of distress and wondered if the sheriff heard Matt's gasp.

"Pardon me, ma'am, for my lack of proper clothes." He rubbed a thumb over a button on his undershirt, then absently tucked a lightweight green-and-blue quilt more securely around his waist. "And for not getting up." A ghost of a smile, tinged with bitterness, touched the lawman's face. "It may be a while before I can do that without a struggle."

A doctor grabbed his bag and nodded to them as he hastily exited the room, plunking his bowler hat on his head as he went through the doorway.

Sheriff Starr shot an angry glare at the man's back. "According to that quack, maybe never."

The reality of the pain and damage they had inflicted on this poor man left her stunned.

His eyes narrowed, and she was certain he hadn't missed her reaction. She grasped the first thing that came to mind. "I thought you only had a concussion. I didn't think anything was broken."

The sheriff raised an eyebrow, a hint of curiosity lighting his eyes as he adjusted the quilt again. "Not sure if anything is, but something is wrong with my back. Doc Wilson doesn't know if it's broken or just twisted all out of shape. Either way, my right leg is numb and hard to move. Won't hold my weight. That's why he asked that idiot from Dallas to come take a look at me."

He studied her so intently that Lily wondered if he recognized her. When his speculative glance took in her brother's height and bulk, she was almost positive of it.

"I appreciate your concern…Miss Chastain, was it?"

Lily nodded, dreading what was coming.

"You two seem to be a mite more upset about my welfare than I'd expect, given that we've never met."

"I'm sorry, Sheriff," blurted Matt, pushing his way past Lily. Squaring his shoulders, he moved closer to the lawman. Lily hustled over to stand beside him, cringing when the sheriff frowned. "I never meant to knock you off that balcony. I was just trying to protect Lily."

Anger flashed in Sheriff Starr's eyes, and a dark flush colored his pale cheeks. In a voice cold as death, he asked quietly, "You're the one who did this to me?"

Lily thought her heart would pound right out of her chest. She moved in front of her brother, knowing it would annoy him, but unable to help herself. It was her fault they were in this mess, not his. "Matt didn't know you were the law. I didn't, either, until you stepped into the moonlight, and then there was no time to warn him or you."

The lawman frowned thoughtfully, digesting her words, possibly thinking through the events of that night.

"I thought you were his partner," said Matt.

The sheriff shifted in the chair and grimaced in pain. Closing his eyes, his face turned white. "Whose partner?" he asked, the words strained.

"The man in the hotel room," said Lily. Sweat beaded on his forehead and upper lip. "Do you need to go back to bed? You're awfully pale."

"Yeah, I'd better."

"I'll help, sir." Matt moved beside the rocking chair.

"All right." He met Lily's gaze. "If you'll look the other way, I won't feel obliged to hang onto this cover."

Lily turned around, facing the door. She knew Matt could handle it but not being able to supervise made her anxious. A minute later, she heard the sheriff groan.

"Lift my legs up onto the bed as I turn around."

"Yes, sir," said Matt quietly.

Sheriff Starr cried out in pain, causing Lily to peek over her shoulder. It was difficult not to try to help, but she was afraid she would only anger him more. When her brother pulled up the sheet, covering the lawman from the waist down, she turned around.

Matt braced the sheriff's shoulders with his arm, helping him lie back against a pile of pillows. He closed his eyes, breathing rapidly, his hands curled into fists beside him. After a few minutes, he reached for a couple of pillows lying near his head.

Lily nudged Matt aside. "Where do you want them?"

He opened his eyes, looking at her in relief. "Under my legs, from the knees down." Bending his left leg, he managed to give her space for the pillows under his knee. But he could barely move his right leg. When he did, he gasped, then clenched his jaw.

"I'll do it." Lily reached beneath the sheet and carefully lifted his leg, sliding the stack of pillows beneath both of them. Then she eased his right leg back down.

Mrs. Franklin came bustling into the room, frowning at Lily. "I thought I heard you call, Sheriff Starr."

"Just one of my yelps." He took a deep breath and seemed to relax. "It's better now. You can go on with your baking."

"Humph." She cast a baleful eye first at Lily, then Matt. "You two should leave. Let the sheriff sleep."

The lawman waved away her words. "Got things to talk about."

With another "humph" and a shake of her head, she turned on her heel and left.

His face glistened with sweat. Lily dipped a washcloth in the basin of water on the night stand and wrung it out. She started to wash his face, then hesitated. "May I?"

"Please. I'm hotter than a two-bit pistol."

Brushing his dark brown hair off his forehead, she gently wiped his face, carefully avoiding the large dark blue lump near the hairline. She was amazed that he hadn't snapped his neck in the fall. The thought made her shudder.

The sheriff's hand closed over her wrist. "You're trembling."

"It's a wonder you didn't break your neck. We could have killed you."

He pushed her hand aside and released it, turning his head to stare out the window. "Might have been better. End it all right then and there instead of being half a man the rest of my life."

"Don't think that way. You'll get well." She dropped the washrag into the basin. "You have to," she added in a whisper.

"Feelin' guilty?" There was no sympathy in his voice.

"Yes."

"You ought to. Now, pull up a chair and tell me what you were doing in that hotel room."

Lily scooted the rocking chair closer to the bed, sinking down onto the seat. Despite his pain, his eyes and mind were sharp. She didn't want him to notice that her knees were practically knocking.

Starr looked at her brother and nodded to a chair on the other side of the room. "You might as well sit down, too. Close the door first."

Matt shut the door, moved the chair beside Lily and took a seat.

She paused to collect her thoughts.

When a light knock sounded on the door, the sheriff sighed. "Better see who it is."

Grateful for the moment's reprieve, Lily hopped up and crossed the room. When she opened the door, her heart sank. The man waiting in the hallway wore a shiny five-pointed star on his shirt. She'd seen him around town and recognized him as the deputy sheriff, though she didn't know his name. Now she and Matt couldn't run if they wanted to.

The man removed his hat, nodding politely. "Good mornin', ma'am." He looked over her head. "I'll stop by later, Ransom."

"Come on in," said the sheriff. It was clearly an order, not a request.

Curiosity flashed across the other lawman's face. When Lily stepped back out of the way, he walked in. She closed the door and returned to the chair by the bed.

"This is Deputy Sheriff Quintin Webb," said Starr. "Quint, meet Lily and Matt Chastain—the ones who almost killed me."

Lily cringed at the fury roiling beneath his quiet words. She glanced up at the deputy. For a second, he stared at them in disbelief. Anger quickly replaced it.

"It was an accident." She looked back at the sheriff. "Please believe me. We never meant to do you any harm."

The deputy went around to the other side of the bed and leaned against the wall, scowling at them. Lily noted that he stayed between them and the doorway.

Sheriff Starr pinned her with his gaze. "You were about to tell me what you were doing in that hotel room."

"Retrieving the money he stole from us," said Lily.

"He robbed you, so you crawled through his window to get your money back?" The sheriff stared at her for a second, then shook his head. "Lady, now I know you're *loco*. What were you going to do if he woke up?"

"I knew he wouldn't. He'd been drinking heavily all night. Matt had been watching him."

"He'd been playing poker at the Senate Saloon," said Matt. "He was so drunk he was flashing money around. *Our* money. I followed him back to the hotel. He fell twice going up the stairs. I went up on the veranda to see if I could tell which room was his. He made it real easy by opening the window before he fell on the bed. In less than a minute he was snoring like a tired ol' hound."

"He'd lost some of the money," added Lily. "But I got about half of it."

"Why didn't you come to me?" asked Sheriff Starr.

Lily hesitated. After three days of considering her actions, she was embarrassed by her impulsiveness. She didn't understand how she could have done something so foolish. "We came to town to talk to you. We left our wagon at the wagon yard and started to your office. When we walked past the saloon and saw him sitting there, playing poker with Papa's money and acting like he was somebody important…" She closed her eyes and caught her lower lip between her teeth to keep it from trembling.

"We didn't know how we could prove to you that the money was ours," Matt explained.

Sighing, Lily opened her eyes. "I was so angry, I couldn't think straight. It was stupid for me to go after it."

"Yes, it was. If he'd waked up, he likely would have shot first and asked questions later."

"I moved his pistol out of reach."

A hint of approval drifted across the sheriff's countenance. "Since he was so drunk, you figured you could outrun him."

She shrugged. "I knew I could. Going after the money wasn't so risky, but we scared him off. Now I may never find him again, or his partner."

Sheriff Starr looked at Matt. "You mentioned a partner earlier."

"Yes, sir." He glanced at his sister. "We're kind of coming at this story backwards."

Lily frowned at him. "I was answering his questions." At the fleeting hurt on his face, guilt and grief rose swiftly. When she reached for his hand, he held hers tight, giving her the strength to tell the lawmen all that had happened.

She looked back at Sheriff Starr. He watched her closely, waiting patiently. "Matt's right, I am going around the mulberry bush." Taking a deep breath, she tried to keep her voice steady. She didn't succeed. "Two days before we came to Willow Grove, the man in the hotel and another man rode into our camp. They robbed and shot our father. Killed him in cold blood."

The sheriff exchanged a startled glance with the deputy. "You didn't go to Quint to report it because you knocked me off the balcony."

Lily nodded. "We were so rattled and scared, we didn't know what to do. We were afraid that if we went to Deputy Webb about them killing Papa and stealing our money, he might figure out that we'd hurt you." She turned to the deputy. "We were afraid you'd throw Matt in jail."

"Did they take anything besides the money?" Sheriff Starr asked.

"Papa's watch. Mama gave it to him for a wedding present. It has their first names and the date engraved on the back."

"Did you retrieve it, too?"

"No, I had to leave it. I hated to, but he had it in his vest pocket. I wasn't about to try to take it. The way he was waving the money around in the saloon, anybody could have robbed him. I don't think they know about Matt and me, but I didn't want to risk making him suspicious if they do."

"If he still has it when we catch him, it will help tie him to the crime. You saw them shoot your father?"

"Yes," said Lily, dragging in a harsh breath.

"I was out hunting," said Matt. "Looking for a rabbit for supper. I barely heard the gunshot. By the time I got back to camp, they'd already lit out."

"I had gone to the creek for a bucket of water. I dawdled a while." Why hadn't she hurried back? If only she'd had the foresight to carry a gun. "I didn't see the men until I went back to camp. They must have taken Papa by surprise because the shotgun was propped up against the wagon wheel. I didn't have a gun, and they were between me and the wagon. I couldn't get to it to help him. So I hid behind some rocks." *Like a worthless coward.*

"You couldn't have done anything else."

"I should have tried something." Papa had always protected her and Matt, even at the end. Couldn't she have somehow done the same for him?

"And been killed, too. What did they say?"

"They wanted to know if anyone else was with him, and he said no. They seemed to accept that as truth. They demanded his money, and he refused. That's when Price shot him."

"How do you know his name?"

"The other man, the one who was here in the hotel, called him that before they left." She closed her eyes, picturing the scene in her mind, wishing she couldn't, yet grateful that the man's face was burned into her memory. "They both had their pistols drawn, and Price just shot him." Looking back at the sheriff, she didn't try to hide her pain, couldn't. "Like he was nothing."

"That kind of man has no respect for life. They didn't take the horses?"

"No. They didn't seem interested in them. They rode hard when they left."

"Didn't want to risk anything slowing them down," said Deputy Webb. "Or folks asking questions. The man at the hotel registered as John Smith. He didn't report anything stolen, and he hightailed it out of town before I had a chance to talk to him."

Matt grimaced. "I saw him leave around dawn."

"You didn't follow him?" asked the sheriff, obviously growing weary.

"We started to, but we needed to see how you were," said Lily. It had been a difficult choice.

"Took your time comin' to check on me."

"We gleaned what we could from talk around town. It's taken this long to work up the courage to come see you," Lily admitted honestly. The lawman's eyes drifted closed, giving her a chance to study him for a minute. Regret filled her soul, adding to the burden of her already aching heart.

He looked up at her. "Sorry you didn't leave town?"

Lily squared her shoulders and met his gaze directly. "Are you going to arrest us?"

"I ought to throw your brother in jail for assault." Starr glared at Matt. "Or maybe attempted murder."

Matt tensed. Lily hoped he wouldn't try to bolt.

"As for you…" Sheriff Starr turned his scowl on her. "A few days in the calaboose might make you think twice about climbing through a possible murderer's window."

"He didn't kill Father. The other man did."

"That doesn't mean he's not a killer." He let that sink in, let her blood run cold. Rubbing his right thigh, he sighed wearily. "If I don't hogtie you, you'll go tearing off after them and get yourselves killed."

Lily decided he wasn't going to throw them in jail. If he intended to, he would have had the deputy haul them away already. Her compassion overcame her frustration—for the moment. "I'll find them someday. Right now we have another obligation."

"What?"

"To pay your medical bills."

"The county is paying the doctor, so you can keep your money."

"And to take care of you or help around here however we can."

An unnerving light flickered through his eyes. "You plannin' on playing nursemaid, Miss Chastain?"

"Part of the time. Matt can do the rest." She thought she saw his lips twitch.

He looked over her head out the window, the hint of amusement vanishing. "For how long?"

"Until you don't need nursing anymore."

He kept staring out the window, gazing off into the distance, his countenance carefully shuttered. When

Chapter Three

They stayed anyway.

Ransom wasn't told what kind of arrangement they made with Mrs. Franklin, but he suspected they agreed to take care of him and do jobs around the house in exchange for meals. He couldn't blame his landlady for accepting the offer. Nursing him added to her already full load. Appreciation for their help warred with resentment and anger because they'd put him in such a fix. Pain and an unexpected attraction to Lily Chastain didn't help any.

He was thirty-five. He figured she was around twenty. Too young for him. Too stubborn. Too independent. But then, he'd never been interested in clinging vines. He admired independent, intelligent women. Maybe that was the problem. Going after her money was about the dumbest thing Lily could have done, short of calling the man out for a gunfight. Payback. Impulsive and dangerous, but given what she had been through, almost understandable.

He'd had her look through all the wanted posters at his office, but she couldn't pick out anyone for certain. A few resembled the man who shot her father, but when Quint sent telegrams checking on them, he found they both had been in jail in other parts of the state for a few weeks. There was an unidentified killer roaming his territory, and Ransom couldn't do a thing about it. That only added to his bad mood.

Since they'd been there, Matt had fixed a leak in the roof and painted half the storage shed. During the day, if Ransom needed help getting in or out of bed, he came running whenever Lily called.

Matt slept on the floor in Ransom's room at night, coming to his aid anytime he needed something. He tried not to wake the young man, but occasionally he had to have help getting into the chair when he simply couldn't lie in bed any longer.

He learned from Matt that Lily slept on a pallet in the kitchen pantry. Her sleeping on the floor and where any of the tenants could walk in on her didn't sit well with him. He doubted that any of them posed a real danger, but he would have felt better if she had a room with a bed and a lock on the door.

Lily stayed close at hand during the day, tidying up his room, bringing his meals, wiping his face with a cool cloth when the pain made him break out in a sweat. He couldn't decide whether or not he liked being fussed over so much, though she seemed to sense when he needed to rest or have time alone. He'd seen her walk by the open door with a broom, then later with the mop. He also thought she must be doing some of the cooking. When she'd brought his bowl of broth for supper the night before, he'd caught a whiff of vanilla as she handed him the tray.

He, on the other hand, had smelled like he'd been on the trail for a month. That was enough to send him down the hall to the boarding house bathroom. Wearing a robe that had belonged to Mrs. Franklin's husband, he made what felt like a mile-long trek leaning heavily on the cane, with Matt's arm around his waist to support him. Cold water was piped to the tub from the outdoor cistern, but the boarders had to carry hot water from the stove in the kitchen. Matt and Lily hauled several buckets of hot water to fill the tub halfway. Ransom figured they probably emptied the reservoir.

Undressing and climbing into the tub was difficult, but the hot water did wonders to ease his aches and pains. He'd barely had the strength to haul himself out of the tub, but he was too proud—and too stubborn— to call Matt to help him. If Lily hadn't had the foresight to move a chair next to the bathtub ahead of time, he would have landed in a heap on the floor. Putting on a clean undershirt and drawers was harder than he'd expected, but he managed that, too, without help.

When he finally got back to the room, he found that she had changed his bed, too. Clean and exhausted, he slept fairly well considering he woke up every time he moved.

On Saturday morning, Ransom had Matt bring some clean clothes over to the bed. He sent the young man off to breakfast, then painstakingly got dressed.

He hadn't realized how much the bath had loosened his muscles the night before. It was a benefit that, unfortunately, did not remain until morning. Lifting his leg to put on his pants made him want to scream, and he was sweating like a blacksmith by the time he had them on.

March wasn't hot, but he struggled out of his undershirt anyway. By the time he had his shirt on, he was too tired to worry about buttoning the top three buttons or tucking it into his pants. He collapsed on the bed—hot, worn out and downright cranky.

A few minutes later, Lily came in, pushing the door open with her hip as she carried in his breakfast. She wore a rust-colored calico wrapper, belted at the waist instead of flowing loosely like some women wore. The color and style made her more attractive than ever.

As usual, the tray was covered with a large cloth napkin. The dishes would be covered, too, hiding any hint of what was inside. Not that it mattered. Nothing he'd eaten lately had much of a smell, anyway.

"If that's more milk toast, you can take it away. Leave it, and I'll throw it at you," Ransom growled. "Five days of slop for breakfast and broth for dinner and supper is more than any man can tolerate."

"Good morning to you, too." She balanced the tray in one hand and moved the water pitcher and glass aside on the bedside table. "No milk toast." She set down his breakfast. "Mrs. Franklin and I decided you'd never regain your strength if you didn't have something more substantial."

"Oatmeal mush?" He shouldn't be grumbling at her, but he just felt plain ornery. His stomach had been gnawing on itself since the middle of the night, and his face itched from almost a week's worth of whiskers. He wanted a good breakfast, a shave and a change in scenery.

There were one hundred and two nails in the ceiling, five small spots that needed touching up with paint, and two pictures that weren't level. The eyelet ruffle on the curtain had forty-nine pleats and two flyspecks. He'd run out of things to count.

"Oatmeal sticks to your ribs." Was that a twinkle in her eye?

"Don't like it." The scent of fried potatoes and onions came from the kitchen, making his stomach rumble.

She handed him a cloth and waited for him to spread it across his lap. "Do you want another pillow behind your back?"

"What I want is to sit in the kitchen with everybody else."

"There are still a few people eating." Her gaze flicked over him, and she smiled. "And you're dressed. That blue is a good color for you, by the way. Brings out the color of your eyes."

Which was why he'd bought it. Her compliment shouldn't have meant as much as it did.

"There's no reason you couldn't join them."

Even when burdened by sorrow she was pretty. But when she smiled, her whole face lit up. Ransom felt a strange little twist in the vicinity of his heart.

He shoved a lock of hair back from his forehead, annoyed that his hand shook. More annoyed that she noticed.

Her smile vanished, her expression filled with concern. "You're shaking. Do you want me to help you into the kitchen?"

Ransom snarled at her. "What I want is to get out of bed like a normal person, stand up straight and walk in there on my own two feet. Without a cane. Without help." Rage and frustration boiled to the surface. He had the urge to shoot something...somebody. A pretty somebody with wheat-colored hair and big dark brown eyes would do for a start. He settled for throwing the hand towel at the foot of the bed.

Then wished he hadn't. Wincing at the pain shooting across his lower back, he tried to relax against the pillows.

Lily didn't say a word as she retrieved the towel, but he saw her swallow hard. Regret nudged him at his outburst. It wasn't her fault—well it was, but in all fairness, his being hurt was an accident. There, he'd admitted it. It wasn't right to blame her or Matt for his injuries.

Avoiding looking at him, she handed him the towel. He dropped it on the bed and grabbed her hand. Her gaze flew to his. "Lily, I'm sorry. I know Matt didn't mean to hurt me. This whole situation is driving me crazy. Sometimes I have to let off some steam or I'll explode. But it's not right to take it out on you."

"Better me than Matt." She slowly eased her hand away. "He has a gentle heart. This is eating him up inside."

Ransom spread the towel over his lap, taking the tray when she handed it to him. As he set the napkin aside, she lifted the metal cover from the plate, revealing scrambled eggs, biscuits and gravy. Breathing in the aroma of real food, Ransom's mood quickly improved. "What about you? Do you have a gentle heart?"

"No." She backed up a step. "Do you want some coffee?"

"Yes, ma'am. Black."

She nodded and hurried out.

He was too hungry to ponder her answer at the moment. He tucked that project away for later. After sprinkling salt and pepper over the eggs and gravy, he set the shakers on the bedside table and dug into the food. He was half-finished when she returned a few minutes later with a cup of hot coffee.

"You probably should let this cool." She set it on the table and started to leave again.

"Sit down and rest a while, keep me company." Ransom swallowed a bite. "I'll mind my manners and not talk with my mouth full."

She hesitated, then sat down in the rocking chair near the bed. "Bet you slurp your coffee though."

He smiled, cutting another bite of biscuit and gravy with his fork. "Not if I take your advice and let it cool. This is the best food I've ever had. My thanks to you and Mrs. Franklin." He glanced at her, glad to see her relax a bit. "Where are you and Matt from?"

"Des Moines, Iowa. One day Papa came home and said he'd sold the store and the house. He told us to pack our belongings because we were headed for Texas. He planned to open up a mercantile like we had in Iowa."

"Did you want to come?"

"Yes and no. I didn't like leaving my friends behind."

"And a sweetheart?" Ransom glanced up from his food to see her reaction.

"No." His question obviously didn't bother her a bit.

He settled back to rest a minute. "So are all the men in Iowa blind?"

That put a spot of color in her cheeks. "There were a few who showed an interest in me, but I wasn't interested in them."

Ransom nodded. "Too independent to be saddled with a beau."

Frowning, she gave the rocking chair a little push. "Too busy keeping house for Papa and Matt, as well as helping in the store."

"So other than leaving your friends, you didn't mind moving?"

"I'd lived in Des Moines my whole life, never been more than fifty miles away. I was ready to see more of the country, to do something adventurous." Sighing, she looked away. "I got more than I bargained for."

"We'll find the man who killed your father, Lily."

She looked back at him, her expression hard. "I'll find him myself."

The hatred in her eyes sent a chill down Ransom's spine. "And then what? Are you going to kill him?"

Her chin lifted in defiance. "Yes."

"You'll be tried for murder. Do you want to hang or wind up in prison for the rest of your life?"

"A jury wouldn't convict me. Not when they hear how he killed Papa in cold blood."

"They might not, but you can't know that for certain. They would only have your word on what happened."

"Matt's, too."

"Matt didn't see who did it. If you let the law take care of this and bring him to trial, then the district attorney can help you convince a jury. Our prosecutor is good. We might be able to turn Smith against Price or find other evidence to convict them."

The determined glint in her eyes remained. "He has to pay for what he did."

"Yes, he does, but don't take matters into your own hands. Think about Matt. From what I've seen, he won't let you handle this by yourself. Do you want him to hang, too?"

"No." Her gaze skimmed along his bed, flitting to the cane, then the door.

He had a good idea what she was thinking. That she was too polite to say it surprised him. "I won't be laid up forever. In fact, after I eat, I'm going to venture out to the front porch."

"Can't catch a murderer there."

"No, but Quint is a good lawman. He should be back from your campsite in a few days, unless he finds something to lead us to them."

"What can he find? They were only there a few minutes."

"For one thing, he can track them. See if both men came to town or if they split up. If they did, he might be able to trail the killer."

"I'm sure we walked all over any tracks they might have left. We weren't thinking about following them or catching them right then."

"Of course not."

She stared at the flowered wallpaper beyond the bed. "We buried him out there on the prairie."

"I know," he said quietly. He'd asked Griggs, the undertaker, to go with Quint and see if he could bring the body back to Willow Grove for a proper burial. In case Griggs decided he couldn't move their father for some reason, he hadn't mentioned it to Lily or Matt.

She continued as if she hadn't heard him. "We didn't know how far it was to town. He's out there all alone."

"His body is there. But your father is in Heaven." At least he hoped he was a Christian. If he wasn't, it would still be better for her to think of it in that way.

Lily blinked and nodded, looking back at him. "Yes, he is. He was firm in his beliefs."

Ransom had the feeling she wasn't so firm in hers. "You planning on going back to Iowa after things are settled?" The thought bothered him.

"I don't know. I might travel a little."

"See more of the country."

She shrugged and quickly looked away. But not before Ransom caught the sheen of tears in her eyes. He'd lost his parents to illness and a brother in the war. He could only imagine the pain of seeing a father she dearly loved gunned down in front of her. Maybe that was one reason she was bent on finding his killer. It gave her a reason to keep going, to hold herself together.

He picked up the coffee cup and gingerly took a sip. Just the right temperature. "My thanks for the decent breakfast. I feel stronger already."

A smile touched her face, warming his heart. "Mrs. Franklin said you had a knack for telling tales."

"I do feel stronger." He chuckled at her skeptical reaction. "Well, fuller anyway. Reckon it will take a few more good meals and getting out of this bed to regain my strength."

"My granny always said keeping a sick person confined to bed was the worst thing you could do to them. But you have been sitting up quite a bit."

"I'm still going stir-crazy. I have to get out of this room, go outside for a while."

"A shave might make you feel better, too. The few times Papa tried to grow a beard, he gave up after about a week. Said his face was itchy."

"I do believe you want to see how I look without the whiskers."

"It doesn't matter to me."

"Not at all?"

A slight blush touched her cheeks. "Are you fishing for a compliment, Mr. Starr?"

His grin was unrepentant. "I take 'em where I can get 'em." Right then, he'd take all the reassurance he could get.

"Well, I'll admit to being curious to see if you are as handsome as all the ladies say you are. Personally, I find the beard rather appealing." She studied his face, her brow wrinkling thoughtfully. "Though I really don't know why. I've never liked whiskers before."

"Maybe you just like the person wearing them."

Her gaze met his. "I like him sometimes."

"When I'm not snarling at you."

"That pretty well sums it up."

Chapter Four

Ransom laughed and his back muscles spasmed, making him clench his jaw.

She jumped up and took the cup from his hand, setting it on the table. Moving the tray, she set it on the table, too. "What can I do?"

"Rub my back when I roll over on my side." As he rolled over, gritting his teeth to keep from groaning, she pulled away a couple of pillows, allowing him to lie flatter. That eased the cramp a bit. Then she began to knead the tight muscles. Her strength surprised him. "You must make a lot of bread."

"Am I rubbing too hard?" She paused.

He took the second to catch his breath. "It hurts, but it's the only way to work out the knot."

She rubbed his back for several more minutes, until it relaxed. "Better?"

"Yes. Thanks." He breathed a sigh of relief, staying on his side. "Don't make me laugh."

"I wasn't trying to."

He pushed himself up to a sitting position, swinging his legs over the side of the bed at the same time. It was a technique he had discovered the day before and made getting out of bed much easier. "I know. I'll just have to smile big for a while."

Looking down at his bare feet, he wiggled his toes. "I don't think I'll bother with socks. I'm not even going to attempt boots."

"It's warm out already, and it's sunny on the porch."

"Do I look presentable?"

"You should probably comb your hair and finish buttoning up your shirt." A frown creased her forehead as she gently pulled back one side of the upper opening on his shirt. Her breath caught. "Oh, Ransom," she whispered.

He'd noted the bruising when he took his bath. It went halfway down his chest, but he didn't know how far up it extended. He'd been too tired to look in the mirror. Judging from the soreness, he was probably purple from one collarbone to the other. He was thankful they weren't broken. "It's all right."

"No, it's not." Her gaze met his, moisture shimmering in her eyes. "I'm so sorry. For everything."

"Don't worry about it. Nothing is broken, and I'm healing up." *Please, God, let that be true.* He fastened a couple more buttons. "I'll be right as rain before you know it. Now, help me to the dresser, and I'll comb my hair."

She handed him the cane. "Can you stand by yourself?"

Matt had always helped him in and out of bed, so she wouldn't know the routine. "Yes. Once I'm up, put your arm around my waist and walk with me. You don't need to worry about trying to bear any of my weight. I just need you to keep me steady."

He might be able to do it by himself, but he wasn't going to pass up the opportunity of having her tucked nice and close to his side. Especially since he had a legitimate excuse.

She moved beside him, watching him carefully. Pushing himself up off the bed with one hand, he leaned on the cane with the other, letting it and his left leg support him as he stood. She stepped close, sliding her arm around his waist as he slowly straightened. He paused, letting her touch and fresh, clean scent distract him from the pain.

"Are you okay?" she asked quietly.

He looked down, seeing concern—and awareness—in her dark eyes. She wasn't any more immune to him than he was to her. "Doin' fine, sugar. You keep hanging onto me, and I'll stay that way." He meant more than merely keeping his balance. The flash in her eyes and the blush coloring her cheeks told him she understood.

"Careful, Sheriff, or I might step on your toe."

Ransom grinned and started toward the dresser. The trip was slow and painful, but he did a little better than he had the night before. "Told you a good breakfast would help."

She stared at him in the mirror. "You mean that was better?"

"Not by much, but at this point, I'm grateful for the

smallest improvement." He propped the cane against the dresser and looked at his reflection, trying not to laugh. His hair stuck up in the back on both sides. "You didn't tell me I had horns."

"I thought those were normally there," she said with a remarkably straight face.

He chuckled, then winced at the pain. "I told you not to make me laugh."

"Sorry." Her gaze met his in the mirror, her expression softening. "But it's such a nice sound."

Lassoed. If he wasn't careful, he'd be hogtied before he knew it. He had to force himself to look away. Picking up his hairbrush, he smoothed down the wayward locks. She moved her arm from around his waist but stayed at his side.

Tipping his head, he checked his beard in the mirror. Looking mighty shaggy. "Maybe Matt could go ask the barber if he'll come over and give me a shave later." He rubbed his fingertips over the whiskers. "I'm a little shaky to try to cut down this timber."

"It looks soft."

"It's not." Turning carefully, he rested his arm on the dresser, leaning on it, and gave her a teasing smile. "But you can check it if you want."

The blush returned to her face. "I'll take your word for it."

"Coward."

"Yes, I am." Her voice cracked and anguish filled her eyes before she quickly looked way.

He was certain her words had little to do with him. "Lily, there's nothing you could have done for your father."

"I could have distracted them, drawn them away so he could get the shotgun. I should have tried to help him. I should have done something." Her voice broke on a sob.

Ransom gently gripped her arm and pulled her toward him. He wanted to soothe her broken heart, to protect and defend, to convince her that she wasn't to blame.

The ache in his back grew worse, and his legs felt as if they would buckle any second. Anger and frustration threatened, but he determinedly pushed them down. She needed gentleness, not him fighting his own demons. *Lord, keep me standing, for however long it takes. Please.* He turned farther, leaning his back against the dresser, slightly bending his knees. Thankfully, that lessened the pain. He felt more solid.

At six foot one he was just about a foot taller than her. He drew her into his arms, holding her close. Tears poured down her cheeks as she rested her face against his chest. He gently stroked her hair and let her cry. "Let it out, sugar. Don't hold your hurt inside."

Matt walked by the doorway. A second later, he stepped back and looked into the room. His face etched with pain, he met Ransom's gaze, nodded and slipped quietly away.

Ransom murmured words of solace, taking his own comfort in her nearness, in the way one hand gripped his shirt and the other slid around his waist, holding onto him. Despite his infirmity, she turned to him, needed him. Despite being a cripple—*Please God, not for long*—he had strength to share.

He had never been lacking for feminine attention.

Since he had been hurt, Mrs. Franklin had been plagued by lady callers wanting to cheer him up with their smiles and prattle. Thankfully, she had turned them all away without even asking if he wanted to see them.

Except for Lily Chastain. He suspected Mrs. Franklin had been as intrigued as he had by the appearance of a woman he didn't know saying she had a debt to pay.

He couldn't help feeling that there was more at work than mere curiosity. Maybe it was as simple as her needing his help to find her father's killer. Or to try to keep her from doing something rash. Rescue the damsel in distress. During his career, he'd played the shining knight to plenty of fair maidens, but none had ever touched him on the same level as Lily. Of course, he'd been on an emotional buckin' bronc lately, so maybe he shouldn't put too much credence in the way she made him feel.

His friends Ty and Cade McKinnon, both newlyweds, often teased him about needing a woman of his own. Ransom admitted to himself, never to them, that seeing his old friends so happily married cracked open a door that he'd kept firmly shut. Being sheriff wasn't filled with the excitement and adventure he'd been used to. It left him with too much time to think, to watch his friends and realize how lonely he was. Either he had to get back to his old life or settle down in the new one and change his ways.

Under the present circumstances, neither one was an option. It took a whole man to chase desperadoes. And to be a husband. He would never ask a woman to marry him if he wasn't, especially not Lily. He wanted a wife tied to him by love, not guilt.

Ransom had already proved that Dallas doctor wrong on one count. He was walking, even if it was probably the biggest challenge he'd ever had. Whether he could ever walk normally remained to be seen.

Lily raised her head and wiped her eyes. He didn't know if she'd cried her fill or sensed his sudden tension. She didn't seem in a hurry to leave the circle of his arms.

"I got your shirt all wet."

"It will dry soon enough. Feel better?"

She nodded, meeting his gaze. "I guess I needed a good cry."

"I hear it does wonders." Though the tears he'd shed in the darkness since his fall hadn't eased his heartache and fear any. He released her. He didn't want to, but if he didn't sit down, he was going to fall down.

Picking up the cane, he started toward the extra chair near the dresser. She was instantly at his side, her arm around his waist. She didn't let go until he was safely seated. He caught her hand, keeping her close.

"It's not your fault, Lily. The man who killed your father is solely to blame. You have to accept that fact or it will destroy you."

"It's hard to do."

"Yes, it is. It will take time and probably a lot of prayer."

She tipped her head, her expression thoughtful. "Are you a praying man?"

"I have been this past week. Before that, I talked to Him on occasion." And not just when he was in trouble.

"I suppose most people turn to God more when they're hurt."

"What about you?"

She hesitated. "I used to talk to Jesus a lot. It used to be easy."

"Some people turn their backs on Him when things go bad."

"Do you think that's what I'm doing?" She tried to pull away, but he kept a firm grip on her hand.

"You tell me. Do you honestly think God would want you to track down your father's killer and murder him?"

"What difference does it make whether I do it or you? Or your deputy?"

"When we go after someone, we go with the intention of bringing them back to trial."

"And you always bring them back alive." Her tone and expression plainly said he was being a hypocrite. She tugged on her hand, and he released it.

"Can't always. Most outlaws don't give up without a fight. Sometimes I don't have a choice."

"How many men have you killed?"

"Too many. It won't ease your pain. You may gain momentary satisfaction from your revenge and from knowing he can't hurt anyone else, but that won't last." He looked away, not wanting her to see too much. "If you have any decency at all—and I know you do—taking a man's life never leaves you." He looked back at her. "Believe me, Lily, you don't want him haunting your dreams."

Her eyes rounded with surprise, then she frowned. "You dream about the men you've killed?"

"Sometimes. Even a few who probably deserved to die. I'm a hard-hearted, thick-skinned lawman, but it's not my place to act as judge and jury."

"Maybe you aren't as hard-hearted as you think you are."

"Neither are you." Though her frown darkened, he didn't give her a chance to reply. "You couldn't walk up to a man, even your father's murderer, and shoot him any more than I could. That's what makes us different from him, why you're here taking care of me instead of trailing his partner. That's why God will see him brought to justice."

"You really believe that?"

"Yes. I've been doin' a lot of thinking since I went flyin' off that balcony." Not all of it good.

She flinched, and he mentally kicked himself. "Sorry. A lot of thinking lately. When Ty was here day before yesterday, he reminded me that even when bad things happen, God can still bring good out of it. He quoted some Scripture, told me to remember it when I'm feelin' low. He said it helped him after his first wife and their baby died several years ago. Would you bring me my Bible? It's in the drawer of the nightstand."

With a troubled expression, Lily retrieved the Bible and brought it to him. It was more worn from roaming the country in his saddlebag than from actual use. He knew the words Ty had pointed out by heart, but thought it might sink in better if he read them to her. He'd marked the verse with a scrap of paper. "It's the first part of Romans, chapter eight, verse twenty-eight. 'And we know that all things work together for good to them that love God…'"

He rested the Bible on his lap. "I've never been much for goin' to church, but I've loved God for a long time. I've believed in Jesus as my Savior since I was a boy." He was coming to realize there needed to be more to the relationship. Maybe that was why God hit him over the head with a two-by-four to get his attention. "So I know He's going to work some good out of this situation."

Her angry, disbelieving gaze swept over him. "How can you say that? Do you honestly believe that something good can come from my father's death or you being hurt?"

An odd peace settled over him, an overwhelming sense of rightness. "Yes, I do. I met you."

Chapter Five

Mrs. Franklin peeked out the front window, chuckling softly. "I declare, you'd think the man was a king holding court."

Lily looked at the handful of townspeople gathered around the sheriff. She'd lost track of how many had come and gone. She stepped back from the open window, speaking quietly, though with all the laughter and chatter on the porch, she doubted Ransom would hear them. "Folks are mighty happy to see him up and about."

Her landlady snorted. "About is a long stretch. But he does seem to be enjoying the fresh air and sunshine, as well as the company."

"Enjoying all the attention, if you ask me," muttered Lily as she watched a pretty young blonde flirt shamefully with Ransom. The cad flirted back. Just a little, she admitted silently. He shifted in the chair for the third time in the last five minutes. "He's getting tired."

Mrs. Franklin glanced at her, then back at Ransom. "Been out there almost two hours. 'Bout as long as it's taken you to dust here in the parlor."

Lily's face grew hot. "I thought I should stay close in case he needed something."

Mrs. Franklin grinned. "Something besides the glass of iced tea and plate of cookies you took out to him?" She patted her on the shoulder. "You could go out and check on him again."

"I'm not sure he'd appreciate it." Lily smiled ruefully. "I've already been out there three times."

"Well, you stay in here and keep an eye on him. You might as well sit down and rest a bit while you do it. I'll go finish dinner."

Lily nodded and took a seat near the window. The group of people slowly drifted away. She looked down the street. For the first time all morning, it was empty.

"Lily, are you still there?" asked Ransom, turning his head slightly to speak over his shoulder.

"I'm here."

"Come rescue me before anybody else shows up."

Lily dropped the dust cloth and hurried out the front door. Lines of pain and weariness bracketed his mouth. She glanced up the street. "Don't dawdle. Somebody just turned the corner."

"That's Mrs. Peabody. She's too nearsighted to see me sitting here. She won't stop unless I'm outside when she walks by."

Ransom braced his cane firmly on the porch and

pushed himself up from the rocking chair. Lily slipped her arm around his waist. "Just get me into the parlor and call Matt. I don't want to risk squishing you."

They slowly moved toward the door. He seemed a lot weaker than he had been when he came outside. Lily tightened her hold. "Put your arm around my shoulders and lean on me. I won't break."

As he lifted his arm and rested it on her shoulder, he drew in a sharp breath, but he didn't complain. He let her bear a little of his weight, but not much.

"You shouldn't have visited with Miss Clark so long."

"Prissy likes a captive audience."

"You didn't seem to mind." She had to move away from him to hold the screen door open.

Ransom inched through the doorway into the house. The instant she stepped beside him, he put his arm back around her shoulders. "Jealous, sugar?"

"Don't be silly." She'd only wanted to smack the woman with the broom because she was tiring him out. Lily tried to shrug off his endearment. It didn't mean anything. But he hadn't called Miss Clark sweet names. She guided him carefully into a side chair. "I'll get Matt."

Racing down the hall and out the back door, she called to her brother. "Ransom needs you to help him back to bed."

Matt climbed down the ladder and set the paint bucket and brush on the ground. "Is he still out front?"

"No, he's in the parlor. He wore himself out."

"He knows his limits, Lil." He started toward the kitchen.

"I doubt it. He's just like Papa. Always pushing himself too hard."

"Maybe that's one reason you like him so much."

Lily followed her brother through the back door. "Who says I like him?" she mumbled.

Matt turned around with a grin, walking backward. "You always hang onto a man you don't like?" He slowed and leaned toward her, laughter lighting his face. "And let him hang onto you?"

Lily rolled her eyes and stopped in the kitchen. "Just go get him into bed. I'll check on him in a few minutes."

"Yes, ma'am." He winked. "You could do a lot worse, big sister." He spun around and trotted toward the parlor.

Lily muttered under her breath, then noticed Mrs. Franklin taking a cake out of the oven. "Smells good. What kind is it?"

"Sponge cake with a bit of lemon flavoring." Mrs. Franklin set the pan on a rack to cool, then turned to Lily. She studied her for a minute. "Every single woman in town has tried to catch Sheriff Starr's eye. He hasn't shown interest in anybody until now."

"He did seem to enjoy Miss Clark's company." Lily tried to keep her tone light. "She's pretty and seems nice."

"Prissy Clark is a man-chaser. Hear tell she's done more than flirt with a few of them, too. If the sheriff hadn't been stuck out there, he wouldn't have done more than say good morning." Her voice grew quieter. "*You're* the one he's interested in, dear."

Lily thought of how he had comforted her and tried to convince her that her father's death wasn't her fault.

Of how he held her with tenderness that went beyond kindness. He cared about her. She didn't know in what way—or how he could—but she'd felt it, seen it in his eyes. It would be easy to fall for Ransom Starr, but she couldn't let herself. She had to avenge her father's death. Ransom wouldn't want anything to do with her then.

"That's just because he's been shut up in his room and is bored," said Lily. "Once he gets back to work, he'll forget all about me." Even though she would never forget him.

"Not likely." Mrs. Franklin glanced at the clock. "You'd better set the table. Folks will be coming in for dinner before we know it. They count on me not to keep them waiting."

"Yes, ma'am." Lily was thankful for the reprieve. She went into the dining room and carefully took the dishes from the buffet. Mrs. Franklin used fine blue-and-white china at her table, with the addition of large handled white mugs for the coffee. All of her boarders were men, and her philosophy was simple. Treat them like gentlemen, and they'll behave like gentlemen. It worked for the most part. Lily laid out the place settings, including a linen napkin at each one. She set Ransom's dishes aside to take into the kitchen. He wouldn't feel up to sitting at the table today.

She also left Deputy Webb's place empty. He hadn't spent much time at the boarding house since Ransom was hurt, but he had a room there. Mrs. Franklin said he sometimes joined them at dinner, but he was still gone, investigating her father's murder. Lily wondered if he would find anything of use.

Plucking a drooping flower from the centerpiece, she blinked back tears. Her mother had set a fine table, too, and had trained her to do likewise. Lily's father had always appreciated how well she'd carried on her mother's tradition. *I'll use your china again someday, Mama,* Lily thought sadly. *If I can ever do it without my heart breaking.*

Before going back to the kitchen, she peeked in on Ransom. A breeze blew through the open window, billowing out the thin curtains then sucking them back against the screen. He was curled on his side, facing away from the window, fast asleep. Annoyed at the little tug at her heart, she quietly pulled the door closed and went back to her chores.

The boarders arrived at noon, hungry and in good spirits. They cleaned up at the washstand on the back porch, then took their places at the table. Lily and Mrs. Franklin carried in the food, minus Ransom's portion, and poured coffee for everyone except Matt. He drank milk. The men fell silent as the ladies joined them.

Mrs. Franklin bowed her head. Everyone followed suit. "Lord, thank You providing this food," she said quietly. "And thank You that Sheriff Starr is mending. We ask You to continue healing him. In Jesus's name, amen."

Lily noticed that all the men added an "amen," even the ones who usually didn't.

Alvah Crutcher, the town's photographer, dished up a helping of chicken and dumplings. "Heard the sheriff sat outside for a while this morning." He handed the chicken to Ed Bennett, who was a clerk at McKinnon Brothers general store.

"He stayed out on the porch for a couple of hours," said Mrs. Franklin, putting some green beans on her plate and passing the bowl to Matt. "He's sleeping now."

"I lost count of the folks who said they'd dropped by to see him," Ed said, starting a bowl of peaches on its way around the table. "Even the ones who didn't were cheered to hear he's feeling better. They're hoping he'll be back in the office soon." He frowned as he added some sweet cucumber pickles to his plate. "Mr. McKinnon doesn't think that's too likely."

"Won't be soon." Mrs. Franklin glanced at Lily. "But he's a determined man. I reckon he'll get back to work eventually."

Lily desperately hoped so, and it wasn't only to alleviate her guilt. She was afraid of what might happen to Ransom if he couldn't continue being sheriff. She couldn't imagine anyone being better suited to the job. Despite his pain, he had considered aspects of her father's murder that she hadn't even thought of.

They focused on the food, chatting about other happenings in town. The new opera house, courthouse and jail were almost finished. Lily and Matt had watched the workmen complete the new city hall the previous week when they had been waiting to hear about the sheriff. All the brick buildings were impressive, from the outside anyway. They hadn't seen the inside.

Two of the boarders, Reuben and Claude Driver, were bricklayers working on the courthouse. Reuben set his fork on the side of his plate and looked at Mrs. Franklin. "We'll be done with our job this afternoon. We'll be heading to El Paso tomorrow like we expected."

"I hate to see you leave," said their landlady. "You've been good tenants." She smiled at Lily and winked at Matt. "That means you will each have a room."

"I thought you had a waiting list." Having a room of her own and no longer sleeping in the pantry would be wonderful, but Lily didn't want Mrs. Franklin to lose out on paying customers.

"Well, I did. But a couple of gents decided to go back east and the others are moving into the Parker Boarding House when it opens up tomorrow. So this will work out just fine."

"I'll need to keep sleeping in Mr. Starr's room," said Matt. "Until he doesn't need me at night anymore." He smiled at Mrs. Franklin. "But it will be nice to have a place to change clothes and stuff. It's a little crowded in the wagon."

"What's the matter, son? Can't balance between the trunks and the boxes?" Ed nudged him on the shoulder with a grin.

"That about sums it up." Matt cast an impish glance at his sister. "Lily could stock the women's department at McKinnon's Store."

Lily shrugged. "That's what happens when your father owns a mercantile."

The words hung in the air as she realized what she'd said. Her gaze flew to Matt's, her eyes filling with tears at the pain in his. For a moment, everyone seemed at a loss for what to say.

Ed cleared his throat. "That's the way of it, all right. Cade and Ty see to it that their wives have the best wardrobes in town. You know, Miss Chastain, once the sheriff is healed up, you should talk to Ty about working at the store. Sometimes the ladies are more comfortable with a woman helping them, especially one who has a knack for fashion. The cowboys buy more when a pretty lady helps them, too."

"Cowboys aren't the only ones who appreciate a pretty lady helping them," Claude mumbled around a mouthful of food as he looked at Lily. Everyone, including his brother, stared at him. Other than a shy nod and a "thank you, ma'am" now and then, she had never heard the bricklayer say a word.

Claude glanced around and ducked his head, his face turning bright red.

"Thank you, Mr. Driver," said Lily.

He met her gaze with relief in his eyes. "You're welcome, Miss Lily." He turned his attention to his food and didn't look up until they'd finished with the meal. When the other men stood, he did, too. "I'll miss your cookin', Mrs. Franklin."

Mrs. Franklin nodded with a smile and started stacking the plates. "And I'll miss your harmonica playing. Would you play for us this evening?"

Lily hadn't heard him play, but she didn't think Mrs. Franklin would encourage him if it sounded bad.

"Don't want to bother the sheriff."

"I'm sure he would enjoy it." Lily picked up a couple of empty serving bowls, thankful that she'd saved some food for Ransom. "I would, too."

Claude smiled shyly. "After supper." He followed the other men from the dining room and out the front door.

Matt helped Lily and Mrs. Franklin carry the dishes into the kitchen. "That's the most I ever heard him say."

Mrs. Franklin chuckled as she poured hot water into the dishpan. "He did more talking at dinner than I've heard in the six months he's been here. Too bad they're leaving. I expect Lily would find herself with another suitor." She glanced meaningfully down the hall toward Ransom's door.

"I'm not interested in a suitor." Lily plucked the dishrag from her landlady's hand. "You go sit a while and read your new *Harper's Bazaar*."

"I'll do just that. Think I'll sit on the front porch and watch the world go by while I'm at it. You'll keep a listen for the sheriff?"

"Yes, ma'am." It was the only reason she volunteered to do the dishes. And she knew Mrs. Franklin knew it.

The trouble with mundane chores was that they gave Lily too much time to think and not enough distraction to keep her grief buried. By the time she got through the cups to the plates, tears began to fall.

"I miss you, Papa," she whispered. "Did you know how much I loved you?" She'd told him, tried to show him. But she'd let him down, too. "I shouldn't have fussed when you forgot the milk. Or tracked in mud. Or were late to dinner. I should have baked that coconut cake more often." She closed her eyes against the pain and leaned against the work table, choking back a sob. "I should have tried to save you." *Oh, God! Why did You let them kill him? He trusted You. Believed You'd watch over us. Why, God? Why did You let him die?*

The heavens were silent. So was the quiet Voice she sometimes heard in her heart and soul, the Holy Spirit that had guided her for as long as she could remember.

Lily dragged in a deep breath and wiped her eyes on her apron. She dug a hankie from her pocket and blew her nose, determination rising above her pain. Or was it hate? "Yes, I hate them," she whispered fervently, picking up the dishrag and scrubbing a plate.

"Love your enemies...pray for them which despite-fully use you, and persecute you...."

Lily barely resisted the urge to throw the plate against the wall. "I pray they rot in hell," she muttered through gritted teeth. "And that my bullets send them there."

Chapter Six

When Ransom woke up, he couldn't decide whether he felt better or worse. The rest had restored some of his strength, but his back was so stiff he could hardly move. Clenching his jaw, he scooted up to lean against the pillows. They weren't piled quite right, but it was the best he could do. He waited a bit and caught his breath, listening to his stomach rumble. "Wonder if Lily saved me any dinner." Maybe not. When she helped him inside, she'd been put out with him for some reason.

Just as he opened his mouth to bellow, the door opened and she poked her head around it. "You're awake."

"You noticed."

Frowning, she pushed the door aside and walked into the room. "Grumpy, too."

"Me or you?"

"Both." She stopped beside the bed, her frown deepening. "You want the other pillows behind your back?"

"Yeah. And one under my knees. I can't manage it."

She stuffed two more pillows behind him as he leaned forward with a grimace. "You overdid it this morning."

"Can't even sit in a chair for a couple of hours." Not worth spit.

"You've sat that long in here." Lily gently lifted his right leg, sliding the pillow beneath the knee. He moved the left one where he needed it. "Maybe you shouldn't have tried to walk that far so soon."

Ransom bit back a snarl, determined not to take his frustration out on her again. "It's a sorry state of affairs if I can't even walk to the front porch and back. I won't stay cooped up in here."

"Nobody said you had to. You need to build up your strength. Chicken and dumplings should help."

"Reckon I picked the right day to gripe about the broth. Did you save me anything else?"

"Who said *I* saved it for you?"

"Well, whoever did, I appreciate it." He studied her as she straightened the things on the bedside table. Her eyes appeared puffy and her nose a little red, like she'd been crying. He started to ask her about it and decided not to. If a woman had a reason to cry, it was her. She wouldn't want him questioning her about it, either.

"Anything interesting happen while I was asleep?"

"The Driver brothers are leaving tomorrow. They're finishing up their job on the courthouse today. Claude is going to play his harmonica for us tonight. Is he any good?"

"Yes."

"Good. He was afraid it would disturb you, but I told him you'd enjoy it."

"Then I'll do my best not to make a liar out of you." Ransom felt almost irritable enough to gripe at her for telling Claude what he'd like or dislike. Since she hadn't brought dinner, he decided he'd better keep his mouth shut.

Later, when he was comfortably full and the barber had given him a shave, he was glad he hadn't picked a fight with her. He wondered why he'd considered it in the first place. He seldom argued with anyone. Usually, he stated how things were and that was it, though he doubted that would be the case with Lily. They would have wasted time and energy bickering.

He much preferred teasing banter, but she had plunked down his dinner and left before he had a chance to say more than thank you.

An hour later, Matt stopped by his room and helped him into the rocking chair.

"Where's your sister?" Ransom asked, hoping he sounded casual.

"Shopping. Mrs. Franklin said Lily needed a change of scenery and invited her to go along to the grocer's and mercantile." Matt sat down on the foot of the bed. Taking off his wide-brimmed hat, he combed his fingers through his light blond hair. "I hope it helps."

"She seemed out of sorts."

"Been kind of up and down all day. I appreciate you comforting her this morning. I try, but it does more good comin' from you."

Ransom nodded, studying him. "What about you, Matt? How are you doing?"

Tears misted the young man's pale blue eyes. He pressed his lips tightly together in an attempt to hold them in. It took a minute before he could speak. "I miss Papa. Sometimes I forget that he's gone. I'll think of something I want to tell him or say something about him and then remember that he isn't here. That's what happened to Lily at dinner." Matt took a deep, shuddering breath. "It's powerful hard, Sheriff Starr. It was real bad when our mother died, but she was sick for about a year, so we knew it was coming. With Papa, it was so sudden."

He met Ransom's gaze. "I wish you could have known him, sir. He was kind and generous and did his best to make us happy. He missed Mama something terrible, but he didn't wallow in his sorrow. He'd talk about the good times we'd all had together, remind us of how special she was and how much she loved us. He grieved plenty for her, but he'd point out that she wasn't sick anymore and that she was in Glory with Jesus. He said someday we'd all be together again. That comforted him a lot, I think."

A tear slipped down the boy's cheek. He quickly wiped it away. "Now, he's with her. I can picture them walking hand in hand down those golden streets. They used to hold hands a lot." Matt looked away and cleared his throat.

"I'm sure they were fine people," said Ransom. "You and Lily are proof of it. When did your mother pass on?"

"Four years ago. I was twelve and Lily was sixteen. She'd quit school about six months earlier to take care of Mother and everything else." He shook his head, his expression thoughtful. "Lily just stepped in and did what had to be done with nary a complaint. After Mama was gone, she even worked at the store three afternoons a week."

"You must have helped out, too. You've been handy around here, painting and fixing the roof."

Matt shrugged, a tiny smile brightening his face. "I'm better suited to things like that. I helped unload the freight and stock the shelves in the store, but I'd rather be outside."

"When I get to feelin' better, I'll take you out to McKinnon Ranch. Cade could probably use another cowboy."

Matt wrinkled his face. "I'd like to see a ranch, but I'm not interested in riding a horse for a living."

Ransom chuckled and shifted his leg. "Had enough of that on the trip from Iowa?"

"Yes, sir. I've been thinkin' about talking to some of the carpenters, see if somebody will teach me the trade. When you don't need my help anymore," he added quickly.

"You like building things?"

"Yes, sir. I worked with a neighbor some last year, adding a couple of rooms to his house."

"I'll ask Ty to check around, see who might need a helper. Then as soon as I'm stronger, I'll cut you loose so you can do something more interesting."

"I'd appreciate that." Matt's expression grew somber. "I'll stay right here until I'm sure you don't need my help anymore. Even that won't be enough to make up for what I did to you."

"It was an accident, son. I'm as certain of that as I am of the sun comin' up in the morning." Ransom decided it was time to change the subject, lighten the gloomy mood in the room. "I understand Claude is going to serenade us tonight."

"Yep." A twinkle lit Matt's eyes. "Only I think it's Lil he's serenading."

Ransom frowned. Claude was making a play for Lily? "Why do you think that?"

"'Cause he paid her a compliment at dinner. It was just one sentence, but it shocked everybody so much, they stopped eating and stared at him."

Bet that made him feel like crawling under the table. "What did he say?"

As he listened to Matt tell about the incident, Ransom wondered if Lily had just been kind or if she'd been impressed by the shy bricklayer. Claude was a decent-looking man when he was cleaned up, which he usually did every evening. He wouldn't be one to pick arguments with a woman. And he could walk, even do hard physical labor, thought Ransom bitterly.

"Lily said they're leaving tomorrow." Ransom suddenly realized he was gripping the chair arm. He forced his fingers to relax.

"Moving to another job in El Paso."

And playing that sweet, mournful music the night before he left. What better way to keep Lily thinking about him? Ransom considered stealing the man's harmonica, which was silly since he couldn't climb the blasted stairs. He couldn't even throw him in the calaboose for raising a ruckus. Claude was as quiet as a church mouse and as peaceful as any lawman could hope for. And his music could make a grown man cry. Maybe that was enough to lock him up for disturbing the peace. Ransom's peace, anyway.

"Mrs. Franklin is giving us their rooms. Said all her prospective boarders have gone somewhere else." Matt picked up his hat.

"Good. I don't like Lily sleeping on the floor."

"It's better than the ground. Drier, too." Matt stood, plopping the hat on his head. "I'd better get back to painting."

"Thanks for the visit."

"Thanks for letting me talk."

"Anytime."

After Matt left the room, Ransom's thoughts went back to Claude Driver and his attraction to Lily. She'd be spending one more night in that pantry. All the man had to do was come downstairs and open the door....

"Stop being ridiculous," he muttered. "Claude wouldn't hurt Lily." But sometimes the quiet, shy ones were the ones you had to watch. Ransom sighed heavily. It was going to be a long night.

Later that evening, Ransom joined the others in the front parlor. He silently gave Claude credit for playing only cheerful tunes on his harmonica. He was concerned that the lively music raised the man's esteem in Lily's eyes even more than something poignant might have, but at least it made her smile. For that he was thankful—and jealous every time she turned her sparkling gaze toward Claude.

But Ransom hadn't been an excellent Texas Ranger and private investigator simply because he was good at digging up information. He'd learned long ago to hide his feelings. He smiled and tapped his fingers on the arm of the chair, keeping time to the music along with everyone else.

Weariness and pain took their toll, and he left the party less than an hour after it began. After Matt helped him to his feet, Ransom turned to Claude. "I'll to have to listen from down the hall, but don't stop playing."

Claude met his gaze with a slight frown. "You sure?"

"I'm enjoying it. I just need to lie down." Ransom nodded to both the Driver brothers. "Take care of yourselves out there in El Paso. It can be rough. There's a reason it's called the Six Shooter Capital." He saw a worried frown flit across Lily's face. He was tempted to mention that it was also called "Sin City" but decided against it.

"We'll be fine." Reuben smiled wryly. "Since we've been following the railroad, most jobs take us to towns that aren't quite settled yet. Even Willow Grove was rowdier when we first came here."

"It's settled down because of Sheriff Starr," said Mrs. Franklin. She glanced at Ransom, then spoke to Lily. "Our former sheriff was good, but Sheriff Starr's reputation has kept most of the riffraff away."

"With that bit of flattery, I'll head on to bed." Ransom nodded to the room in general, his gaze briefly settling on Lily. "Y'all have a pleasant evening."

After a chorus of good-nights, Matt helped him down the hall. Once he was settled in bed, Ransom pondered Mrs. Franklin's words. They weren't merely flattery, but the truth. As word spread about him being hurt, he worried that trouble might come to Willow

Grove—and about Quint getting caught in the middle of it.

"He can't handle it alone, Lord. Please heal me pronto." A particularly sharp pain stole his breath for a second. "Or send somebody to help him."

Ransom listened to the music, picturing Lily's happy face. The pain in his back and leg settled into a throbbing ache, almost as deep as the ache in his heart. *She'd be better off with Claude,* he thought. *Driver's a decent man. He'd provide her with a good home and quiet adoration. But he wouldn't be able to keep her from trying to find her father's killers.*

"And I think I can?" he whispered to the darkness. He hated being unable to take care of things. Frustration and a wave of self-pity brought moisture to his eyes. "You'd better send somebody to take my place, Lord. As sheriff and with Lily. I'm no good to anybody like this."

A shadow fell across his door. A second later, Lily stopped in the doorway. "Are you awake?" she asked quietly.

"Why aren't you still in the parlor?"

"I wanted to see if you needed anything."

Gentle arms to hold him. Someone to chase away his fear. He cleared the huskiness from his throat. "I'm fine. Thanks."

"You don't sound fine." Lily came over to the side of the bed. Instead of laying her hand on his forehead as she sometimes did to check for fever, she gently cradled his jaw. Resting her thumb on his cheek, she touched a tear that he hadn't realized had slipped from his eyes. Her breath caught.

He froze, mortified that she saw his weakness.

She gently wiped away the moisture with her finger-tips, then pulled the rocker close to the bed and took his hand in both of hers. "Are you in terrible pain?"

"Hurts pretty bad." He hoped she would think he only meant his back.

"Is there anything I can do?"

"You're doin' it." He pressed his fingers against hers. "Talk to me a while."

"About anything in particular?"

"What were you like as a little girl?"

She chuckled. "A know-it-all. Some of the time I was even right."

"A lot of the time, I expect. I bet you were good in school."

She shrugged. "In most things. I didn't like geography very much. Why should I care exactly where England is? I'll never go there."

I'd take you. He almost said the words out loud. "You don't want to see castles and great cathedrals?"

"We have great cathedrals here that I've never seen. Why risk going across an ocean to see one?" She shook her head. "I won't travel anywhere without dirt beneath my feet."

"There's dirt beneath the ocean."

"There's lots of wet between the boat and the ground." She withdrew one hand, sitting back in the chair.

He was glad that she kept her other hand tucked around his. Though he had given comfort at times, he hadn't been on the receiving end of it much. "I sailed up the coast of California once. Spent about half the time hanging over the side of the ship."

He could see her frown in the moonlight. "What was so interesting to watch in the water?"

Ransom grinned. "Nothing, but it was better to lose my breakfast, dinner and supper there than on the deck or in my cabin."

She made a face. "Now I know for certain I don't want to go on a ship."

"You sounded pretty certain before."

"Now, I'm positive."

"Matt said you quit school when you were sixteen."

"Not quite sixteen. I only had one more year anyway. Mama needed me at home, and it gave me more time with her."

"Then it was a good thing. What do you want out of life, Lily?"

"Justice."

At least she hadn't said revenge. "After that?"

She looked away. "To take care of Matt, until he gets tired of me bossing him around." He barely heard her sigh. "I expect that won't be long. Then I'll think of something."

"Claude is sweet on you."

"Trying to get rid of me, Sheriff?"

"Just lookin' out for you."

"Don't work so hard at it." Her voice dropped almost to a whisper. "Mr. Driver is a nice man, but I'd go crazy having conversations with myself."

Ransom shouldn't have been so relieved. "You'd always win the arguments."

Lily laughed. "Guess there's something to that."

They sat for a few minutes. The pain in his back and leg had eased. Yes, sir, there was a lot to be said about a woman's caring touch. When she started to absently rub the tip of her finger against the back of his hand, he wondered if she was thinking about a lifetime of quiet talks and holding hands in the dark.

"Are you afraid?" she asked softly.

The question surprised him, then he decided it shouldn't have. She had a knack for sensing his moods and feelings. And she'd caught him crying. He was tempted to let her think his physical pain caused it, but Ransom wasn't a liar. If there was any chance of a future with Lily, it had to be built on truth and honesty.

"Yeah, I am. I try to have faith that God won't let me stay like this, but I reckon He might have a reason for me not to get well. Something only He understands. I know that sometimes happens to men who are a lot closer to the Almighty than I am. I'll do everything I can to get back to normal."

"And if you don't? What will you do then?"

"Probably buy a little ranch. Hire a good outfit to do the work. I don't know much about ranching. I've been chasing men instead of cows for a long time now. But I figure I can make a go of it as long as I have a good foreman.

"Of course, I'd resign as sheriff first. I may do that before long anyway." He hated to pull his hand from hers, but he had to shift his position. He gave her fingers a quick squeeze before moving. "Trouble will show up, probably sooner than later. The county can't afford to pay me and hire another deputy, too. It's not a job Quint should attempt on his own."

"I heard you did it alone for months."

"I've had years of experience, and there were no big

problems. Ty and Cade are good to help out, like they're doin' now, but they have their own businesses and lives to lead."

"Don't do anything hasty. I haven't heard a single person talk about you quitting."

He settled more on his side. "You don't get out much."

"True, but Mrs. Franklin's friends keep her informed of what's going on. If anyone was complaining she would have been pounding the bread dough extra hard."

Ransom smiled wryly. "True." His smile faded. "If you hear any rumblings about people thinking I should quit, tell me. I don't want to get blindsided."

"All right. But wouldn't Mayor McKinnon say something if folks were demanding your resignation?"

"Maybe. Though it's not up to him. The county commissioners hired me. They're the ones who'll fire me. If anybody complains to Ty or Cade—he's one of the commissioners—more than likely they'll tell them to quit bellyachin' and give me time to heal."

"Which is exactly what they should do."

The staunch conviction in her voice warmed his heart. "The second thing I'd do is release you and Matt from your promise." When she started to protest, he raised his hand, halting her. "If you remember, I never accepted your offer. Don't get me wrong, sugar. I appreciate everything you do for me. You help me in ways you probably don't even realize. Just having you here now, talking like this, means more than I can say." He already depended on her too much. "If that doctor from Dallas is right and I won't ever be whole again, I don't want you to feel obligated to me."

"But we are."

"I won't have you bound to me out of guilt, Lily. Not for a lifetime. Not now."

"I want to take care of you." She sounded like she was about to cry.

Ransom remembered Matt's comment about her up-and-down emotions earlier in the day. "I'm glad you are. But if I'm not showing improvement in a couple of weeks, I'm going to make some changes. Move into a house and hire an old cowboy or a woman old enough to be my mother to take care of me. It's not right to make everyone here tiptoe around because they're afraid they'll disturb me."

"According to Mrs. Franklin, her boarders are usually pretty quiet anyway. She said having a waiting list had worked out fine because it gave her a chance to see how a person acted in town. If she heard about them causing trouble, she just kept moving them to the bottom of the list."

"Or had me tell them they weren't welcome to stay here. That only happened once," said Ransom. He stifled a yawn.

"I'll let you get some sleep." She stood and pushed the rocker back into its normal place.

"Thanks for visiting with me. When I'm back on my feet, I'd like to spend more time with you. Show you what I'm like when I'm not moanin', groanin' or gripin'."

"You mean that's not your normal disposition?"

He liked the teasing lilt in her voice. "No, ma'am." He exaggerated his Texas drawl. "I'm easygoin' and charmin'."

"I think you'd better stay grumpy."

"Why?"

"Charming would be very dangerous."

While he was trying to think of an acceptable reply, she skedaddled, pulling his door almost closed. He'd always had a way with the ladies but never went beyond light flirtation, at least not in the last ten years or so. He'd sown some wild oats when he was younger, but illicit liaisons really weren't his style. His parents had raised him to be a better man than that and his conscience—or perhaps it was the Holy Spirit—had doggedly reminded him of it.

Ransom gazed out at the starry sky, remembering the gentle touch of her fingers on his cheek. He'd never take advantage of Lily, and he'd do everything in his power not to hurt her. "Lord, I sure would like the opportunity to sweet-talk her just a little." He paused. "All right. Sweet-talk her a lot. Tell her how pretty and special she is. Let her know how much I care about her."

He frowned, not sure he liked the feelings she stirred in him. "Independent, hardheaded, not a lick of sense…sweet, gentle and kind. Pretty, too." He sighed heavily and closed his eyes. "Nothin' but trouble."

Chapter Seven

On Sunday evening after the Driver brothers caught the train to El Paso, Lily and Matt moved into the upstairs rooms they had vacated. They only carried in some clothes and toiletries for the time being. It would take a while to sort through the boxes in the wagon for other things.

It hadn't taken long for Lily to learn what chores Mrs. Franklin expected her to do—take care of Ransom, keep the parlor and dining room clean and tidy, and help with the cooking and dishes as she had time. She tried to stay busy during the day and not dwell on her father's death, but she wasn't always successful. At night, she didn't even try to hold back the tears.

Since nights were the worst, she worried about Matt because he was still sleeping in Ransom's room. At least now her brother had a place where he could go during the day if he needed to be alone. A few times they had gone out on the back porch by themselves in the evening where they talked and cried together. He said he was doing all right, that building a new shed for Mrs. Franklin helped work off some of his anger.

She decided if she were the one pounding the nails it might have helped, too. Especially if she pictured Price's face with every smash of the hammer.

On Monday morning, a Mr. Griggs came by to see Ransom. They talked in his room for a few minutes. When he left, Ransom called her.

"Yes?" She walked over to the side of the bed.

"Sit down for a minute." Ransom nodded toward the rocking chair.

"All right, but I can't stay long. I have a cake in the oven." Lily sat down and looked expectantly at Ransom.

"Do you know who Griggs is?"

"No."

"He's the undertaker. I asked him to go with Quint last week and see if he could bring your father's body back here for burial."

Lily's heart started pounding and her mouth went dry. "Did he?"

"Yes. He's in a coffin at the undertaker's. Griggs said Reverend Brownfield could hold the service this afternoon if you want. Under the circumstances, he recommended against trying to ship your father's body back to Iowa."

"He hadn't expected to be buried next to Mama if we stayed here." He would have wanted a proper funeral with something spoken by a minister, not the sobbing jumble of grief and anger and snippets of Scripture from her and Matt.

Tears filled Lily's eyes, and she covered her face with her hands. Leaning forward until her forehead rested on the mattress, she wept. She felt Ransom's gentle hand stroking her hair. He didn't say a word until she brought her tears under control and straightened, looking at him.

His expression was as gentle as his touch had been. "I thought it might help to have him here, not all alone out on the prairie."

"It does. Thank you."

"You're welcome. At least I've done something."

She reached for his hand and brought it to her face, touching her cheek against his knuckles. "I can't tell you how much it means to us." It meant even more because he had still been angry at them when he sent the undertaker with Quint. She lowered their hands, still clasped, to the bed. "You have no idea how you've helped us, not merely with this but with your forgiveness, words of wisdom and comfort."

"Have to do something to make up for the times I'm ornery."

Lily laughed and released his hand. "Right now you're running even."

One corner of his mouth lifted in a lopsided smile. "Guess it could be worse."

"Definitely." She smoothed out a wrinkle at the edge of the sheet and stood. "I'd better get that cake out of the oven."

He tipped his head up and sniffed. "So far, so good. Doesn't smell burned. Spice cake?"

"Yes. My mother's special recipe."

"If it's as good as it smells, save me half of it."

"I'll see what I can do." With a smile, she left him to rest. Her smile faded when she reached the hallway and went in search of Matt.

The graveside funeral for their father was a simple one, but Lily thought he would have been satisfied. Mrs. Franklin and all her boarders—except for the sheriff and deputy—attended, a thoughtfulness that deeply touched both Lily and Matt. She was surprised by Ty McKinnon's presence, but perhaps in his position as mayor, he felt it his duty to attend funerals. Reverend Brownfield was kind and sympathetic, a good choice for the task. He asked Lily a few questions about her father beforehand so the thoughts he shared were appropriate.

At least she assumed they were. Fighting a dual battle against grief and rage at her father's senseless death, she only heard portions of the reverend's words. When the final prayer was over and she tossed a handful of dirt onto the pine coffin, she did so with a silent promise. *A life for a life. The man who killed you will pay, Papa.*

During the rest of the week, Ransom got out of his room for a while every day. Sometimes he sat on the porch, sometimes in the parlor. He still wasn't up to joining them at mealtime. Sitting in a chair and then trying to move up to the table was impossible, even with someone else pushing it. They tried it one day at dinner, and he turned white from the pain.

Ty and Cade McKinnon came by every day to see
how he was and to fill him in on what was happening
around the town and county. The brothers were taking
care of the law enforcement while Deputy Webb was
out of town. Ty told her that there wasn't much happening at the moment. Most of the cowboys had gone
out west toward the Pecos River to round up the cattle
that had wandered during the winter storms.

Ransom had so many visitors that Lily didn't see
him as much as she had the first few days. She tried to
guard his rest but wasn't always successful. Not only
was he very well-liked, people respected him, too. They
often stopped by for his opinion on something as well
as to see how he was faring. Lawyers came by to ask
questions on cases and citizens stopped by to consult
on petty annoyances. One day the district judge, attor-
neys, an accused horse thief *and* the jury marched into
his room to hear the sheriff's testimony.

The week drifted by with no repeat of the tender moments Lily had experienced with Ransom. He wasn't
unkind or distant, just either occupied or sleeping. She
concluded that it was probably for the best, though at
times she desperately needed his understanding and
comfort.

She waited impatiently for Deputy Webb to come
back, hoping that his long absence meant he was on the
killer's trail. He finally returned late in the night on Saturday, over a week after he left. His room was on the
first floor, along with Ransom's and Mrs. Franklin's.
It was right below Lily's, so she'd noticed when he
came in and turned on his lamp.

The next morning Mrs. Franklin and a few of the

tenants went to church, but Lily stayed behind to take
care of Ransom. It was a good excuse. She didn't know
if she could ever enter a house of God again. Why
should she bother? God didn't care about her or Matt.
He had taken the two people they loved most in the
world.

Yet when she heard the faint melody of a hymn
drifting on the wind, her heart ached even more. Losing the faith that had sustained her most of her life left
her empty and dejected. Matt busied himself with rearranging what was left in their wagon. If he missed at-
tending church, he didn't show it.

Other than breakfast, Mrs. Franklin didn't cook on
Sundays. The boarders usually ate at one of the local
restaurants with friends or sometimes fixed themselves
a sandwich or cheese and crackers.

Lily finished organizing the things in her room, then
thumbed through Mrs. Franklin's magazines. By midmorning, she was ready to go pound on the deputy's
door. He saved her the trouble by wandering into the
kitchen a few minutes after ten. "Good morning, Miss
Lily. Is there any coffee left?"

Lily nodded, motioning toward the stove. "Some
biscuits and fried salt pork, too. I kept them warm for
you."

"Much obliged."

He poured himself a cup of coffee while Lily took
the plate of biscuits and meat from the warming oven
and set it on the kitchen table. She'd left his place setting and the jars of jam on the table after everyone else
finished breakfast. He sat down as she headed for the
icebox to retrieve the butter. When she turned back to-

ward the table, she was surprised to see him bow his head in silent prayer. She paused until he looked up and reached for a biscuit.

Giving him the crock of butter, Lily went back to the stove and poured herself a half cup of coffee. She didn't really want it, but she needed something in her hands. She sat down across from him. "Did you find anything?"

"Not much at the campsite." He buttered a biscuit. "I followed their trail for a while. They went west and camped about five miles from where y'all were. They split up there. One came this way and the other went north. I followed him up the Caprock into the Panhandle until a thunderstorm washed away the tracks. I checked with the ranchers in the area, but nobody had seen him. The ranches are spread way out up that way. He may have headed to Mobeetie or Tascosa." He took a bite of biscuit and chewed it, his expression thoughtful.

"Could have gone up into Indian Territory or New Mexico. I'm bettin' on New Mexico. It's easier for a man to hide out there."

"Smith was heading west when Matt saw him leave town."

"He wasn't seen in Big Spring or Midland. I wired the sheriffs. He could have gone just about any direction once he got away from Willow Grove and people." The deputy forked a bite of salt pork. "No way to know except to check with the law around the state, which I've pretty much done already, and try to cover the territory and talk to the ranchers, see if I can track them down."

"Which you can't do with the sheriff laid up."

Webb met her gaze. "No, ma'am. I can't. As much as I want to find your father's killers, my first obligation is to keep the law here in the county and Willow Grove. That's what I'm paid for. We don't even have a town marshal at the moment." He shook his head. "Can't seem to keep them. I'm sorry. I wish I could do more."

Lily sighed and stood, dumping her coffee in the slop bucket. "I understand. I only have myself to blame, Deputy Webb. If we'd gone to the sheriff directly, Smith would be in jail and you might know where Price went. And Ransom would never have been hurt." She set the cup on the counter and gripped the edge of the cabinet, leaning against it. "How could I have been so stupid?" she whispered, sick with despair.

"Folks don't always think straight when they're grieving, especially after what you went through. We won't give up. I just can't go looking for them right now." He took a sip of coffee. "How is Ransom?"

Lily returned to the table and sat down. She'd prefer puttering around the kitchen but that didn't seem polite. "Still in a lot of pain, but better than when you left. He's walking some with a cane and someone to help."

"That's good to hear. I wasn't sure he'd ever be able to take a step."

"It's slow and painful. He can't go far. But he sits on the porch or in the parlor some during the day. He has a lot of company. Too much, I think. Ransom says it keeps his mind off how much he hurts, so I don't shoo them away too often. He was napping when I peeked in on him half an hour ago."

Webb smiled, mischief lighting his hazel eyes. "Ransom, is it?"

Lily felt her cheeks grow warm. "I call him Sheriff Starr sometimes."

The deputy chuckled. "When he's being a pain in the neck? I expect he prefers his Christian name. For that matter, I'd be more comfortable if you called me Quint. Just about everybody else does. Even after a year as deputy, I'm not used to Mr. Webb or even Deputy Webb."

"From what I hear, you earned their respect even before you took the job. Mrs. Franklin said they probably never would have caught those cattle rustlers if you hadn't joined the gang and led the law to them."

He shrugged and buttered the last biscuit. "They would have been caught eventually, at least some of them. The ringleaders might have gotten away, though. Nobody suspected that a lawyer and his assistant were actually in charge of the outfit. I sure didn't have any idea they were involved until I was right in the thick of it." He slathered some peach jam on the biscuit. "I don't ever want to do that kind of thing again. Took me weeks back out at the ranch to get to where I slept soundly again."

"So you didn't become the deputy sheriff right away?" Lily tried to remember if Mrs. Franklin had mentioned that. She didn't think so. But her mind wandered often and she missed some of the conversation.

"Nope. I went back to work at McKinnon Ranch. Been with Cade a long time." He suddenly grinned. "Now he's my brother-in-law, so reckon I'm stuck with him whether or not I'm at the ranch."

"He seems like a nice man." She based her opinion on the way he treated Ransom and the praise she'd heard from others about him and his brother.

"As good as they come. Him and Ty both. I couldn't ask for a better man for Jessie. Her first husband was mean and worthless, so I'm mighty thankful she and Cade got hitched. Have you met my sister?"

"No. I've been staying here most of the time in case the sheriff needs something, but when she came by I had gone to the store for Mrs. Franklin."

"They have a new baby boy, barely a month old. That's another reason Cade's staying in town instead of out at the ranch. With their other kids, Brad and Ellie, in school, Jessie needs to be in Willow Grove. I'm anxious to get over there today and see little Jacob. He's probably grown a foot."

Lily smiled at his obvious affection. "I doubt quite that much. But babies do change quickly."

"You an expert on children, Miss Lily?"

"Not at all, but I have been around a few," she said dryly.

He grinned and pushed back from the table. "Me, too. I'll go peek in on Ransom. See if he's awake."

Evidently he was, since Quint disappeared into Ransom's bedroom and stayed for over an hour. When he left, he headed directly to the sheriff's office.

Ransom's door was slightly ajar. Lily knocked quietly.

"Come in, Lily."

She pushed open the door and walked in. "How did you know it was me?"

He leaned his head against the back of the rocking

chair and smiled. "I recognized the sound of your footsteps. A light *tap-tap-tap*. I've gotten pretty good at fig-
uring out who's coming to the door, if they're regular
visitors. Couldn't do it if the floor was carpeted instead
of wood. Mrs. Franklin's legs are longer, so her steps
are longer, not quite as light as yours. Men's shoes
sound different than boots, so I can usually tell when
it's Ed or the doctor. Matt's work boots have a different sound than cowboy boots. Cade weighs more, so
his steps are heavier. Ty's steps are farther apart than
Quint's. And so on."

"Is that a trick you learned as a detective?"

"Learned it with the Rangers. Perfected it as a detective. Spent time hiding in the shadows in both jobs."
His expression grew somber with a hint of compassion.
"I wish Quint had been able to find them. I hope you
understand why he came back."

"I do." She didn't like it, but she couldn't blame the
deputy. "Do you think a detective could find them? We
have some money in the bank in Des Moines. Papa was
going to have it sent to him when he was ready to order
goods for the store."

"He could try, but you might spend all the money
and still not catch them. Quint is sending a telegram to
an artist in Fort Worth this morning. I've asked him to
come out here right away. If he can draw a good enough
likeness of Price and Smith from your description,
we'll have wanted posters printed up. We'll send them
out across Texas and some other states. Then we'd have
more than one person looking for them."

"All right. I'll pay him."

"No need. Your father was killed in my jurisdiction.

I don't think I'll have any trouble convincing the county commissioners to foot the bill." He glanced toward the doorway. "Speaking of commissioners, I think I hear one of them now."

A second later, Cade McKinnon walked into the room with a grin. "Nothing wrong with your ears. Or mine. What are we going to pay for?" When Ransom explained about the artist and wanted posters, Cade nodded. "Can you give him a good description, Miss Lily?"

"I think so. I'll remember their faces for as long as I live. Especially Price."

"Then we'll take care of it." Cade turned his attention to Ransom. "You need to get out of the house. You feel like goin' over to our place for dinner?"

"You carrying me piggyback?"

"Nope. Got the buggy. I'll drive around back so you won't have to walk too far." Cade looked at Lily. "I promise we'll go slow, and I'll do my best not to jostle him around. We'd also like for you and your brother to come, too. Jessie was already setting places for you at the table when I left. It's only about five blocks but if you don't want to walk, I can come back for you."

"We don't mind walking, but we don't want to be an imposition." She glanced at his Sunday suit, then down at her striped green two-piece everyday dress. "I'm not dressed to go to Sunday dinner."

"You don't need to be. I took Brad and Ellie to church, but I won't stay all gussied up long. We aren't fancy folks, ma'am. Jessie will be real disappointed if you don't come. You can keep an eye on Ransom. I figure you can tell us when he needs to come back."

"I can tell you myself," said Ransom.

"Yeah, but you might not." Cade looked at Lily. "He's a stubborn cuss."

"So I've noticed." She smiled at Ransom's indignant frown. "Matt and I will be happy to join you and your family for dinner, Mr. McKinnon. It will be nice to meet them. Besides, I don't want to miss the chance to order Sheriff Starr around."

"Haven't missed an opportunity yet," grumbled Ransom. The sparkle in his eyes belied his attempted gruffness. "Fetch my slippers, Nurse Lily."

"I'm not a dog, Sheriff." Lily scooted his slippers over with her foot. She knew he could slide his feet into them without help.

"You growl a lot." He grabbed her hand, keeping her by his side as he put on the shoes.

"Only when provoked. I don't know if he's up to polite company, Mr. McKinnon. He's cantankerous today."

"The name's Cade. And he's just gettin' back to normal." Cade grinned and started toward the door. "I'll bring the buggy around."

When he left the room, Lily glanced down at Ransom. How could a man look so handsome in a plain white shirt tucked into dark pants?

"Do I look presentable?" she asked. "I've heard that the McKinnon wives are fashion plates." And beautiful. But she didn't want him making any comparisons there.

"You look mighty fine to me, sugar." His teasing smile vanished, and she couldn't quiet read his expression. It held a trace of tenderness and something else…irritation? "But then you always do."

Her heartbeat did a little flip-flop, even as she silently chided herself against reading too much into his comment. "You sound like that annoys you. Maybe I should rub bear grease into my hair and wear the same clothes for a month."

"And smoke a corncob pipe while you're at it. That might take care of the problem." He picked up his cane and stood with a grimace.

She slid her arm around his waist as he settled his free arm across her shoulders. They'd done it so many times the last week that their movements were almost automatic. "What problem?"

They took a few steps before he answered, his voice quiet and deeper than normal. "How attracted I am to you."

She caught her breath but somehow kept moving, afraid that if she stopped suddenly, she'd cause him to trip. "You've just been stuck here for too long. Pretty soon, Mrs. Franklin will start looking good to you."

He gently squeezed her shoulder. "She's a handsome woman, but I don't daydream about kissing her."

Lily gulped, hoping and praying—no, not praying, she didn't believe in that anymore—hoping that he didn't realize she'd had the same daydreams. "Cade's right. You need some time away from here and to see other people."

"Been seeing other people all week. After I sorted out their various problems and they left, my thoughts went back to you." He stood still, leaning on the cane, waiting until she looked up at him. "I will kiss you, Lily," he said softly. The creak of Cade's buggy briefly drew his attention out the back window before he met

her gaze again. "Not right now. Maybe not even tomorrow. But one of these days…"

Caught up in the conversations and laughter of the
McKinnon family, Lily tucked Ransom's words into a
corner of her mind. She hardly thought of them at all
except when his gaze met hers, which happened far too
often for comfort.

The McKinnons were a loving family, and they extended that affection to Ransom. Cade and Jessie's
children treated him like a favorite uncle. Brad gave
him a detailed account of helping his father round up
some wayward cows. Ransom responded with appropriate comments and real interest.

When Ellie stood beside his chair, propped her book
on the chair arm and proudly read him a story from
McGuffey's First Eclectic Reader, he listened with total
attention. Stumbling over a word, she turned the book
so he could read it, and he helped her pronounce "might."

She frowned and turned the book back around. "It
looks funny. How come it's spelled that way?"

"Somebody decided that a long time ago, sweetie.
Reckon that's the way with most words."

Ellie shifted, turning so he could read with her. He
put his arm around her. As she read, he glanced up,
looking across the room at Lily and smiled.

Her heart did that silly flip-flop again.

Jessie sat down beside her, baby Jacob in her arms.
"Ransom will make a good father. Our kids adore him."

Lily hid a smile. Did all of Ransom's female friends
want to play matchmaker? "The feeling obviously goes
both ways. You have delightful children."

"Thank you. We think so, too. Though they can be a handful, especially Ellie. That child has a mind of her own." She shifted the baby, letting his bottom rest on her lap. "How is Ransom doing?" she asked quietly.

"Improving. Though it's slower than he'd like, he's walking better today and a little stronger. He didn't seem any worse for the ride over here. Perhaps that will encourage him to get out a bit."

"Walking is painful for him."

"Yes. Sometimes so is sitting, standing, or lying in bed." Lily sighed, guilt suddenly a heavy burden again. "At least he's not in constant agony." Now.

"Cade says he looks much better than when it first happened. I wasn't up to visiting him then. I was sorry we missed you when Camille and I stopped by to see him last week. Mrs. Franklin said she had sent you to the store."

"Yes." Lily adjusted her skirt in the chair. "Sometimes I think she forgets things on purpose when she shops so she'll have an excuse to send me after it."

"Her way of encouraging *you* to get out a bit," said Jessie. "This must be a hard time for you."

"It is," Lily admitted. "But it would be worse if I didn't have anything to do."

"Ransom keeps you hopping?" Jessie lifted Jacob to her shoulder, patting him on the back.

"Not too much, now. He even moved around his room a little without help yesterday. This morning, Matt said he got out of bed by himself."

"Most of the time he wants you right there beside him so he can lean on you," said Jessie. The baby burped, then snuggled against her shoulder.

"He won't let me bear any of his weight, unless he's

really tired. Most of the time he just needs someone to steady him."

A knowing smile touched Jessie's face. "I expect he'll keep that up as long as possible. It's a good excuse for him to put his arm around you."

Remembering Ransom's comment that morning, Lily blushed.

"Oh, dear, I didn't mean to embarrass you. It's just so good to see him interested in someone."

"I'm afraid you're reading too much into the situation. I'm only taking care of him for a while, until he doesn't need me anymore."

Jessie laughed softly. "Lily, I'm not sure that time will ever come. Ransom is a charmer and could have his pick of any eligible woman in town. I've never seen him look at anyone the way he looks at you. I think he's smitten. He's a fine man."

"I'm sure he is. But I'm not looking for a husband." Not yet.

"Neither was I, but one found me anyway. The same thing happened to Camille. Texans can be very persuasive."

"I'm sorry Ty and Camille couldn't be here today. I wanted to meet her, too."

"She's expecting a baby. Ty lost his first wife and baby in childbirth, and the poor man gets more nervous every day. He thought she seemed a little tired this morning so insisted she stay home and rest. We'll try to drop by to see you one day this week. She's anxious to meet you, too." Jessie moved the baby to her other shoulder. "Would you like to hold Jacob? He doesn't have a problem going to strangers."

"I'd love to." Lily carefully took the baby, cradling him in the crook of her arm, smiling as he grabbed hold of her finger. She cooed at him for a minute, until she felt Ransom's gaze. When she looked up, the tenderness in his eyes took her breath away.

Chapter Eight

The next afternoon, Ransom sat on the front porch eyeing the new jail and sheriff's office a block down the street, wondering if he could make the walk. He'd never been a coward. Never backed down from anything. Until now. He didn't have the guts to risk falling down in front of the whole town. When he spotted Quint heading in his direction, he made up his mind. "Matt, would you bring me my badge and boots, please?"

Matt stopped chopping weeds in the front yard and leaned the hoe against the porch. "You goin' somewhere, Sheriff?"

"Down to see my new office." To see if he had any right to call it his office.

Quint arrived just as Matt came out the front door with Ransom's boots. "I heard back from Burns in Fort Worth. He'll be in on tomorrow's train."

"Good. We need to get those wanted posters out pronto." Gritting his teeth, Ransom leaned forward. Holding the top of the boot, he raised his leg and pushed his foot into it. Breathing hard, he leaned against the back of the chair, hoping the pain would settle down. It took a few minutes, but it did ease up. He put on the other boot and leaned back in the chair to rest.

Quint had watched him without saying a word. "The office is ready for us to move in."

"Figured it might be. I thought I'd mosey over there and see how it looks. Do you have somebody lined up to move the furniture?"

"Yep. Sam and Joe Kit are loadin' up their freight wagon right now. It'll take me a few minutes to get a buggy."

"I aim to walk over there." Ransom looked at Matt when the younger man took the badge from his pocket and handed it to him. "I should have asked for my hat, too."

"I'll get it." The young man hurried back into the house.

His expression skeptical, Quint took off his hat and smoothed his hair before putting it back on. "Are you sure about this?"

"Nope." Ransom pinned the star on his shirt. "That's why you're going to walk with me and keep me from making a fool of myself. Help me down the steps, then be ready to catch me if I trip or my legs buckle."

Matt came back out, letting the screen door slam shut behind him. "Here you are, Sheriff Starr. You want me to walk with you?"

"No, thanks. Quint's going to play nursemaid." He tried to keep his tone light but didn't quite make it. After settling the hat on his head, he pushed himself up to stand, leaning on the cane. Interestingly, he felt more solid with his boots on.

Quint peered around him and looked through the parlor window. "What does Lily say about this?"

"She's not my keeper," snapped Ransom. Though he expected she'd put in her two cents' worth if she saw him hobbling down the street. "She's upstairs changing sheets. Let's hightail it before she gets wind of this."

Quint quickly moved to Ransom's side.

"Just let me hang on to your arm, support a little of my weight and catch me if I get off balance."

With Quint's help, the trip down the stairs wasn't quite as hard or as painful as Ransom expected. Still, by the time he made it down all four steps to the street, he'd broken out in a sweat. He glanced at Quint. "Give me a minute."

"We got all the time you need." Quint looked over his shoulder. "Matt, go on ahead and borrow a chair from the county clerk's office in the courthouse. I saw them moving some furniture in there a while ago."

"Yes, sir."

Ransom made a face as he watched Matt hustle across the street. "I didn't think about there not being anything to sit on."

"This way you can supervise the moving, tell us where you want everything."

"Not much to tell. Put the desk here and a couple of extra chairs over there." Ransom started across the street, and Quint fell step in beside him. *He could crawl faster than I can walk,* thought Ransom.

Carefully watching where he put his feet, he crossed the dusty street without any major trouble. By the time they reached the boardwalk on the other side, folks were popping out of the stores up and down the street, pointing at him and scurrying in their direction.

"Folks sure are easily amused around here," he muttered, wishing nobody had noticed them until he was up on the sidewalk. "Don't know why they think they have to hurry. I'm not going anywhere fast."

"How you doin'?" Quint scanned the gathering crowd. "You want me to scatter them?"

Ransom shook his head. "That'd cause more talk." He took a deep breath and paused, waiting for the pain to settle down. *Please, Lord, help me into the office without making a fool of myself.* Then he could collapse without anybody noticing.

"Good to see you, Sheriff Starr."

"Afternoon, Sheriff. Good to see you walking again."

Ransom nodded and spoke to several people as they called out greetings and encouragement. Most of them meant well, though he figured some were there out of curiosity. "Quint, you'd better help me."

Quint gripped his forearm with both hands, allowing him to lean heavily on him as he struggled up the steps. Ransom was grateful his friend understood that he needed more than just a steadying hand.

Once he was on the boardwalk, he paused again, turning around and leaned against the side of the building. "Little different view from over here." He glanced back at the boarding house and saw Lily standing in an upstairs window. He hoped she was cheering him on, not chewing him out. "Thanks for the welcome. Y'all can go on about your business."

The crowd slowly dispersed with a mix of good wishes and a few muttered complaints that he was still ordering them around.

Matt had a chair waiting in the office. As soon as they were inside, Quint shut the door, and Ransom dropped into the chair with a groan.

"You made it." Quint grinned at him.

"Yeah, I did." Ransom was surprised by a sudden swell of emotion. *Thank You, Lord.* Maybe he wasn't doomed to life as a cripple. *Don't get your hopes up*, caution warned. *It was only one block.* But that was a lot farther than from the bedroom to the front porch.

He looked around the room, which was larger than the old one. A potbellied stove stood in one corner, and someone had already hung a hook and the keys by the calaboose door. Through the open doorway, he noted that the cells finally had locks on them.

Ransom pointed to the wall across from him. "Put the desk over there. That will give us a good view of the street on one side and the jailhouse on the other."

"That's what I'd figured," said Quint. "It's gettin' warm in here. Do you mind if we open the windows and front door?"

"Go ahead. I don't feel like I might keel over now."

Matt opened the alley window, and Quint opened the two facing the street as well as the door. All the windows had bars on them for added protection. They'd never had a jailbreak, but it didn't hurt to discourage the idea. A nice breeze flowed through the room. "I think this office is going to work out just fine. Won't be nearly as hot as the old one."

"Maybe the prisoners won't gripe as much," added Quint.

"Not about the heat, anyway." Ransom smiled, glad to be back where he belonged. Even if he couldn't haul anyone into jail, he could keep an eye on the prisoners—when they had any.

He made a couple of suggestions about where to put the gun cabinet, coatrack and bookcase. "Think that will work, Matt?"

"Yes, sir. I reckon I should get back to work." He didn't appear too excited about the prospect.

"I'd appreciate it if you'd stay around here in case Quint has to leave. Don't want to get stranded. Of course, if you're anxious to go chop weeds…"

Matt grinned. "They won't go anywhere." He stuck his head through the jail doorway, looking at the cells. "Do you ever put any real outlaws in there?"

"We've had a couple of horse thieves and a few cattle rustlers. One man accused of murder, but he wasn't convicted. Mostly, we deal with drunks and petty thieves."

Quint leaned against the wall by the front door and crossed his arms. "It was rougher around here before Ransom became sheriff last year. Had plenty of mean characters riding through, but the country is getting more settled. In another few years, it will be downright tame."

"There will always be men—and sometimes women—who'd rather steal than earn an honest living," said Ransom. "Always a hothead who thinks the way to settle an argument is with a gun. That happens in big cities and small towns."

"Or out in the middle of nowhere," said Matt quietly. "Do you really think you'll find the men who killed my father?"

"Yes, I do, but there's no telling how long it will take. If Lily can give us good descriptions, we'll send wanted posters out all across the country. It's as much to protect other people as to try to catch them. If that doesn't turn up anything, we'll just have to bide our time. Men like that don't change their ways. They'll commit another crime, probably sooner than later. I don't like it, but sometimes that's the way criminals get caught."

"I can help with Smith's description. I watched him most of the night he was playing cards." Matt looked at Ransom and shook his head. "We sure made a mess of things that night."

"Everybody makes mistakes, son." Ransom stood, leaning heavily on the cane. "I think we need to move outside and see what's going on in the big city. Would you take the chair out front for me?"

Matt nodded and carried the chair outside, setting it in front of a window, well out of the way of the door. When Ransom was settled, Matt sat down on the sidewalk and leaned back again the building. "It's a lot quieter around here than the first few days we were in town."

"Wait until the cowboys get back from roundup. It'll be about three weeks before they're done, but they'll be bustin' at the seams to let loose and have a good time." Ransom fervently hoped he'd be back to normal by then, or at least well enough to help Quint keep them under control.

The Kits arrived with the furniture. They parked the wagon and started unloading. Quint showed them where to put things, then grabbed a chair and joined Ransom and Matt on the sidewalk.

After about an hour, Ransom decided that everybody who had missed his grand walk had managed to come by and say hello. The stores were doing a good business. Matt did his part by going over to McKinnon Brothers for some taffy.

Ransom saw Prissy Clark coming their way and glanced at Quint. His deputy had never said anything specifically, but Ransom had a feeling Quint was sweet on her. He thought his friend could do better, but he'd learned in the last few weeks that a man didn't always choose who caught his eye.

When Quint noticed her, he straightened in his chair. A minute later, he casually stood up and walked into the office to see how the movers were doing.

Prissy stopped and gave Ransom a smile, though it wasn't her usual flirtatious one. He thought she looked a little tired.

"Why, Sheriff Starr, how nice to see you here. You must be feeling much better."

"I'm making progress."

Quint stepped out of the office. "Good morning, Miss Priscilla." As far as Ransom knew, Quint was the only person in town who called Prissy by her full name.

"Good morning, Deputy Webb." Her smile for Quint was warmer. It struck Ransom that it was the most sincere smile he had ever seen her give anyone.

"Are you feeling all right?" Quint took a step closer. "You look a little pale."

"It's just a headache," she said. "But Mama needs a few groceries."

"So she sent you after them." Quint frowned as if he'd like to tell her mother a thing or two.

"Have to keep Mama happy. I'd better get going."

"I could come along and carry them home for you," said Quint.

Ransom nonchalantly looked down the street, trying hard to pretend he wasn't hearing every word.

"That's kind of you, but no thanks." Prissy sighed, drawing Ransom's gaze. Sadness drifted across her face, then she resolutely squared her shoulders. "Baron Millborn might see us, and I mustn't do anything to put him off. He's been calling on me, and Mama is set on us getting married."

"And you have to keep Mama happy," Quint said angrily.

"Yes, I do, Quint," she said softly. "I'm sorry."

He stepped out of her way. "Then you'd better ask Millborn's servant to carry your groceries because his high-and-mighty lordship won't stoop that low."

She winced, then lifted her chin and walked away without looking at him.

Quint sat down, slumping in his chair. "I give up. Until Millborn came along, she was sweet and friendly. Now, I'm not good enough for her."

"You aren't rich or an English lord." Ransom glanced at Quint. "I got the impression this is more her mama's doing than what Prissy wants."

Quint shrugged. "She's always set her sights on

wealthy men. A couple of big ranchers and then Ty before Camille came to town."

Ransom chuckled. "She must have thought I had a lot more money than I do."

"She probably figured you'd go places bigger than Willow Grove. Maybe this time, she'll catch her man. Millborn bothers me. It's not just because he is part of a ranching syndicate, or that he's English and thinks he's better than everybody else. My gut tells me not to trust him. I think he can look you straight in the eye and lie through his teeth."

"You believe he's lying to Prissy."

"I hope I'm wrong."

"I hope so, too, for her sake. She can be nice when she wants to be. You'd think by now she'd figure out that chasing a man is likely to stampede him." Ransom considered the situation for a minute. "Maybe she knows it, but her mother's pushing her."

"Her mother has high ambitions. There's no love lost between them. I don't know why Prissy puts up with her."

"Could be that she likes having a roof over her head."

"She could have moved out plenty of times. Three or four years ago, any number of men would have gladly asked her to marry them. More than a few did, but she was always after someone with money."

Ransom didn't mention that she'd ruined her reputation in the process. Ty had warned him about Priscilla his first week in town, said she had actually crawled through his bedroom window one night in her nightgown. Ty wasn't one to spread gossip, but it had been obvious that Prissy had set her cap for the new sheriff. He told Ransom that the only other person who knew about it was Camille. Even if Quint wasn't aware of that particular incident, there were other stories about Prissy, enough to make most men shy away from her. Or at least any kind of commitment with her.

"What about Mrs. Grissom's niece, the one who's helping her at the dress shop? Have you met her?" Ransom stretched out his legs for a minute.

"The day you got hurt. Seems nice. I hear she already has a couple of gents calling on her."

"Maybe you should pay her a friendly visit, too."

Quint shook his head. "Not interested. She's cross-eyed."

Ransom stared at him, then laughed. "You're kidding."

"Yep. But she's shy. I like a woman who can carry on a conversation." Quint stood. "Let me know when you're ready to go back."

Ransom pulled his watch from his pocket and flipped it open. "Any time now. Dinner is in half an hour. It'll probably take me that long to walk over there."

"I'll see how the boys are doing with the furniture, then we can go." Quint moved toward the doorway but stopped when he saw Prissy coming back down the sidewalk, carrying a small bundle of groceries. Lord Millborn stepped out of the Senate Saloon, blocking her path. Muttering under his breath, Quint went on inside the office.

Ransom watched the meeting between the Englishman and the young woman. Given their rigid stances, it was not a pleasant exchange. Their discussion only lasted a few minutes. Millborn went back into the saloon, and Prissy continued on her way home. She walked past the sheriff's office without even looking in Ransom's direction.

He figured she wouldn't have seen him anyway. She was too busy trying to hold back tears.

Chapter Nine

"His nose was narrower." Lily studied the drawing Mr. Burns had made of Price from her description.

The artist erased the nose, redrawing it slightly narrower. "How's that?"

"That's better, but the eyes aren't quite right. They were colder, meaner."

"I'm not sure any drawing could depict that clearly, ma'am," Burns said kindly. He handed her the sketch pad. "Are they the right size and shape?"

Lily stared at for a minute, closed her eyes and again saw the scene slowly unfold in her mind—the men's confrontation with her father and the hard, calculated expression on Price's face when he pulled the trigger. She shivered and looked at the artist, handing the drawing back to him. "Yes. It's a very good likeness."

Ransom sat beside her on the small settee in Mrs.

Franklin's private sitting room where they wouldn't be disturbed. "Let Matt work with Burns for a while on Smith. Then you can add something if you need to."

Lily nodded, more shaken than she wanted to admit, yet satisfied that she was doing something to find her father's killers.

Burns turned to Matt. "Let's go sit on the back porch and work on it. It's a nice morning. I like to be outside whenever I can." Matt glanced at Lily, waiting for her nod of approval before he stood and walked out with the artist.

Lily suspected the man wanted to give her time to clear her head. She had finally accepted the fact that she could not search for them on her own. "If these posters provide any leads, I want to hire a detective."

"That would be the time to do it. If we come up with anything, I'll contact the company I used to work for. If all their men are on cases, I know of some others who are good." He reached for her hand, threading his fingers through hers. "How are you holding up?"

"Better now that Price's picture is done. Thinking about Smith doesn't bother me quite as much as him." She met his gaze. "I want to see them dead, Ransom. I know it's wrong, but I can't help it."

"That's understandable." He caressed the back of her hand with his thumb. "I hope, in time, you can put it aside. If you don't, it will turn you into a hard, bitter woman. You're too gentle and good to let that happen. From what you and Matt have told me about your father, he would want you to find peace."

"How can I when I have so much anger and pain inside?"

"Maybe you need to go out on the range and scream until you're hoarse."

"I did that before we came to Willow Grove."

"Didn't help?"

"Not much."

He looked down at their hands. "Praying might."

"Waste of time."

He looked up with a frown. "Do you truly believe that, Lily? Or do you say it because you're mad at God?"

"Yes, I'm mad at God."

"He didn't make Price shoot your father. He did that all on his own."

"And God let him die."

"Your father was shot in the heart, Lily. No one can live with that kind of wound."

"God should have saved him," she said stubbornly. "He could have jammed the gun or hit Price with a bolt of lightning. He should have done something!"

"God is the giver of life. Isn't He the one who determines when it ends? He's all knowing and all seeing. Isn't He always right?"

"What's right about taking my father?" She choked back a sob, determined not to cry in front of Ransom again.

"I don't know. We can't always make sense of things, but maybe we aren't supposed to. Sometimes we have to quit trying to understand why things happen and just accept that they do. We have to go on with our lives, Lily, and make them the best that we can." He gently lifted her chin until she reluctantly raised her eyes to look at him. "Holding on to your anger and hate isn't going to make for a very good life."

"I know." She turned her head away. "But it's where I am right now."

"I'm planning to go to church on Sunday, if I'm able. You should think about going, too. It might help."

"I'll think about it." She had no intention of setting foot in the church building, but she needed the conversation to end. "I think I'll go see how Burns and Matt are doing. You want to go outside?"

"I could use a little sunshine." It seemed to take more effort for him to stand. He swayed, almost losing his balance.

She slipped her arm around his waist to steady him. "Careful."

"Ah, that's better." He stood still for a minute, putting his arm around her shoulders and shifting until she was firmly against his side. "A man could get used to having you tucked in close like this, sugar."

"It could prove awkward when you're facing down an outlaw."

He grinned and took a step toward the door. "Afraid you might get hit?"

"Just wondering how you'd draw your pistol. I'd be in the way."

"I'd figure something out."

"Don't you have to go into saloons sometimes?"

"Every so often to bust up a fight or something." He waited while she gave the screen door a shove.

"So it wouldn't work. A lady can't go into saloons."

He walked outside, shaking his head. "That's a fact. Guess I'll have to handle things on my own once I'm all healed up."

Please, God, let that happen. Let him heal.

Lily mentally groaned. She'd just prayed, and she meant it with all her heart.

The wanted posters were printed up right away, and Lily spent two days addressing envelopes. They sent them to every county sheriff in Texas, plus the Texas Ranger headquarters in Austin and lawmen in New Mexico, Oklahoma and Colorado and a few in states to the east.

Ransom went to the office three times that week but didn't feel good enough to go to church. He rested all weekend, sleeping much of the time. On Monday, he spent a good portion of the day at the office, telling Lily that he napped in an empty jail cell since there was no one there to disturb him. After that, he went to the office every day, sometimes staying several hours, sometimes coming home after an hour or so. He was slowly improving, but by Saturday, he was tired and decided to stay in bed.

Jessie and Camille came calling that morning. Lily opened the front door, inviting them in with a smile. Mrs. Franklin had told her that Ty's wife was lovely, but Lily instantly decided that was an understatement. Even several months pregnant, Camille was the most beautiful woman Lily had ever seen.

Jessie made the introductions, then glanced down the hallway. "I noticed he wasn't in the office. How is he?"

"Generally, he's better. He's getting in and out of bed by himself, and last night, he insisted that Matt sleep in his own room. But he was too ambitious yesterday and walked too much, I think," Lily said quietly. "He was hurting worse earlier, but he only admitted to being tired. He's sleeping now."

"Then we'll visit with you and let Ransom rest. If it's convenient for you," said Camille.

"The stew is cooking, so I have about an hour before I need to start on the rest of dinner." Lily pointed toward the parlor. "Let's go in here. I'm afraid you missed Mrs. Franklin. She's gone calling this morning, too. Would you like some tea or coffee?"

"No, thanks." Jessie looked at Camille who nodded in agreement. "We're meeting our husbands for an early dinner at Talbot's Restaurant."

Lily turned to Camille. "I've been enjoying your articles in the *Gazette*. Your attempt at making a pie was delightful."

Camille laughed, glancing at her sister-in-law. "Jessie can vouch that every word of it was true. Thankfully, Ty knew before we married that I couldn't cook. I enjoy writing about everyday things that are amusing."

"Such as the great pig fracas," said Jessie. "Ransom wound up involved in that one. There was a man on the outskirts of town who let his pigs run free. He ignored the citations and fines imposed by the town marshal. Then the marshal decided he didn't like the job and quit."

Camille pursed her lips and shook her head. "We've had three marshals since I've been here. One of them was good, but he and his family decided to move back east. The others took the job because they wanted to feel important and the pay is decent. They're supposed to handle the minor things and leave keeping the peace up to Ransom and Quint."

"Which is what the pig situation became because the marshal wouldn't haul his friend off to jail. The neighbors got tired of the pigs ruining their gardens and yards and went after the culprit with shotguns."

"Oh, my! What did Ransom do?"

"He arrested the man and threw him in jail before his neighbors filled him full of buckshot. He still wouldn't pay the fines or promise to pen up his animals. So Ransom and Quint set out to round up the pigs." Jessie's eyes danced with merriment. "Which was a sight to behold."

"Even funnier when Ty and Cade got involved." Camille absently rested her hand on her stomach, and Lily wondered if the baby could feel its mother's touch. "We had pigs—and men—running all over town. The pigs squealing, the men shouting, all of them covered in mud. We'd had two inches of rain the night before."

Lily joined in the laughter, picturing the rambunctious scene. "I don't suppose pigs herd like cattle."

"Not even close. It's not easy to rope a pig, especially a little one," said Jessie.

"They succeeded a few times with the sows," added Camille. "Mainly they had to resort to catching them by hand…over and over again. The pigs were so slick with mud that they couldn't hang on. They ran down Main Street and along the sidewalk. One even dashed into the grocery store."

"Oh, no! What did he do when he saw all that food?"

"Stopped to eat. He spotted a big basket of apples and dove right into it. The grocer dragged him out with an apple in his mouth."

"And threatened to have roasted pig, apple and all, like the people do in the Hawaiian Islands." Jessie grinned at Camille. "There had been an article in the *Gazette* the week before about the islands."

"Timely. I don't think it would be easy to hang onto a pig even if it wasn't muddy." Lily laughed so hard that her eyes watered. "Obviously, they finally caught them?"

"Half that day. They penned them up and waited a few days until the mud dried before they went after the others. The owner still refused to pay the fines, said he hadn't voted for the mayor or city council so they didn't have any authority over him and his property."

"But he lived within the city limits?" asked Lily.

"Yes. So the judge gave him a stern lecture on the law and our rights and obligations as citizens. Then he ordered Ransom to sell the pigs, withhold the amount of the fines and give the rest to the owner."

"That was that? Did the owner buy any more pigs?"

"We don't know," said Jessie. "He packed up and moved to Abilene after he spent two weeks in jail."

Lily wiped her eyes, her smile slowly fading. It had been good to laugh, to feel lighthearted for a few minutes. "You write serious things well, too. I appreciate the obituary for my father and the article you wrote about his murder."

Camille's expression grew somber, sympathy softening her eyes. "Quint gave me the information. I didn't want to trouble you at such a painful time."

"I sent a copy to the newspaper in Des Moines so Papa's acquaintances would know what happened." Lily had written to his close friends first, but it was a simple way of letting others know, and a relief that she didn't have to compose something herself.

"Neither Quint nor Ransom thought it wise to tell people that you witnessed your father's murder. A few of us know, of course, but not too many. That's why I was deliberately vague about the details, saying he was killed in an apparent robbery and only that he was survived by a son and daughter. We didn't want the killers to have any inkling that you were there at the time.

"But it was also important to give some of the facts. News spreads quickly around Willow Grove, and like anywhere, I suppose, if people don't know the facts, they make them up. I'm sure it has been picked up by several major newspapers in Texas," said Camille. "That type of thing usually gets wide distribution. Unfortunately, there isn't much in the article that might lead to their arrest."

"There isn't anything there that would put Matt and me in danger, either. I'm very grateful for that."

"I've had a good teacher. Mr. Hill—he's my partner at the paper—says reporters and editors aren't always careful about what they write and cause plenty of problems." Camille suddenly blinked and caught her breath.

"What's wrong?" Lily scooted to the edge of her chair, wondering if the baby was going to arrive early.

"Nothing." Camille smiled and patted her stomach. "Junior gave me a swift kick. I think he's going to be tall like his daddy and needs more room."

Lily relaxed and eased back in her chair. "How do you know it's a boy?"

"I don't, of course. But Heaven help me if a girl kicks this hard. She's destined to be a tomboy."

They visited for another half hour, then the McKinnon ladies left to shop a little before meeting their husbands for dinner.

Lily stopped by Ransom's room on her way to the

kitchen. When she peeked around the edge of the door, he scowled at her.

"What was all that squawking?"

"Jessie and Camille came by. They were telling me about the great pig chase."

"Oh." A tiny smile eased the edge of his frown. "Looking back on it, I reckon it was funny."

"But not when you were in the middle of it."

His smile won out. "Actually, I remember laughing a couple of times. Once after I spit out some mud and another when Cade did a belly flop off the sidewalk and landed in the middle of Main Street. Not on purpose, of course. His foot slipped. It was frustrating as all get-out, but so ridiculous I had to laugh. Otherwise I might have filled the old coot with buckshot myself."

Lily laughed again, picturing Cade plopping into the mud. "I have to finish dinner. Do you need anything?"

"Nope. I'm going to be lazy for a while longer and read some of the paper."

"Holler if you change your mind."

"According to you, I don't holler, I bellow."

"Yes, you do. I was trying to be polite."

"Always a first time, I guess." He winked and sent her out of the room with a wave of his hands.

Feeling more lighthearted than she had since her father's death, Lily set the table and mixed up the biscuits.

"Blessed are they that mourn, for they shall be comforted."

Even if it took a silly story about a bunch of pigs to do it.

Chapter Ten

On April twelfth, Ransom went to church for the first time since Christmas, but no one made mention of it when he and Matt walked in. Cade had brought him over in the buggy. Matt came on his own two feet since everything in town was within walking distance—for someone who didn't have a problem walking.

Everyone made such a fuss over Ransom that he was a little embarrassed. He didn't know if they were glad to see him because he was getting better physically or they thought he was finally on the road to redemption.

His friends and Reverend Brownfield knew where he stood with the Lord. He didn't figure it was anybody else's business. When they started singing the first hymn and he knew the words and melody by heart, the ol' sourpuss across the aisle almost dropped her hymnbook. He winked at her and kept on singing, wishing Lily were there to share his amusement.

She had walked out to the buggy with him but stubbornly refused to accompany them. He half expected her to fuss at Matt for going, but she hadn't said a word to discourage him.

While the minister made a few announcements, Ransom's thoughts turned more fully to Lily. He felt bad about leaving her at the boarding house alone, but it was important for him to make the effort to attend church.

His heart ached for her. He'd noted the sadness and loneliness in her eyes as they drove away. *Please, Lord, forgive Lily for being angry at You. Comfort her today. Show her Your love.*

Glancing at Matt, he silently prayed for him, too, especially when the minister directed them to the next song, "Shall We Gather at the River." Brownfield indicated it was a special request from Mrs. Johnson, whose husband had passed on the week before.

Ransom's throat tightened as the pianist played a few lines and the congregation began to sing. It might bring comfort to Mrs. Johnson, but judging by Matt's painful expression, it wasn't helping him any.

> Shall we gather at the river,
> Where bright angel feet have trod,
> With its crystal tide forever
> Flowing by the throne of God?

By the time they reached the chorus, Ransom could only read the words silently.

Yes, we'll gather at the river,
The beautiful, the beautiful river;
Gather with the saints at the river
That flows by the throne of God.

Tears rolled down Matt's face. He pulled a handkerchief from his pocket and bent forward in the pew,
ducking his head. His own eyes misty, Ransom put his
hand on Matt's shoulder and leaned close. "Do you
want to leave?" he whispered.

Matt shook his head.

Ransom was afraid the young man stayed because
of him. He couldn't simply get up and slip out. If they
tried, every eye in the church would be on them. He
supposed that would happen even if Matt left by himself, but it wouldn't be so prolonged.

He kept his hand on the young man's shoulder, of-
fering what comfort he could. A few minutes after the
song ended, Matt took a deep breath and straightened.
Ransom gave his shoulder a gentle squeeze and handed
him the hymnbook to put in the rack on the pew in front
of them.

Reverend Brownfield thanked the piano player and
began his sermon. It didn't take long to understand that
the message was about walking with Jesus and trusting in Him.

Ransom wondered if somehow the minister had
known he and Matt would be there. If anyone in the
congregation needed to be reminded about trusting in
Jesus, they did.

"If we abide in the love of Jesus, we have nothing

to fear," said Reverend Brownfield. "He is our foundation, our source of courage no matter what happens, no matter what changes life brings."

You know I love You, Lord, but some changes are still frightening. Ransom tried to listen to the preacher's words, but his thoughts drifted. He didn't want to have to depend on other people, whether it was to take care of him or run his business if he bought a ranch. He wanted a wife and family, more than he ever had. He didn't want to grow old alone with only friends who included him in their family activities because they felt sorry for him. He wanted to be strong and healthy, to do a day's work like any other man. Not have people look at him with pity.

Maybe it's wrong to worry, Lord, but I do. I don't know how to keep from it.

"Psalms tells us not to fear evil because the Lord is with us," said the minister. "He knows the paths on which He leads us, but we have to walk with Him."

If only it was that simple, thought Ransom. He glanced at Matt. The young man's eyes were dry, and he listened intently. *Matt's father walked with You, Lord.* At least his children believed he did. *But he died. How can we explain that? How do we understand it? How can I help Lily and Matt make sense of his death?* To simply say it was his time was a platitude, yet Ransom believed there was truth to it. But he knew platitudes didn't soothe an aching heart.

"When life seems the darkest, when trouble surrounds you, if your hope is in Jesus, nothing can defeat you. Now, I know that some of you are facing trials far heavier than most of us right now." Reverend

Brownfield glanced at Ransom and Matt, then toward elderly Mrs. Johnson. "You might be dealing with the loss of a loved one or facing an uncertain future.

"God knows what you're going through. To put it simply, friends, no matter how difficult the road, it will be easier to trod if you go with Jesus. It's not just that you walk with Him."

Brownfield's voice had risen and his cheeks were flushed. Ransom hoped he didn't pop a cork. Then he felt mildly ashamed at the irreverent thought.

"He walks with you. He's right there beside you every step of the way. He'll even carry you if He has to." The preacher's voice gentled, and he looked right at Ransom. "Jesus will give you the strength to keep on living." His gaze shifted to Mrs. Johnson. "Or, like Elmer, to face death in peace."

Like I've done dozens of times, thought Ransom. He hadn't sought to die, but he'd risked it because in his work he'd had to. He knew death wasn't the end of the road; a better place awaited him.

That was why Lily's father looked death in the face and accepted it. He had to have known what was about to happen when those men rode into their camp with guns drawn. Mr. Chastain did what he could to protect his children because he trusted that he would live eternally with Jesus. His children also walked with the Lord, so he believed they would have the strength to go on.

He wouldn't have expected Lily to be consumed with vengeance and turn her back on God.

Not that he'd had time to think through all those things, but Ransom was certain he had believed them and that had influenced his actions.

It still didn't explain why it happened. Ransom supposed he would never understand that.

There is evil in this world, and a battle between good and evil, between God and Satan. On this earth, good does not always win. But inevitably Jesus is the victor. He has triumphed over death.

Ransom sat very still, the words echoing in his mind. The minister had not spoken them. Nor was it something he had suddenly concluded on his own. God had given him the answer, the truth he sought.

Thank You, Lord. At that moment, he felt very near to Jesus. He wished he could always be that close. *Please stay right beside me. I can't walk this road alone. Neither can Matt and Lily. Draw them close, Lord. Soften her heart toward You.*

Ransom surreptitiously wiped a tear from the corner of his eye, hoping nobody noticed. If word got out that the sheriff was crying in church, he might as well hand in his badge.

Reverend Brownfield ended his sermon, though Ransom couldn't have said how he concluded it. He'd been having his own private worship for a good five minutes. When Matt opened the hymnal to the closing song, Ransom sang along, the words barely registering. He did note, however, that Matt seemed more at peace than when they'd entered the church. Maybe he'd had some private time with the Lord, too.

When they reached the buggy and Ransom climbed in, Cade asked, "You two want to come over to the house for dinner?" He glanced down the street where his family was walking home. "Jessie always has plenty."

"I'll pass this time," said Ransom. "I'm ready for a nap. But you go ahead, Matt, if you want."

"No thanks. I thought I might see if Lily wanted to go for a ride. Get her out of town."

"Good idea." Ransom wasn't surprised by Matt's thoughtfulness. Lily had been right when she said her brother had a gentle heart. The young man took off at a brisk walk, cutting through the alley.

Ransom and Cade chatted about ranching on the way back to the boarding house. "Have you gotten anymore word on the roundup?"

"They've gathered most of the cattle and are headed back with them. I'm glad we've started fencing in the ranch. We won't have to worry about going clear to Pecos to round them up next year." Cade grinned as he stopped the buggy by Mrs. Franklin's porch. "I hear the folks in Midland have been griping about all the cattle wandering around their new town."

"That's what happens when you put up buildings in the cattle's stompin' grounds." Ransom slowly climbed out of the buggy. He was tired, but not as much as he'd expected to be. Going to the church and back had hardly bothered him at all. "Thanks for the ride."

"Let me know if you want to go next Sunday."

"Will do." Ransom waited at the foot of the porch steps, scanning the town as Cade drove away, and Matt walked up. "Would you mind some company this afternoon?" Ransom asked quietly.

Matt's face brightened. "Not a bit. You could take Lil in a buggy, and I could ride Papa's horse. Taffy hasn't been getting enough exercise."

Ransom wondered if he was excited about riding the

horse or playing matchmaker between him and his sister. "Taffy's a sweet horse?" he asked with a grin.

"Yep. Sweet and gentle as they come."

Lily stepped out the front door. "What about Taffy?"

"I'm going to take her out for a ride this afternoon."

"You don't know where to go." Lily frowned, started to say something, then obviously changed her mind. "I suppose you could find your way back."

Good girl. Give the boy a little breathin' room. "Actually, I was thinking about renting a buggy and inviting you for a drive. There's a nice little creek not too far from town with some big ol' pecan trees for shade."

"Are you up to driving a buggy?" She walked to the edge of the porch, looking out across the prairie with a glint of interest in her eyes.

"If I'm not, can you drive one?"

"Yes."

"Then, let's go. If I get tired, you can bring me back. I'd like to eat a sandwich first and rest for maybe half an hour. Then I think I'll be all right."

She came down the steps, slipping her arm around his waist. Ransom glanced at Matt, who didn't say a word. He appreciated the younger man not telling her that he had been going up and down by himself for a couple of days.

"I've already made some sandwiches." She met Ransom's gaze when he looked down at her. "I figured you'd be hungry."

"I'm starved. Thanks for thinking about us."

When they got inside, Ransom decided to eat in bed and rest his back at the same time. He hoped he wasn't making a mistake with the afternoon's excursion, but he needed to get out of town as much as Matt and Lily did. Normally, he rode out to one of the ranches for some reason or another almost every week. If nothing else, he'd go out and see Cade just to give his horse, Rooster, a good run. Cade had been riding Rooster at least once a week so he got some exercise.

While he took a nap, Matt and Lily went to the livery for Taffy and a buggy. When he got up about half an hour later, they were waiting for him in the front parlor. "Y'all ready to go?"

"All ready." Lily stood and put on a wide-brimmed straw hat decorated with little pink silk flowers. She looked as pretty as a picture of springtime in her rose gingham dress. "I'm bringing some cookies and a couple of jars of water."

"Good."

Matt picked up the food and walked out, holding open the screen door for them.

Ransom put on his hat and followed Lily out. He hid his smile when she waited to help him off the porch. She slid her arm around his waist and they walked carefully down the steps.

"You're doing much better." She looked up at him when they reached the ground. "I don't think you need my help anymore."

"Oh, but I do." He grinned at her.

"But not Matt's." When he started to speak, she held up her hand. "I watched you go up and down those steps by yourself yesterday without any trouble at all."

"Just takes one miss, and I'd hit the dirt. Or the porch, depending on which way I was going."

"That's true for anyone." Lily waited beside the

buggy until he was settled in the seat, then went around to the other side. Matt put the water and the box of cookies beneath the seat.

Ransom tucked his cane alongside them and picked up the reins, waiting until she sat down next to him. "Reckon that means you won't be hanging onto me anymore."

"Reckon so." She looked up the street, her nose slightly in the air.

He leaned close to her ear and whispered, "At least not when we're going down the steps."

"Drive the buggy, Sheriff Starr," she said dryly.

"Yes, ma'am." He grinned and flicked the reins, urging the horse to a walk. As the buggy rolled down the street, Ransom checked on parts of town he hadn't seen in weeks. The stagecoach sat in the wagon-yard at Ty and Cade's livery, ready to leave for San Angelo first thing Monday morning. Across the alley, Jake Forrester's saloon was closed until later in the day.

Lily pointed to a small strip of singed wood on the building next to the saloon. "Was there a fire? Or are the saloon and livery just newer than the other building?"

"Both of them burned to the ground a year ago. A freight wagon bumped a lantern at the livery and started the fire. Ty and Quint went in after the horses. They rescued them all, but for a few minutes, I thought Ty wasn't going to make it out of there."

"I'm surprised you didn't go after him."

"I was about to. I was heading toward the door with a wet blanket wrapped around me when he and a little horse named Buttercup came out. I'm not sure which one of them was staggering more, though I guess he was since he was hanging onto her for dear life."

"Did the horse make it?"

"Yep. She wasn't burned, but she'd breathed a lot of smoke. Had trouble with her eyes for a while, but the doctor fixed up some ointment for her that took care of it." He smiled at her sigh of relief. "The doctors in this town take care of man and beast when they need it."

Turning up Fir Street, he called to Matt, who was riding alongside them. "I'm going to take the long way out of town, see how things are a few streets over."

"Fine with me. It's a good way to get Taffy warmed up."

Bright flowers lined the picket fence around Mrs. Peabody's house. Things were quiet at Nate and Bonnie Flynn's. Ransom absently wondered if Bonnie had ever convinced her saloon-owner husband to go to church with her. He made a wide turn at the corner to avoid a handful of chickens scratching in the dirt at the Smoots' place. Mr. and Mrs. Smoot waved at them from the front porch as they went by. Across the street, Mrs. Simpson sat on her front porch swing, chatting with the gentleman beside her.

When Ransom chuckled, Lily looked at him. "What's so funny?"

He nodded toward the elderly couple. "Mrs. Simpson had that swing installed when Jessie was living with her. Said it made a good place for Cade and Jessie to sit when he came courting. Ty and Camille used it a few times when Camille stayed there. Now, it appears Mrs. Simpson is putting it to good use herself. Mr. Armstrong is a nice, eligible widower. Maybe that's why she hasn't suggested you move in with her so she could play matchmaker. She's busy making a match for herself."

"They do seem to be having a good time."

He'd thought she might bristle a little at the suggestion someone would try to find her a husband. Then again, she was probably used to it. Seemed like gettin' people hitched was a primary occupation of most of the women in town. He supposed Des Moines hadn't been much different. "Maybe we should ask Mrs. Franklin to put up a swing at the boarding house."

She looked at him, amusement crinkling her eyes. "Why would we want to do that?"

"So we could sit this close more often. Of course, it would be better if it was on the back porch. Wouldn't attract so much attention."

He followed Lily's gaze as she glanced at a couple of ladies chatting over a fence. When they drove past, the conversation halted—probably in midsentence—as they stared at them.

"I think we're drawing our share of attention as it is," she said, looking back down the street.

"Bound to happen. Folks can't get away with much around here. But it's a good town." He glanced at her. "A good place to put down roots."

"I thought you liked excitement and adventure, didn't stay in one place long."

"What makes you think that?"

"The work you've done. I'm sure a Texas Ranger didn't sit still much. A detective, either."

"Nope. Not much at all." He paused, thinking about how his life had changed, how he had changed. He turned back onto Main Street near the bridge over Willow Creek. The folks from the Baptist church were having a picnic at the Willow Grove City Park. He expected they'd be holding a baptism service in the creek later in the afternoon.

He drove the buggy across the bridge, being careful to keep the horse at a walk and observe the posted five-miles-per-hour limit on the structure.

"I think I'll ride on ahead," called Matt. "Give Taffy a run."

"The creek's about three miles ahead. It's the first one you come to. Turn left when you reach it, stop when you get to the big trees. Basically the only trees."

"See you there." Matt moved to the edge of the road, riding in the grass so he wouldn't cover them with dust. Within minutes, he went over a little hill and disappeared from sight.

Ransom flicked the reins again and the horse moved to a nice steady trot. "Right before I got hurt—that very night, in fact—I'd decided to tell Cade and the other commissioners to find another sheriff."

Lily turned to him with a stricken expression. "You were going to leave?"

He nodded, regretting that he'd even mentioned it. "When I took this job, life around here hadn't exactly been peaceful. I'd expected a lot more action. Instead, I spent the most boring year of my life."

"What were you planning to do? Join the Texas Rangers again?"

"Probably not. I'm not interested in chasing banditos down in South Texas or spying on fence cutters everywhere else. I thought I might go back to being a

detective. It's rarely dull work. There's a lot of satisfaction in tracking down criminals and bringing them
to justice. Or finding someone who has an inheritance
and doesn't know it or a father who wants to acknowl-
edge the child he just found out he had.

"I liked walking into danger and knowing I had a
good chance of coming out the winner because I could
think clearly and analyze the situation. There are some
parts of that job I really hated though." At the questioning lift of her eyebrows, he explained. "Misleading
people, mostly. Pretending to be someone I wasn't.
Going into disreputable places."

"Like saloons?" She waited for his nod, hesitated
then added, "And bordellos?"

Ransom felt his face grow warm. He hoped she
didn't notice. "Nosy woman."

Her pretty coffee-brown eyes grew wide. "You did
go to parlor houses?"

"Just for information or keep an eye on my suspect." He glanced at her. She was trying to decide
whether or not to believe him. "Sugar, I was wild in my
younger days, but that was a long time ago."

"You're not old," she said with a frown.

"Old enough—or maybe wise enough—to know I
don't want to spend my time with soiled doves. Or
have an affair."

"I'm so sorry we ruined your plans. Though I suppose you could always leave when you get well."

"I could, but now I don't want to. It's funny how I've
come to appreciate the folks here a lot more since I've
been laid up than I ever did when I was well and looking out for them."

"They're very open with how they feel about you. They adore you."

Ransom grinned. "Now, that's a word a man wants a woman to use when she's talking about her feelings. Not a town."

She rolled her eyes. "Very well, the women have you up on a pedestal, as if you didn't know it. And the men respect and admire you. Besides that, they all like you."

"There are a few hombres who'd just as soon see me leave town. But that's not going to happen, unless I don't get well enough to do my job. Even then, I'll stay in the area. I've realized there are more important things in life than danger and chasing down criminals."

"Such as putting down roots in a town?"

"Yes." He reached for her hand, threading his fingers through hers. "And taking a pretty lady for a buggy ride."

Chapter Eleven

Ransom leaned against one pecan tree and Lily against another, enjoying the shade. Taffy and the livery horse grazed contentedly on the green grass along the bank. Matt waded in the creek, trying to catch a frog. He made a dive for the creature and almost fell into the knee-deep water. Laughing, he gave up and climbed out, sprawling on the grass. "He's too quick for me. Don't guess we'll have frog legs for supper, Lil."

"We wouldn't have frog legs for supper even if you caught him." Lily shuddered at the thought. "I'd like to eat at one of the restaurants tonight." She looked over at Ransom, smiling as he lazily waved a blade of grass at her. "Which one is best?"

"All three of them are good, though Wallace's has the best desserts. I have a hankerin' for a piece of apple pie."

"How can you want pie after all those cookies?"

"I only ate six." Ransom grinned. "There'll be plenty of room for pie whenever we wander back to town." He scanned the area and sighed contentedly. "Feels good being out here."

"Yes, it does. You had an excellent idea."

"Can't take credit for it." He nodded toward Matt. "Your brother was going to take you for a drive until I asked if I could tag along."

"That's sweet of you, Matt. Thanks."

"You're welcome." Matt shifted so his lower legs and feet were in the sun to dry. "I figured it would do us good to get out of town for a while. Having Ransom come along was even better because Taffy got some exercise."

That wasn't the only reason it was nice to have him along, but Lily didn't voice her thoughts. It was wonderful to see him feeling well enough to enjoy the outing. It gave her hope that he truly would heal up completely.

Matt pulled on his socks and boots. "Is it all right if I follow the creek a little way and see what's there?"

He asked Ransom, not Lily, and she didn't care. He knew whether it was safe or not, she didn't.

"Sure, but watch for rattlers. I've never seen any around here, but it always pays to be alert. If you run across an area of big rocks, stay clear of it. That's usually where they'll have a den. I don't think there is anything else that could cause you trouble. Just don't stray too far from the creek and you won't get lost."

Matt hopped to his feet. "I won't be gone too long."

"Take your time. There's lots of daylight left, and

I'm not tired." Ransom glanced at Lily, making her catch her breath.

Being with him like this, even with Matt along, lifted her spirits and made her dream a little. What would it be like to always have him in her life? To spend not just one Sunday afternoon with him, but every one?

Foolishness, of course. Once he was well and back in his normal routine, his interest in her would wane. If it didn't, she couldn't let her attraction to him shift her attention away from finding her father's killer. *Don't you think he would remain focused on that, too? Especially if he truly cares for you?*

She dared not hope for anything lasting, even if she longed for it. How had he become so important to her? By being her friend, by comforting her when she needed it, chiding her when she deserved it, understanding her anger when she didn't quite understand it herself. No other man had quickened her pulse simply with a look or the light touch of his fingers on her cheek. His promise rang in her heart like a clear, singing bell. *I will kiss you, Lily…one of these days.*

She watched Matt walk away with a combination of excitement and dismay. Stealing a glance at Ransom, she knew he was thinking the same thing she was. She rose quickly. "I think I'll pick a bouquet of wildflowers. They're starting to bloom nicely."

"They'll wilt if you pick them now. Wait until right before we leave."

"I'll put them in some water. One of the jars is empty."

"Lily," he said softly, holding out his hand. "Come sit by me."

Oh, how she wanted to. She could barely see Matt's head as he followed the creek around a bend. A second later, he was completely out of sight. Unless he ran into something that scared him, he would be gone for a while.

Stop being a ninny. Lily walked over and sat down beside Ransom, hoping she looked calmer than she felt. "It's good to see Matt relax and have fun. Sometimes he seems like he's twenty instead of sixteen."

"He's more man than boy in many ways." Ransom slipped his arm around her shoulders. "It's good for him to play a little—wading in the creek, going exploring. Helps him to learn about the country, too. I've never been to Iowa, but I don't expect it's much like West Texas."

"No, it's not. Mostly farms, with everything fenced. The cattle don't roam around like they do here."

"They won't be doing that much longer. The days of free range are quickly ending. More and more ranchers, like Ty and Cade, are fencing their land so they can improve their herds and keep better track of them."

Caressing her cheek, he gently tilted her face toward his. "But I didn't ask you to come over here so we could discuss cows."

He lowered his head slowly as if to give her the opportunity to tell him to stop. But she didn't want him to stop. She wanted to see if the real thing was anything like it had been in her daydreams.

It was all that and much more. Desire, yes, but carefully tempered. Tenderness. Sweetness. Caring. This was not a kiss he would give just any woman. At least she desperately hoped that was true.

He lifted his head slowly. When she looked at him, he searched her eyes. Approval gleamed in his, and he kissed her again, a little longer, a little more thoroughly.

When he finally eased away—reluctantly it seemed—and rested his head against the tree, she laid her head on his shoulder. She didn't think she could stand up even if she had to.

"That's strange."

"What?" She looked up at him with a frown.

"I didn't see a cloud or hear thunder."

"What are you talking about?"

"Lightning, sugar." He winked and tucked her back against his shoulder.

Lily giggled. "Why, Sheriff Starr, I didn't know you were so eloquent."

"Fits, doesn't it?" he said quietly, threading his fingers through hers.

"Yes, it does. But then I'm no expert. I've only been kissed once before and Harvey Jones and I bumped noses."

"Then I don't have to worry about him?"

"Harvey? Not at all. He waited a few more years and married Mary Dempsy."

"Good." He rubbed his thumb over her hand. "You suit me just fine."

Lily didn't know what to say. She thought of plenty of things: That he suited her just fine, too. That she'd never dreamed a kiss could be so wonderful. That she wished she could stay right here beside him forever. That she was perilously close to falling in love with him, if she wasn't already.

She couldn't say any of those things, so she asked the next thing that popped into her head. "How was church this morning?"

He sighed and shifted, loosening the hold he had on her shoulders.

"Am I hurting you?"

"Not at all. I just had to move a bit. How was church? Folks were pretty excited to see us. I expect several of them were shouting silent hallelujahs that this wayward sinner had seen the error of his ways. Mrs. Doolittle almost dropped her hymnbook when she noticed I knew the first song and the words by heart."

Lily leaned back against his arm, looking up at him. She didn't want to admit that she'd felt wretched being home by herself while everyone else at the boarding house had gone to church. The loneliness had been almost unbearable.

"She came to visit Mrs. Franklin last week, and I had to bite my tongue. She didn't talk about you but had something to say about half the people in town. Most of it bad. Mrs. Franklin kept replying with good things about them, most of them anyway. A few times she couldn't come up with anything. She kept trying to change the subject to recipes or fashions or the latest Ladies Aid project. Sometimes she succeeded."

They sat in silence for a few minutes before Lily asked quietly, "How was Matt?"

"The second song hit him hard. Mrs. Johnson had requested 'Shall We Gather at the River.'"

"Oh, no."

"I suppose it encouraged her, but it tore Matt up."

"He cried?" Poor Matt! But it must have been good for him. He seemed fine now.

"Some. He leaned forward and ducked his head, so I don't think many people noticed. Cade was on one side of him and I was on the other. I offered to leave, but he didn't want to. By the time Reverend Brownfield started preaching, Matt had regained his composure. He seemed interested in the sermon. At least it appeared he was listening intently."

"What was it about?" Lily didn't really care, but she wanted to be polite.

"Walking with Jesus and trusting Him no matter what happens."

"How convenient. Did the minister know you were going to church this morning?"

"Don't think so. I only mentioned it to Cade last night when I asked for a ride. Hadn't said anything to anybody else." He brushed his finger back and forth across her thumbnail. "I figure God knew what I needed to hear. I missed some of it because He and I were having a private conversation."

She glanced at him. "About?"

"Me and the worries I have about the future. About you and Matt and that I didn't understand why your father was killed."

Lily pulled her hand from his. "You and me both."

"This may sound strange, but I think He explained it to me."

Lily hoped her expression wasn't as cynical as she felt. "He just spoke to you?"

"Something like that, though not out loud. I would have keeled over right there if that happened. Haven't you ever been talking to the Lord about something and suddenly you have the answer in a way that you know wasn't just your mind working it out?"

She hesitated. "Yes, at least it seemed that way. So what did He tell you? For everything there is a season? It was just Papa's time to die?" she asked bitterly.

"No, though maybe there's something to that. He said there is a battle going on between good and evil, between Him and Satan. That in this world, meaning here on earth, good doesn't always win. But ultimately, Jesus will be the victor because He has triumphed over death. Over Satan. If you think about it, that makes sense because bad things happen to good, God-loving people. Not just your father, but other people, too."

She turned her head away, unable to hold back the tears that slipped from her eyes. "When Mama died, Papa reminded us that Jesus didn't promise us a life without pain or sorrow, only that He would help us through it. Papa said if life was wonderful all the time, we wouldn't appreciate it because we wouldn't have anything to compare it to." She cleared her throat and pulled a hankie from her pocket to wipe her eyes.

Ransom waited patiently, his arm gently around her.

"I realize that bad things happen. I guess I even understand it as a spiritual battle." She stopped and blew her nose. "Both sides lose people in a war. But I don't understand why this time my father was the loser and not the other men."

"When your father died, he went to Heaven to spend eternity with Jesus." Ransom hesitated. Lily wondered if he was afraid to say what he was thinking.

"Maybe God wants to give them another chance for redemption," he said quietly.

She twisted away from him and scrambled to her feet, glaring at him. "No! How can you say that? They don't deserve another chance."

"It's just a possibility."

"Not one I can accept." But Papa would have. Papa was a God-loving man. If he'd had a choice, he would have told God to take him instead of them—and expected Lily and Matt to pray that his killers would find salvation. I *can't,* she silently wailed.

She stormed along the creek bank, heading the opposite direction from Matt.

"Lily, where are you going?" There was a hint of panic in Ransom's voice.

She looked over her shoulder. He was struggling to stand up. She stopped and faced him. "Stay there. I won't go far. Please, Ransom. I need to be alone right now."

Scowling, he slumped back against the tree, muttering something she couldn't hear. It was probably just as well that she didn't.

She went a few more steps before he called, "Watch for snakes."

"I will."

"And red ants."

She merely nodded.

"And scorpions."

That gave her pause, but she didn't stop until she believed he couldn't see or hear her. Despite her churning mind and the anguish in her soul, she still had the sense to inspect the ground before she sat down. "God, it was hard enough knowing Papa died protecting us, telling those men that he was alone. But to think that You might have taken him instead of them because they didn't know You?" Sobbing, she laid her arms across her bent knees and leaned her forehead against them. "He didn't have a choice. Price had no remorse after he killed him. They're too wicked and cruel to change.

"I can't pray for them. I can't forgive them." *You'll never have peace.* "I don't want peace. I want revenge." Her declaration didn't hold as much fervor as it had a month ago. The need for vengeance still burned inside, but it had lessened.

"I do want peace," she whispered. "I want the pain to go away." She knew it never would completely fade. Her mother's death had taught her that.

Lily lifted her head and dried her eyes, looking for the first time at the countryside around her. Her walk had taken her to a little secluded valley sheltered between hills on each side of the creek. The whole valley and the hill on the other side were covered in grass sprinkled with wildflowers—purple, white, yellow and red. Sunlight glinted off the clear, bubbling stream, threading a glittering ribbon through nature's tapestry.

A mild breeze offset the warmth of the sun. A sparrow perched on a small shrub near the water's edge and sang a sweet melody. When the bird darted off on some unknown quest, only the faint rustle of the tall prairie grass and the buzz of an industrious bee broke the silence.

The quiet wrapped around her, calming and peaceful. She thought of her parents and their faith, never wavering even in light of her mother's long illness. Many were the hours Lily had read Scripture to her mother in those last months. "It eases my pain," she would say, "and brings me comfort."

He father had found the same refuge after her mother's death. Forcing herself to be honest, Lily acknowledged that she too had found consolation in the Bible and in God's love after her mother died.

Why had she denied herself that comfort since her father's death? She had let anger and bitterness control her instead of turning to Jesus and the Holy Spirit for understanding and strength. She had blamed God when it was Price, in his own sinfulness and of his own free will, who had gunned down her father.

By turning her back on God, she not only hurt herself but her brother as well. In her selfish anger, had she deprived him of the comfort of God's love? Or had Matt sought the Savior in the quietness of his heart? Ashamed and contrite, Lily closed her eyes and hung her head, leaning it against her knees again. "Forgive me, Father, for blaming You, for being so angry with You. I can't forgive Price and Smith, not on my own. But with Your help, I'll try. I can't pray for their salvation, Lord. Maybe some day, but not now.

"Protect everyone else from their evil. Please bring them to justice. Make them pay for what they did." Perhaps then, she could pray for their souls.

When Ransom and Matt had gone to church that morning, she'd been annoyed because they left her alone. She'd been angry with her brother because she wanted him to be mad at God and irritated with herself because her heart yearned for the Prince of Peace. She had been too stubborn and too prideful to give in to the Holy Spirit's call. She had spent a terrible morning because of it.

I love You, Jesus. How miserable I've been without You.

She sat there a short while longer, resting in Christ's love. His comfort wasn't easily explained, but she felt it in her heart and in her mind, a nurturing tenderness that soothed her soul and gave her a measure of peace.

After gathering a small bouquet of flowers, she went back to where Ransom waited. Somehow he'd managed to get to his feet. He stood beside the creek. "Tired of waiting?"

"Gettin' worried about you. I was debating about going after you. I'm sorry I upset you and made you cry."

"I needed to cry." She laughed when he gave her a disbelieving look. "That's one advantage women have over men. It's acceptable, a good way to ease pain, anger, frustration and numerous other things. It's a shame men have to be so stoic.

"You forced me to face up to how I've been feeling and acting." She looped her arm through his. "It was my turn to have a personal discussion with the Lord, only most of it was me talking to Him."

He studied her face, searched her eyes, looked into her soul. "You made peace with Him."

"I think so. I still have some things to work out."

He brushed a kiss across her temple. "Don't we all."

Chapter Twelve

A week later Lily went to work four days a week for Ty at McKinnon Brothers, the largest general merchandise store within a hundred miles. They supplied provisions to most of the ranches across the area as well as the townspeople. Ty hired her to work primarily in the ladies department. Within a few days he was singing her praises to Ransom.

"She knows fashion and has a knack for helping the women find what they want or what goes together if their judgment is off," Ty said, as he and Ransom stood near the office at the back of the store. "Believe me, some of them don't have any idea what looks good. She's the best ladies clerk I've ever had."

"I'll tell her that you're bragging on her. The encouragement will do her good."

"I was glad to see her in church yesterday. You, too.

You'd better watch it or you'll become a regular." Ty nodded a greeting to a customer a few aisles over.

"That's my intention, except I don't want to hog all the Sundays. Have to switch out with Quint so he can go part of the time, if he wants to." He didn't figure that would happen often. Quint was a believer, but he didn't hold much with sitting in a pew.

"I see you're taking the late shift tonight." Ty glanced at Ransom's cane. "You up to that?"

"You mean am I up to handling things if somebody gets rowdy?" Ransom shrugged. He had some doubts, but he wasn't about to admit it. "Reckon we'll find out. Things are still quiet. Quint deserves some time off. Dozing at the office isn't a good night's rest. When the cowboys get back to town, we'll both be working night and day."

"I know you're not up to that." Ty absently straightened a display of work gloves. "You're going to fool around and wind up back in bed. Or worse, do permanent damage."

"It may already be permanent," Ransom said quietly.

Ty's gaze shot to him. "Doc still thinks that?"

"He says it's a possibility." Probability had been the word he'd used, but Ransom wouldn't admit or accept that. "Only time will tell. My leg still won't totally bear my weight. But I'm working on it. I can hobble around my room without the cane as long as I have something else to lean on."

"How's the pain?"

"Tolerable most of the time. Occasionally, I wish somebody would just shoot me and put me out of my misery."

"I hope you don't go into dangerous situations thinking like that."

Ransom grinned. "When I'm thinking like that, I couldn't go into a dangerous situation if I wanted to." He'd kept his eye on Lily while they talked. She finished with her customer and sent the lady on her way with a new dress, new shoes and a new hat. No wonder Ty was impressed.

"Now, I think I'll go say good-night to Lily before I go to work."

"Careful, you might not get to the office on time." Ty's eyes twinkled merrily.

"Quint will come lookin' for me if I don't." Ransom walked up to the counter, warmth sweeping through him when Lily smiled at him. "Evenin', sugar."

"Good evening, Sheriff Starr. You're out late in the day." Lily came around to the front of the counter.

"Headin' off to work."

A frown touched her brow. "You're working tonight?"

"Yep. I normally give Quint a few nights off during the week."

"But things aren't normal."

"Close enough." He leaned against the counter beside her. "I need to see if I can handle it," he said softly. "If I can't, then it's time for Cade and the commissioners to give the job to Quint and find him another deputy." When she started to protest, he shook his head. "I'll probably wind up sleeping in the cell anyway. There hasn't been a ruckus in over a week."

"Then something's bound to happen tonight." She laid her hand on his arm. "Ransom, I know you need to prove to yourself—to the town—that you can do the job, but aren't you rushing things?"

He grinned, knowing it would rile her. He could handle her temper right now but not too much gentle concern. "Worried about me?"

"Of course not. Why should I worry?" She crossed her arms and looked away from him. "My granny used to say that a stubborn man was worse than ten mules. You're going to do what you want to no matter what I say."

"That's right." He hid a smile. Her granny must have had a saying for everything. He gently nudged her chin around with his knuckle until she looked at him. "But I'd appreciate it if you'd remember me in your bedtime prayers."

"What if something happens before bedtime?"

"Maybe you'd better say a prayer before then." He ran his fingertip across her cheek. "Like when I leave."

She sighed and shook her head. "You know I will. And later, too."

"Once is probably good. Don't sit up all night worrying. God has a long memory. He won't forget what you ask Him."

"I wish we were back out under the pecan tree," she whispered.

"Me, too." His gaze dropped to her lips. "I could kiss you right here."

"Too many windows. Big windows."

Ransom glanced toward the storefront where three women and two men had stopped to peer inside. "Yep, and half the town is watching us."

She cast a quick look toward the window, her face

turning red. "Not half the town, but within an hour the whole town will know you're flirting with me."

"I don't care if you don't."

Her expression was thoughtful for a second, then she looked up at him. "I don't mind."

"You'd care if I kissed you right now." He forced a hint of humor into his voice.

She laughed. "I'd be too embarrassed to enjoy it."

"Then I'd better save it. I'll see you in the morning before you leave for work."

"All right." She reached down and squeezed his hand. "Be careful."

"Always am." Giving her the smile he saved just for her, he walked out the front door.

Three hours later Ransom quietly eased through another doorway, this time in the White Buffalo Saloon. A terrified salesman was pinned against the bar by the wavering aim of Elton White's six-shooter. Elton was drunk and looking for a fight, and he didn't care who it was with.

The saloon owner, Nate Flynn, stood in front of the shattered mirror behind the bar, blood oozing from a small cut on his face. He held a shotgun with one hand, resting the barrel on the counter and pointed at Elton. His other arm hung at his side, blood on his sleeve, the cloth punctured by a round bullet hole.

Scanning the room, Ransom confirmed that the rancher was all on his own. Every other man in the place, with the exception of the piano player, hid behind overturned tables. The ivory tickler cowered at the end of the piano, watching the drama play out.

Ransom walked slowly across the room, his cane adding another tap to those made by his boot heels on the hardwood floor. "Looks like you boys have a stand-off. What's all the ruckus about, Elton?"

"This uppity drummer won't give me no perfume samples for my missus."

Ransom edged closer to Elton. He put his weight on his good leg and switched the cane to his other hand. Gripping the back of a chair for support, he glanced at the object of Elton's ire. "I thought you sold cigars."

"I do." The salesman glared irritably at Elton. "I told him that, even offered him one, but he doesn't have the mental capacity of a termite."

Now he'd done it. Elton wasn't stupid. He was originally from Boston and probably had more education than anyone else in the saloon. Even three sheets to the wind, he knew that he had just been insulted.

"You arrogant pipsqueak." Squinting, Elton tried to steady his pistol, pointing it in the general direction of the drummer's heart.

Ransom tossed the cane straight up, sliding his hand along it to hold it as a club. He hooked the curved handle over Elton's wrist, pulling his arm downward and to the side just as he squeezed the trigger. The bullet splintered a floorboard in front of the bar several feet away from the salesman. Ransom brought the cane upward with a snap, hitting Elton in the jaw.

The man's head jerked backward, and he dropped the pistol. He swayed, then regained his balance and took a swing at Ransom. He didn't come close.

"You don't want to take me on," Ransom warned quietly, his voice edged with steel.

The rancher grumbled under his breath and plopped down in another chair, barely staying on the seat.

Using the walking stick, Ransom shoved Elton's gun across the floor. He relaxed, shifting the cane back to the proper hand.

Nate carefully released the hammer on the shotgun and set it on the bar. He glared at his scowling customer. "I'm sick and tired of you coming in here every couple of months and bustin' up the place. You've gone too far this time." He flinched as he pressed his hand against the wound on his arm. "Now, I'll have to listen to Bonnie bawl and carry on and demand that I close down 'cause I've been shot."

"Didn't mean to shoot you," muttered Elton as the other customers came out from their hiding places. "Just the mirror."

"Your aim is gettin' a mite poor." Ransom glanced at Nate. "You going to press charges?"

"I ought to. He could have killed me." Nate glowered at Elton. "I reckon as long as he settles up for the damages and the doctor bill, I won't."

"I should get something," said the drummer. "He scared me out of my wits."

"Sorry, the city council hasn't set any fines for lost wits." Ransom nodded to the blacksmith and another rancher. "Y'all help me haul him over to the jail." They quickly grabbed hold of the prisoner's arms and pulled him to his feet, half dragging him toward the doorway. Ransom looked at Nate. "Close down for the night and get on over to Doc Wilson's."

Nate nodded, watching his other customers put the tables and chairs back in place and drift toward the door. "Y'all come back tomorrow. We'll be open."

"If Bonnie lets you out of the house." The local feed store owner picked up a dishtowel and tied it around Nate's arm. "Get on over to the doc's. I'll lock up and bring you the key."

"Thanks, Jim."

Satisfied that everything was being taken care of, Ransom followed the men and the now docile Elton down the street to the jail. They took him through the sheriff's office and into a cell, dumping him on a cot.

Ransom locked the cell door and returned to his office, gratefully sitting behind his desk. He hoped the others didn't notice that he was breathing a mite hard.

"Good work, Sheriff," said the blacksmith. "I thought that drummer was done for."

"A couple of us started to stop him, but when he swung that pistol in our direction, we decided against it. He didn't care who he was pointing at." The rancher shook his head. "It's a shame Elton gets so mean when he's drunk. The rest of the time he's not a bad feller. Good to see you back at work, Sheriff Starr. Looks to me like you're up to the job." He chuckled and opened the door. "Never saw anybody use a cane quite like that."

After the men left, closing the door behind them, Ransom breathed a huge sigh of relief. He'd passed his first major hurdle and kept a man from being killed. There was no way of knowing for certain whose life he'd saved. Likely Elton's. Nate had been in the saloon business too many years to let someone shoot him twice if he could help it.

Thank You, Lord.

He reached for his coffee cup and realized his hand shook. Frowning, he curled his fingers into a fist and rested his hand on the table. He couldn't remember when he'd reacted to danger by actually shaking. His insides had trembled plenty of times, usually when everything was over. Even then, the man everyone else saw was calm and in command, both of himself and the situation.

Was it fear? Nerves? Physical weakness? Any one of them could be reason enough to step down from the job. He went over the confrontation in his mind, minute by minute, step by step. Yes, he'd been afraid. A bit of fear was a healthy thing, kept a man sharp. Yes, he'd been nervous walking into that saloon. Concerned that he'd make a mistake and get somebody killed. Worried that he'd stumble or fall. After he'd entered the door and sized up the problem, he had sorted the options and worked out a plan just as quickly as he ever did. Once he was beside Elton and holding on to the chair for support, he'd felt solid. He'd been a little wobbly by the time he got back to the office, but during the confrontation, he'd been confident that he could stand—as long as Elton didn't come after him. If his swing had been on target, Ransom doubted he would have been able to dodge the blow.

He held out his hand again. This time it was steady. "Relief, that's what it was." And all the other things, too. But he'd won this battle. Every victory made the next one easier.

As long as it didn't come too soon.

Chapter Thirteen

Less than an hour later, Lily heard all about it. The feed store owner told the grocer, who told the land agent, who told the insurance man, who told Alvah Crutcher, the photographer who lived at Mrs. Franklin's boarding house. He'd hurried right home to share the news.

"I wish I'd been there with my camera," said Alvah.

"A fine distraction that would have been, Mr. Crutcher." Mrs. Franklin huffed and picked up her knitting again, making the needles fly.

The photographer shrugged. "A man can dream, my dear Mrs. Franklin. Someday we will have cameras that can capture impromptu events such as that." He turned to Lily, his eyes bright with excitement. "They say Sheriff Starr was his old self, completely in control of the situation from the minute he walked through the door."

"Only this time he used his cane," said Ed, who worked with Lily at the store. "Imagine that."

Lily *was* imagining it, and it terrified her. She was angry, too. And very proud of him. How was she supposed to deal with all those emotions at once?

Quint had strapped on his gun belt as he listened to Alvah's story. "I'll go see if he wants me to take over." He smiled at Lily as he opened the front door. "Elton snores like a freight train."

She followed him out, waylaying him on the porch. "You mean this has happened before?"

"Every couple of months. He comes into town, gets drunk and picks a fight with somebody. Up to now, it's always been a fistfight. This is the first time he's had a gun." Quint frowned. "I wonder where he had it hidden. He turned in his six-shooter when he rode into town this morning."

"Well, why didn't you stop him? You let him go to the saloon, knowing he'd cause trouble?" Lily managed to keep her voice down, but she couldn't keep the anger out of it.

"We can't throw him in jail until he does something to deserve it. He comes into town about once a week and most of the time, he's fine. Either doesn't drink at all or stops with a few. We've tried to figure out how to tell when he's going to have too many dippers full, but he always seems the same. You can be sure that we'll search him after this. His word isn't good enough anymore."

"Well, I think not." Lily sat down in the rocking chair on the porch. She would wait right there until he returned or sent Ransom back.

Quint stopped at the bottom of the steps. "Even if Ransom wants to stay at the office, I won't be back for a couple of hours. I'll make the rounds down in the district for him, save him some walking. Should I mention that you're worried about him?"

"The only thing I'm worried about is having to take care of him again if he gets hurt." She rocked harder. "I like working at the store."

Quint looked away for a second, but when he turned back to her, she could still see the remnants of a grin. "That's the only reason you don't want him laid up again?"

"Yes," she snapped.

Quint laughed and went off down the street.

Matt came out on the porch and took the second rocker. Lily was thankful that everyone else stayed inside. Someone had moved the chairs earlier in the day to keep them out of the sun, so they weren't directly in front of the parlor. She doubted anyone would hear their conversation though the windows were open. Especially not with Alvah telling tales about other lawmen he had known.

Lily frowned at her brother. "I don't want to talk about it."

"What? That you're sweet on a man with a dangerous job?"

"It doesn't matter. Half the women in town are sweet on him. Probably more than that."

"He doesn't give a hoot about them. But he does you."

"When did you get to be such an expert, Mr. Smarty Pants?" Lily made a face a him.

Matt laughed. "I'm not a little kid, Lil. I've stayed at the office with him sometimes, remember? He doesn't look at other women the way he looks at you."

His comment warmed her heart. She wished it didn't. "He isn't completely well. He doesn't have his strength back, either."

"Didn't sound like that was a problem tonight."

"If that man had decided to plow into him instead of taking a wild swing, Ransom couldn't have moved out of the way. He certainly couldn't have stood up against it."

"True." Matt frowned, tapping his foot on the porch instead of rocking. "I haven't heard any stories about Ransom getting into fistfights. From what I hear, he just pulls his revolver and that's the end of it. Folks say he's the fastest draw they've ever seen."

"He didn't use his gun tonight."

"He didn't need to. He used the cane. He used his wits. That's one of the best weapons anybody can have. But you'll still worry."

"I suppose so, as long as we're here."

Matt's frown deepened. "You thinking about leaving?"

"Maybe someday, after Price and Smith are caught. What do you want to do?"

"I like Willow Grove, and I like working for Mr. Cox." He had started as a carpenter's apprentice right after Lily went to work at the store. "I've learned a lot already."

"He's a good teacher, then?"

"Yeah, he explains things so I can understand them. If I make a mistake, he doesn't yell at me the way I hear some of the other carpenters chewin' out their helpers. Ransom says he's the best in town.

"Mr. Cox says he plans to stay here even if the town quits growing. There's always work for a carpenter. If he's not building something new, he's repairing something that's broken or remodeling stuff." His eyes glowed with excitement.

Lily had never seen her brother so enthused. He'd always been a hard worker, but building things had fascinated him since he was a tiny boy. "You aren't going to want to go back to school in the fall, are you?"

"Learning a trade will do me more good than two more years of sitting in a school room. I already know most of the math I need for the job, and what I don't know, Mr. Cox said he'd teach me. Papa and I had talked about me working as an apprentice instead of going to school."

That was news to Lily. "When did you do that?"

"Right before we left Iowa. He was in favor of it if I found someone good to work with."

She believed him. Matt didn't lie. Her father had believed in an education—to a certain point. He'd often said that sometimes the best education came from living life and working a job, whether it was a trade or business. "We'll see how you feel toward the end of summer."

"We'll stay here until then?"

"Longer if needed. I hope somebody will capture Price and Smith and bring them back for trial."

It wasn't the only reason she wanted to stay and her brother knew it. But neither of them mentioned a certain handsome, stubborn sheriff.

* * *

"Lily had steam comin' out her ears when I left the house." Quint poured himself a cup of coffee and sat down in the spare chair, propping his feet up on the desk.

Ransom grimaced and poured a cup of coffee from the pot on the stove in the corner. "I'd rather suffer with Elton's snoring than get a tongue-lashing from her."

Quint tipped his head toward the jail cells. "The noise isn't as annoying as it was in the old place. Putting a thick door between here and there was a good idea."

Ransom walked back to the desk, aware that Quint watched his every step. His friend probably noticed that he was leaning a little heavier on the cane. After all the excitement, his back had tensed up into a steady ache, and he was tired already.

"How you doin'?"

"I was a little wobbly when I got back here, but I'd hurried over there as fast as I could." Ransom picked up the cup, blowing lightly on the coffee. "My mind worked fine. Sorted out the best way to handle it as soon as I stepped through the door. After Elton was tucked in the jail I went over the incident, step by step." He looked up, meeting Quint's gaze. "Even congratulated myself on a small victory.

"Then I went over it again and accepted the truth. I'm not ready to handle things on my own, Quint. If Elton had stumbled into me, much less really come after me, I would have been dustin' the floor with my britches. Who knows what might have happened then. I'm going to resign and ask Cade to make you sheriff."

Quint's feet hit the floor. Hot coffee sloshed on his

hand and he bit back a mild curse. "I won't take the job. I'm just finally gettin' comfortable being a deputy. I don't want to be sheriff."

"You need someone to back you up. I've been foolin' myself thinking I could do that. I move too slow. I'm not strong enough, and I'm not steady on my feet." Ransom set the cup on the desk, his heart heavy. "I'm unreliable, Quint. People depend on me to protect them and their property and I can't do it."

"You have more experience being a lawman than anybody around here. There's more to being a sheriff than how fast you can move or how steady you are on your feet."

"True. But all my knowledge doesn't do me any good if I can't chase a thief or dodge a bullet."

Quint sat quietly for a few minutes thinking about it. "Stay on as sheriff, but ask them to hire another deputy until you're up to snuff."

"They can't afford another deputy."

"Then take a cut in pay or something. Ransom, we need you to run things. I've never met anybody who can size up people the way you can. You see things that I don't, spot trouble before I see it. The people of this county picked you because you know how to keep the peace, not just because you're fast with a gun."

Ransom gave him a wry smile. "They didn't pick me at all and you know it." The previous sheriff had turned the job over to him when he became a United States Marshal. Proctor had three years remaining in the term when he left, so Ransom inherited the job for three years. "If you take over now, you'll have a year under your belt by the next election."

"I won't let you rope me into it. And you're not going to up and quit." Quint left his coffee cup on the end of the desk and stood. "I'll check on things in the district. When I get back you can go on home."

"I can stay the night. With Elton tucked away, things should stay quiet." His prisoner snorted particularly loud. "Everywhere but here, anyway."

"Quiet doesn't have anything to do with it. You're hurtin'. I can see it by the way you move. By morning, you'll be too stiff and sore to walk home. Besides, I'm bored. I had a good visit with Jessie and the kids. Left after the kids went to bed because the baby was sleeping. Jessie needed to grab some shut-eye while she had a chance. The folks at the boarding house will be going to bed soon, too, if only to escape Alvah's longwinded stories.

"You think about asking Cade to hire another deputy. Since there's no city marshal, maybe the city and county can go together. We've been doin' the marshal's duties for months already. Might as well get paid for it."

"There's something to that. It's not so bad since the city council decided we didn't have to shoot stray dogs." Ransom and Quint had both refused unless the animal was actually posing a menace.

"That'll work as long as Hiram keeps taking in the ones nobody else wants. Cade's coming into town tomorrow for a special commissioner's meeting."

"I'll talk to them," said Ransom. "Though I'm not sure what I'll tell them. I'll study on it a spell. I'm not anxious to give up my job, but I don't like taking money when I can't do the work properly."

Quint walked toward the door. "You can be the range boss, oversee everything. Of course, on most ranches, they think they should earn more money, not less."

"That wouldn't sit well with the bureaucrats."

"Careful, or I'll tell Cade you're callin' him names." Grinning, Quint left to keep the town peaceful.

The next afternoon, Ransom met with the county commissioners. He didn't mince words. "I'm not in good enough shape to do my job."

"The way I hear it, you handled Elton without any problem," said Tony Birch, commissioner of precinct three.

"I was lucky." Or more likely the prayers of a good woman saw him through. "He didn't do much to challenge me. If he had, things might have turned ugly. I don't know how long it will be before I'm back to normal. I propose that I stay on as sheriff at a quarter of my regular pay to oversee things. You hire another deputy on a temporary basis to help Quint until I get well. If I'm still not able to do the job in six months, then I'll resign and you can choose another sheriff."

"And if we don't accept this proposal?" asked Bob Overstreet, the other commissioner.

"Then I'll resign immediately and suggest you make Quint sheriff."

"He doesn't want the job," said Cade. "He told me flat out that if we try to make him sheriff, he'll resign, too. I think we should do as Ransom asks. We need him to run things, but this will give him time to heal. I talked to Doc Wilson before I came over here."

Ransom glanced at him in surprise. He wondered if

the doctor had been as blunt with Cade as he had been with him—that there was a good possibility that he might never be the man he'd been before.

"Doc says that it could take six months for him to heal." Cade met Ransom's gaze, and he knew Doc had laid things on the line with his friend. "He emphasized that Ransom needed to be free to rest whenever he felt like it as well as work when he was able. He said both were equally important to his recovery. He can do that if we have two deputies."

"Is quarter pay enough for you to live on?" asked Tony.

"It is. I have some money saved up."

"Enough to court Miss Lily?" Bob grinned at him. "She might like to do more than just sit in that porch swing I saw Matt putting up this morning."

Though he wanted to tell the man that his love-life wasn't any of his business, Ransom smiled. "I've got enough." If he decided to court her. He didn't think he should, but he wanted to. Lord help him, how he wanted to.

"You got somebody in mind to help out?" Tony leaned the chair back on two legs.

"Blake Stanton," said Ransom.

"Ty's stage driver?" asked Bob.

Ransom nodded. "He was a deputy for several years down around San Antonio. I worked with him some when I was with the Rangers. He's a good man."

"What's his wife going to think of him being a deputy again?"

"I don't know," said Cade. "But from what I hear, she's not real happy about him being gone so much with the stage. Ty has already hired another driver. I move we ask Blake Stanton to work as deputy, a position to be reevaluated in six months or sooner if Ransom decides he's well enough to handle the job," said Cade. "All in favor say *aye.*"

"Aye."

"Aye."

"Motion carried." Cade turned to Ransom. "I move that we pay Sheriff Starr one quarter of his regular salary for the next six months or until he is well enough to resume his duties full-time, whichever comes first. I also move that Sheriff Starr's main duty will be to oversee the running of sheriff's office and deputies, and that he be given the freedom to work only when he feels up to it. All in favor, say *aye.*"

The other two commissioners voiced their approval.

"Blake will be bringing the stage in later today," said Cade. "I'll talk to him after we settle on a salary."

"Much obliged. Don't be stingy," said Ransom as he stood. "I'm not forfeiting seventy-five percent of my income so you can improve a road somewhere."

"The better the roads, the more people will come here," said Tony.

"All the more reason to hire another good deputy." Ransom bade them goodbye and left them to their deliberations. If Blake would agree to do it, Ransom could follow the doctor's orders—to take it easy—and spend more time with Lily.

However, he wasn't convinced that spending more time with Lily was wise. He was already more than halfway in love with her. He thought her feelings for him ran deep, too.

Glancing down at the cane, he felt like smashing it against the wall. *What if I can't get rid of this thing, Lord?* What would he do if he still needed it in six months? He'd be out of a job. Despite telling her that he'd buy a little ranch and hire someone to run it, he didn't have a good feeling about that. For one thing, he didn't know beans about ranching. For another, it was risky. Ranchers had to contend with drought, bad winters, low cattle prices and any number of calamities that could leave them penniless.

He wasn't rich, but he had a good savings socked away. He'd made a few investments over the years that had paid him well. Surviving for a while wouldn't be a problem. Providing for a wife and family would be.

His heart ached at the possibility of never knowing the joy of a family and a good, loving wife. Even that wasn't as troubling as the thought of permanently being crippled. He tried to have faith and believe that he could handle it with God's help. But his prayers and proclamations rang hollow.

He'd never been so frightened in his life.

Chapter Fourteen

Blake was happy to take the job and started to work right away. On Wednesday afternoon, Ransom, Lily and Matt went out to the ranch to visit with Cade and his family. Ty and Camille were there, too.

The men relaxed on the back porch while the women cleaned up the supper dishes. Brad was teaching Matt how to rope a stump, and Ellie played with a kitten on the end of the porch. Baby Jacob was in the house, asleep in his cradle.

Ransom glanced into the kitchen, smiling as the females discussed recipes. For the first time since Ty and Cade had each gotten married, he didn't feel like the odd man out.

"How's Blake doing?" asked Cade.

"Fits right in," said Ransom. "They've lived in Willow Grove long enough that he knows the town and the business owners. His previous experience gives him confidence, and that prompts respect. Between them, I think he and Quint can handle things."

"Might get more complicated when all the cowboys show up later in the week." Ty leaned back in his chair and propped his feet up on the porch railing. "Holler if y'all need some help."

"Will do, but we should be all right. I'll keep watch on the saloons right downtown, and they'll keep an eye on the district. Most of the action will be down there."

"As long as Elton stays home or sober." Cade watched Ellie and the kitten, his expression tender.

A jolt of envy caught Ransom by surprise. It took him a second to focus on Cade's comment. "He swears he'll stay off the liquor, and he probably will—until the next time he has a row with his missus. She keeps threatening to go back east and stay with her sister. It would be safer for all of us if she would."

"He might do better this time. Nate said Elton felt real bad about shooting him," said Ty. "No wonder, after Bonnie gave him what-for."

"She had good reason." Camille walked out the back door, followed by Jessie and Lily.

Ty jumped to his feet, the front legs of the chair landing with a thump. "Sit here, sweetheart." Taking her elbow he gently guided her into the chair. "You shouldn't have been standing so long. How are you feeling?"

Camille smiled up at him, patting his hand. "I feel fine, dear. I barely stood at all. The only thing Jessie and Lily let me do was dry the silverware and they made me do that sitting down." She rested her hands on her rounded stomach.

A minute later, Camille jumped slightly and laughed. "Junior is wiggling around again. Ty, let's go for a little walk and rock him to sleep."

"Does that work?" asked Lily, leaning against the railing and shaking her head when Cade offered her his seat.

"It seems to." Camille held out her hand and let Ty help her up.

"I need to stretch my legs." Ransom stood, glad that getting up was easier than it sometimes was. "Lily, do you want to go for a walk?"

"I'd enjoy one. I still have kinks from the buggy ride."

"The road isn't that bad." Cade frowned and surprised Jessie by pulling her down on his lap. She squealed, then laughed and put her arm around his shoulders.

"The road was fine. I'm just not used to sitting that long anymore."

"It's not much longer than a church service."

"But at church, we get up and down a few times for the singing."

"She still wiggles around." Ransom winked at her. "Almost as much as Ellie."

"I don't wiggle." Ellie picked up her kitten and joined them. "I squirm."

"That you do," said Cade with a laugh.

Ellie frowned when the other adults joined him. "It keeps my bottom from going to sleep."

When they laughed harder, Ellie's lower lip drooped into a pout.

Ransom held out his hand to the little girl. "Don't let these grown-ups get to you, sweetie. That's the same reason they move around in the pews but they won't admit it. Come on, you can help us show Lily the horses."

"Okay." Ellie carefully placed the kitten on the porch and hopped down the steps. She skipped on ahead a short distance, then came running back as Ransom slowly made his way down from the porch. "Do you go so slow because it hurts?"

"That's part of it." He glanced at Lily as she moved down the steps at his side, but she didn't put her arm around him. He missed that, but he was glad he didn't need the help anymore. "It's kind of tricky going down steps on three legs."

"The cane is like another leg?"

"Yep." He and Lily reached the ground and started toward the barn. Their destination was the pasture beyond it and the corrals. Ty and Camille followed them down the steps, then walked beside them.

"Why do you need it?" Ellie danced backwards a couple of yards in front of them.

"My leg won't hold me up by itself, so I lean on the cane to bear some of my weight."

"Then having the cane is good."

"Yep. I'd be in a pickle without it."

Ellie giggled. "Pickles aren't that big."

"True. And I'd look funny in a green suit."

"You'd smell funny, too," said Ty. "Like vinegar."

The little girl laughed and turned, racing on ahead.

Ransom slanted at glance at Ty. "See what you're in for?"

"Yeah. Ain't it fun?" Ty smiled, but worry hovered in his eyes.

Ransom felt a twinge of guilt for stewing about his own predicament. He couldn't imagine his friend's fear about the upcoming birth. Ty had watched one wife die in childbirth and lost the baby a few hours later. How did a man survive such a loss?

He reached for Lily's hand, holding it so tightly that she looked at him in surprise. He eased his grip but pulled her a little closer to his side. Was loving worth it? Did the moments of joy and love make up for the times of pain and sorrow? Did he want to take that risk?

"Have you picked out names?" asked Lily.

"Sarah Elizabeth if it's a girl," said Ty. "In memory of our mothers."

"William Tyler if it's a boy." Camille leaned her head against Ty's shoulder. "For the two men dearest to me. My father and my husband."

"Your father must be excited about the baby."

Camille shook her head, sadness touching her face. "He died several years ago."

"I'm sorry." Lily was silent for a minute. "Your baby won't have any grandparents?"

"No, just a doting aunt and uncle." Ty waved at Ellie, who raced back around the barn to see if they were still coming. "And a couple of cousins who can't wait for his or her arrival."

"They'll spoil that young'un rotten." Ransom sneaked a peek at Lily. Though she probably seemed fine to the others, he suspected she was dealing with some strong emotion—such as suddenly realizing that her children would never know her parents.

They walked past the barn and corrals, spotting five

horses grazing in the fenced pasture. "Watch out for the barbed wire." Ransom pointed to the four strips of spiky wire stretched between each post.

"Doesn't that hurt them?" Lily lightly touched a barb with her fingertip.

"It can but they don't usually run into it. They're pretty good about avoiding fences, no matter what they're made of." Ty whistled, and a horse and pony trotted toward them. "We use barbed wire around the pastures because railing is too expensive and hard to come by."

"They're using wire some in Iowa, too, but we lived in the city so I've never actually seen any." Lily glanced at Ransom when he released her hand, then smiled as the horses cautiously approached them. "I can't imagine trying to fence a whole ranch with wood railing. I've read they use flat stones in England."

"Don't have any around here. There are some round rocks but they don't stack very well," said Ty.

"I don't expect they would." Lily gently patted the horse on the side of the face when the little mare came up to her. "Aren't you a sweet thing."

"She's Brad's horse." Ellie reached through the fence to rub the pony's nose. "Tater's mine. Daddy says we'll grow up together. She's just big enough for me to ride."

"It must be fun to have a pony of your very own."

"It is. She's sweet. I wanted to ride her out tomorrow to watch them cut out the herds, but Daddy said I should stay in the buggy with Mama." Her mouth curled down and she scuffed the toe of her shoe on the ground. "He's lettin' Brad ride Frisky, but he can't get too close."

"That's right, honey." Ty ruffled her curls. "We'll watch from up on the bluff. The cattle will be tired, but they could still stampede if anything spooks them."

"I don't want to get trampled," the little girl said solemnly. "Don't want Brad to, either."

"None of us do. That's why we'll stay out of the way and let the cowboys do their job."

Ransom rested his hand on the fence post, watching Lily survey the countryside and the sunset paint the sky with orange and gold. "Pretty, isn't it?"

She nodded, her expression peaceful. "It has a rugged beauty, a wildness to it."

"Doesn't resemble Iowa much."

"No, but I like it. I can see why people would put down roots here."

Ty, Camille and Ellie had wandered farther down the fence to check a sagging stretch of wire.

"Are you going to put down roots here, sugar?" Ransom asked quietly.

She met his gaze, a softness in her eyes that made him catch his breath. "Maybe. I'm keeping my options open."

"Good," he said gruffly. He looked away, afraid she might see how desperately he wanted her to stay.

Ellie bounced up, rescuing him from having to say anything else. "Uncle Ty says we'd better go back to the house 'cause it's gonna be dark in a few minutes."

They strolled on back to the house and spent the evening talking. Though Ransom contributed to the conversation now and then, mostly he sat back and enjoyed the company. It was good to see both Lily and Matt laugh at Cade and Ty's stories. There had been a time when he didn't think she would ever laugh again.

Chapter Fifteen

After breakfast, armed with a picnic lunch, they set off on the hour-long trip to where they would watch the herds being separated. Cade had explained that there were cattle from two other nearby ranches moving with theirs. They would halt them in a protected valley with a good stream flowing through it and spend a few days sorting out the cattle.

When they arrived at the bluff, Lily's jaw dropped. "Oh, my goodness!"

"Three thousand or so Longhorns in one spot is an impressive sight, isn't it?" Ransom got a kick out of watching her amazement.

"It's incredible. Even more so when I stop and think that they drove them about three hundred miles."

"Some of them were that far away. They start out near the Pecos and work their way back, picking up cattle as they find them. Each ranch works a different section, bringing them to a central location, then they move the whole herd east from there."

"This is only part of them," said Ty. "Some of the western ranches cut their cattle out long before now."

"They look hungry. You can see their ribs." Compassion flavored her voice.

"It's a long trip, and it was a rough winter. Cade said last night that they'd lost quite a few head, both before the roundup started and on the way back. He rode out to meet them early yesterday. It wasn't as bad as he'd feared but worse than he'd hoped."

Again the thought of buying a ranch seemed much too risky. *Maybe I'll start my own detective agency*, Ransom mused. *If I have to give up being sheriff*. Then he put it from his mind. Today was for enjoying the company of his friends and Lily. Funny, he didn't think of her as a friend. She *was* one, closer than people he had known much longer, but she meant more to him than that. He wasn't sure he wanted to delve too deeply into those thoughts right now, either.

"There's Daddy!" Ellie pointed at Cade and jumped up and down on the floorboard of the two-seat buckboard she shared with her mother and Lydia Noble, who held baby Jacob. Lydia's husband, Asa, worked for Cade. He had been the wagon boss for several outfits during the roundup, which meant he was the one in charge.

Cade had gone down the slope at the far end of the bluff and rode across the flat, grassy valley in an easy lope. Nearing the herd, he slowed his horse to a walk.

"Ellie, quit bouncing," ordered Jessie, turning and

clamping her hand down on her daughter's shoulder. "We don't need to be jostled off the seat."

Though her voice wasn't sharp, Ransom detected the worry there. He didn't blame her. Having that many cattle, some with a six-foot spread of horns, bunched up in one place was dangerous. None of them would rest easy until the cattle were all moved back to their home ranges, happily grazing in small groups or by themselves.

"Is that Asa he's talking to?" asked Lily.

"Yep. He's likely told the crew how he wants things done. Waiting for Cade's approval is more courtesy than necessity." Ransom looked over at Ty and Camille in the next buggy. "Right, Ty?"

"You called it. He'll probably come back up here and watch. Wouldn't want to get all dusty and dirty." Ty grinned at Jessie, knowing she had seen her husband dusty and dirty plenty of times.

At Asa's command, the cowboys fanned out, driving various cows from the herd amid much bawling and stirring up the dust. Calves raced after their mamas, terrified of being left behind.

The horses did much of the work, but the cowboys sometimes added a swat with a rope or a yell. Occasionally, they roped a reluctant critter and led or pulled it to the appropriate bunch. The men who weren't doing the cutting kept the three smaller herds together.

Ty pointed to the group on the left. "Those are ours. The ones back behind the main herd belong to the Lazy J and the ones on the right are John Ridge's." He laughed when Cade started back to join them. "See, I told you he'd skedaddle before they stirred up too much dust."

"Speaking of dust," said Matt, pointing to the east. "Who's that over there? Looks like they're coming this way."

Standing beside his buggy, Ty turned to look at the two buggies and a strange-looking wagon. "That's trouble."

Just then Cade spotted them and took off at a gallop to meet them.

"That's Alvah's photography wagon," said Ransom. "He built a darkroom that he could take along with him."

"He ought to know better than to get down there in the middle of things. Most folks in town do." Frowning, Ty shaded his eyes as Cade reached them. They all stopped, but as Alvah and Cade talked, the other two started up again.

"Isn't that George Houghton, the banker from back east who bragged that he's going to build a cattle empire?" Ransom shook his head. "He hasn't got a bit of cow sense."

"The other one is Baron Millborn," said Ty. "Blast it, he has Prissy with him and he's heading right for the herd." He looked uncertainly at Camille. "I'd better go down and help Cade."

"I'll be fine, dear. But don't go getting yourself shot over some cattle."

"I don't plan on it. Matt, may I use your horse?"

"Sure." Matt dismounted quickly, leading the horse over to him. Ty mounted just as quickly and took off along the edge of the bluff until he could go down the side. As soon as Ty hit the flatland, he kicked the horse to a gallop, riding at an angle to intercept them.

Ransom put his hand on Lily's shoulder. "I'd better go, too. You stay here and keep an eye on Camille."

"Can you get down there in the buggy?"

"I'll manage." Though he wondered the same thing. There wasn't a road of any kind going down the bluff. *Lord, I need a way to get down there pronto.*

Lily quickly hopped out and stepped aside so he could turn the buggy around. "Be careful."

"Yes, ma'am." He smiled, wanting to encourage her so she wouldn't worry too much. At the same time, it was nice having a woman care whether or not he broke his neck.

He had to go farther than Ty did, but he found a spot with a slope gradual enough to accommodate the buggy. The horse balked for a second, then gingerly obeyed his command. Even though the ground was smooth enough not to get stuck, the trip down the hill jarred him plenty. Clenching his jaw, Ransom ignored the pain as best he could.

When he turned toward the herd, he saw that Ty had stopped the banker and the baron, but he'd only done it by drawing his pistol. He didn't dare pull the trigger near the herd. Ransom hoped the other two men didn't realize that. The Englishman was shouting loud enough to start a stampede without a gun. Prissy was tugging on his arm, trying to shush him. As Ransom pulled the buggy up in front of them, Millborn turned his anger on her and drew back his hand.

"You hit her, Millborn, and I'll throw you in jail for assault."

The man glared at Prissy and lowered his hand. "She needs to learn her place."

"She likely just saved your hide." Ransom glanced at the herd, then focused back on the Englishman. "Your noise already has the cattle stirred up. Another minute or two of yelling, and we would have had a stampede on our hands."

The banker's face went white, and he nervously watched the milling cattle. The Englishman stuck his nose up in the air. "An exaggeration, no doubt. And no concern of ours."

Ransom looked at Prissy's wide eyes and pale face. She understood the danger they'd been in. "I don't care if your arrogance gets you gored and squished, Millborn, but I'd hate for Miss Priscilla to be trampled to death because of your stupidity."

"How dare you!"

"I dare because I'm right." Ransom leveled his gaze on Millborn. "And because I'm the law."

The Englishman glanced at the cane propped up beside him and snorted in dismissal.

Ransom barely held his temper. "Don't push me, Millborn, or you'll sit in jail until the judge comes back from his vacation in a month or two."

"As the *law,* you should arrest McKinnon." The baron pointed at Ty. "He accosted us with a gun."

"If anyone gets arrested," drawled Ty, exaggerating his Texas accent, "it's going to be you for trespassing." He pointed the gun right between Millborn's eyes. "Can I shoot him, Ransom? I don't like him."

"Well, he is on McKinnon land uninvited. And he is about as likeable as a cockroach." He glanced at Prissy again, noting a twinkle of amusement in her eyes.

The baron squirmed, but he was still full of bravado. And smarter than Ransom had figured. "He can't shoot me. The noise would stampede the cattle."

Asa rode up beside Ty. A second later he was joined by Cade. Ransom noted that Alvah was heading toward the end of the bluff, where he would be able to drive his wagon up to the top.

"Well, now, you have a point." Ransom turned his attention to Prissy. "Miss Priscilla, can you drive a buggy?"

"Yes." She studied him warily.

"Could you find your way back to town?"

"Yes. But—"

"Good. Then there's no reason for me not to order Asa to use his rope and drag your uppity companion back to town. Or maybe halfway to town. He can go the rest of the way on foot. If he can walk, that is."

"Now, see here—"

Prissy laid her hand on the baron's arm and turned on the charm. "Sheriff Starr, we really didn't mean any harm." She shifted slightly, leaning against the Englishman's side. "We were going on a picnic when we ran into Mr. Houghton and Mr. Crutcher. They said they were coming out to see the herd, and we thought it would be a lark.

"Milly," she crooned, "if we get any closer to those smelly old cows, we'll be all covered with dust. Let's go on to the spring and sit in the shade and have our picnic." She moved her hand from Millborn's arm to trace his ear with her fingertip. "All by ourselves."

"Uh, well…yes, that's a good idea, my dear." Millborn frowned at the others. "No harm done here, after all."

And there won't be if I can help it, thought Ransom. "Miss Priscilla, why don't you join us up on the bluff. There's room in Jessie's buckboard for the ride back to the ranch house. We'd see that you get back to town."

"No, thank you, sheriff. I'll stay with Lord Millborn."

Was that regret he saw in her eyes? She was of age. There was nothing he could do if she stayed of her own free will. "All right. Y'all have a nice picnic."

As Millborn drove his buggy around and went back the direction they'd come, Ransom focused on Houghton. "I'm thinking you had no idea of the trouble you were about to cause."

"You're exactly right, sheriff." The banker turned to Ty and Cade. "Gentlemen, I see I have much to learn about cattle and ranching. I apologize."

"Apology accepted," said Cade. "You're welcome to watch with us. I convinced Alvah that was the best place to observe the men working the cattle. We have plenty of food to share for dinner."

"I'd be delighted. I am getting a mite hungry. Didn't realize it was so far out here."

Shaking his head, Asa went back to supervise the work.

"Come on, Mr. Houghton, I'll show you how to drive up to the bluff." Cade waited for the banker to turn the buggy around, then rode beside him.

Ty put away his pistol and looked at Ransom. "Milly?" They burst into laughter and started back to join the others.

On the way up the hillside, Ransom spotted Millborn's buggy off in the distance, turning toward a picturesque little spot called Breedon's Spring. He thought of Quint and the feelings he held for Prissy. It was too bad that she placed more value on a man's pocketbook than his character.

Chapter Sixteen

Following the trip to Cade and Jessie's, Ransom often thought about the time they spent there. Lily and Matt had been fascinated with the ranch and how things were done. It had been a much needed time of relaxation and diversion, both for them and for him.

He sat on the sidewalk in front of the sheriff's office late Saturday afternoon, sipping a cup of coffee, remembering how proud Lily had been when he'd stopped Millborn and the banker from riding right into the herd. Despite him pointing out that the others had as much to do with it as he had, she refused to give them more than token credit—when she was talking to him anyway. She'd called him a hero, but it wasn't true. The banker would have turned away once he realized the situation, but he seriously doubted that Millborn would have shown him or his badge a smidgen of respect if the others hadn't been there to back him up.

They had all been lazy until midafternoon, eating under the shade of a few mesquites and watching the men work the cattle. Then they'd returned to the ranch house and rested a bit before the drive back to town. Despite Matt's earlier declaration that he'd never want to be a cowboy, Ransom detected some reluctance in leaving the ranch.

Shifting his leg, he surveyed the street. He'd paid for the jaunt with more pain, but it was worth it to have spent so much time with Lily and to see her have fun. Jessie and Camille did their best to be her friends and encourage her to stay in Willow Grove. He appreciated their efforts.

Most of the cowboys who had been gone on the roundup had ridden into town Saturday morning. So far, it had been fairly peaceful, but Ransom didn't expect it to stay that way. After the men hit the baths and the barber for a haircut and shave, many headed straight for the saloons to gamble and drink away their pay.

Quint was grabbing some supper at the café while Blake patrolled the red-light district. Ransom kept watch on the downtown area from his chair. He was centrally located, so he'd decided it was smarter to stay right where people could find him.

Activity on the street had picked up during the last hour with the townspeople finishing up their errands and hurrying home to supper. The ranch families who had come in for their Saturday shopping strolled about. Wives visited the mercantile or the grocers while their husbands gathered in small groups along the wooden sidewalks to chat or bought supplies at McKinnon Brothers. Children dashed along the walk or across the street, excited to see their friends or stop for some candy at the confectioners.

More cowboys were roaming around, too, coming from the rougher saloons and dance halls in the district in search of a good meal. Ransom spotted three staggering down the walk two blocks away. He stood, walking toward them as fast as he dared. He went down the steps, intent on stopping their mischief before it started. By the time his boots touched the dirt, however, they'd found it in the form of Winston Sidell, a traveler from back east, who picked the wrong time to leave the Barton Hotel.

"Lookie what we got here." They circled the hapless gent. "A feller from the big city." The cowboy flicked Sidell's bowler hat with his fingertip, almost knocking it off.

"Lefty Joe, back off," Ransom called from the middle of the street.

"Aw, Sheriff, we's jus' havin' some fun."

One of the other cowboys grabbed the man's shoulder and spun him around. "Dance, fancy man."

Sidell stumbled but glanced at Ransom and took courage. "I will not."

Lefty Joe grabbed the bowler and threw it in the air, reaching for his gun—but it wasn't there. He'd checked it in the sheriff's office when they rode into town. Muttering a few choice words when the hat hit the ground, he tried to stomp it, but his brain and foot weren't communicating.

"All right boys, that's enough." Ransom stopped in front of them. "Give the man his hat."

"Nope." Lefty Joe grinned at Ransom. He wasn't much more than a kid and had a habit of being obnoxious. "Can't make me."

"You care to bet on that?" Ransom noted the other two edge away.

Lefty looked down at Ransom's cane, his lips curling into a sneer. "You and who else?"

"My good friend, Mr. Colt." Ransom drew his pistol faster than Lefty could focus on it. "Now pick up the hat, dust it off, hand it to the gentleman and apologize."

Frowning, Lefty Joe bent down and fell right over, barely missing the hat. He rolled over on his back and giggled. "Oops."

Ransom looked at his companions. One of them hurriedly picked up the hat and brushed it off. Handing it to Sidell, he mumbled an apology. Then he and his friend awkwardly hauled Lefty Joe to his feet.

"Go get some supper to soak up some of that whiskey. If you cause any more trouble, you'll spend the night in the calaboose." When they walked away, Ransom holstered his gun.

"Of all the nerve." The visitor glared after the cowboys. "I certainly won't recommend to my acquaintances to stop in this town."

"It's normally not so bad. The men have just come back from weeks on the range. I'd advise you to stay in the hotel this evening after you've had your supper. They're apt to be more rambunctious as the night wears on. Tomorrow will be peaceful 'cause they'll be nursing hangovers."

"Thank you for coming to my assistance, sir. If I

hadn't been so startled, I suppose I could have simply walked away."

"If you were quick." Ransom thought for a second. "Maybe not so quick. They weren't movin' real fast."

"I feared they had guns."

"You're wise to be cautious. They're supposed to check in their weapons when they arrive in town, but a lot of them hide a pocket pistol if they can get away with it. It doesn't feel natural to a man used to wearing a sidearm to be without it. Enjoy your meal." Sidell nodded and hurried across the street to the restaurant.

Ransom peeked though the windows of a couple of saloons before turning back toward the office. When he heard a shriek up the street, he looked toward the commotion and his heart froze. A giant of a man—a freighter, judging by his clothes—had Lily cornered against the wall of DeWalt's Apothecary. He reached for her. She swung at him with her purse but missed.

Ransom took off at what he desperately wished was a run but what might pass for a fast walk. Ignoring the pain shooting across his back and down his leg, he shoved people out of the way and bellowed, "Leave her alone!"

If the man heard him, he didn't pay any attention. He jerked the purse out of her hand and flung it aside. Grabbing her at the waist, he threw her over his shoulder. "I got me a real wildcat," he crowed.

Yelling at him, she pounded his back with her fists and kicked frantically until he clamped a beefy arm across her legs. Bystanders protested and a cowboy tried to help, but the attacker knocked him aside with one punch.

Ransom abandoned the boardwalk for the street, using the cane automatically, almost running, though agony jolted him with every step. Nothing mattered except reaching Lily. He'd beat the man to a pulp. Kill him if necessary. Anything to protect her.

When he was thirty feet from them, the cane snapped in two. His leg gave way and he fell forward, hitting the hard packed dirt with a bone-jarring thud. Stars danced before his eyes, and it took a minute to catch his breath. When his mind began to work again, he realized Lily's screams had stopped. Terrified, he raised his head—and almost wept in relief. Quint had the barrel of his pistol pressed against the freighter's temple. The man slowly and carefully lowered Lily's feet to the sidewalk.

She straightened, swaying a bit until Mrs. Peabody put her arm around her to steady her.

Ransom struggled to sit up, and Ty ran to help him up. Ed was right behind him with a new cane. Once he was standing, Ransom took a step and almost went down again when his good leg partially buckled. If he hadn't been so furious, he might have given more than a fleeting thought to what damage he'd done to his back.

Ty hovered beside him as he walked the rest of the way. Quint still held his gun on the man but had put some distance between them. By the time Ty reached the sidewalk, Lily had regained her equilibrium and her temper.

"You big oaf!" She hauled off and punched her attacker in the nose. He howled and the crowd roared with laughter as Lily grimaced and shook her hand, then rubbed it.

Ransom drew his gun from the holster and pointed it at the man's heart. The assailant's eyes grew round, and his face paled behind the hand holding his nose.

"Ransom, don't…" Ty's words barely penetrated the red haze in Ransom's mind.

"He attacked my woman." Ransom spoke quietly, his voice cold and hard.

The big man sank to his knees. "I didn't know she belonged to you."

"But you could tell she was a lady." He cocked the pistol.

"Don't do this," warned Ty.

Ransom raised the gun, leveling it between the man's eyes.

"Ransom, he didn't hurt me." Lily's soft voice drew his attention, her eyes dark with worry. Then she grinned. "Not as much as I hurt him."

Her surprising change of mood snapped him out of his rage. His gaze shifted back to the villain cowering at his feet. Blood dripped from his nose, and he looked cross-eyed at the barrel of Ransom's pistol. The absurdity of the man's expression pulled him back into focus. He was about to kill a man in cold blood.

Because he hadn't been able to protect the woman he loved.

Ransom took his finger from the trigger and pointed the gun at the sidewalk, carefully easing the hammer forward. He looked at Quint just in time to see relief flash across his friend's face. "Throw him in jail." He scanned the crowd and holstered the pistol. "Y'all go on about your business. We're done here."

In more ways than one. His back and leg were on

fire, his insides shaking like a wet dog. He kept a firm grip on the cane and tucked the thumb of his free hand inside his gun belt. "Quint, I'm goin' home. You and Blake will have to handle things tonight."

"We'll manage." Quint grabbed the freighter's arm and jerked him to his feet. "March." The man glanced sheepishly at Lily and hung his head.

The crowd scattered, but their excitement increased to a low roar.

"Do you need some help getting home?" asked Ty.

"No. I can make it." He hoped.

"I'm going that way, too," said Lily. "I'll walk with you."

Ransom's mind swirled, repeating the whole episode in heartbreaking clarity. He forced himself to concentrate on putting one foot in front of the other. Otherwise, he'd fall on his face—again.

Lily was unusually quiet. Probably in shock now that it all was over. Or maybe it was because he'd called her his woman in front of half the town. That must have embarrassed the life out of her. He had no right to make that claim. He was worthless.

They turned the corner and walked half a block down the empty side street leading to the boarding house. Lily suddenly halted. Ransom stopped, too, leaned against the lumber yard fence and looked at her.

She put her arms around him, holding tight, burying her face against his shoulder. He felt a shiver race through her, then another. Needing to balance with the cane, he put one arm around her and held her close. "You still carrying that gun in your purse?"

She nodded. "But he surprised me. I couldn't get my

purse open. If I'd gotten a good hit with it before he took it away from me, I would have knocked him flat."

"Maybe you should wear a gun belt."

She chuckled and gripped a handful of his shirt. "The cowboys would say you weren't being fair."

"You have a right to protect yourself, sugar." He dragged in a breath. "You can't count on me to do it."

She relaxed her hold and looked up at him. "You did the best you could."

"That's not good enough," he said angrily, lowering his arm, thankful when she released him and took a couple of steps back.

"You'll get better."

"What if I don't, Lily?" Fury and fear made his voice harsh. "It's been six weeks."

"And you've improved. You're walking when that doctor said you wouldn't."

"Barely." He took a few steps, realizing the truth of his comment. The pain grew by the second until it was almost unbearable. Sweat beaded on his face as he leaned against the fence. Nausea turned his stomach upside down. *Please, God, don't let me faint.*

"Merciful heavens!" Lily put her arm around his waist, literally holding him up. "There's a barrel of nails right here. Just one step."

Somehow, he dragged his leg over, and she guided him down to sit on the closed top. "Good…thing…it has…a lid."

"You ninny, I'm a better nurse than that." She checked his face with a frown. "Don't you pass out on me."

"Ain't planning on it." He closed his eyes and leaned

back against the fence, glad to have something to rest against. "Better go get Ty."

No answer. He opened his eyes to see her running toward Main Street. *She's a good woman, Lord. She deserves a lot better man than me.*

Chapter Seventeen

Lily wouldn't have gone to church the next morning, but Ransom flat-out ordered her to go away and leave him alone. Then as she was leaving, he hollered at her to tell Cade to come see him.

I should have stayed in my room, she thought, absently listening to the minister drone on, not making any sense. She thought maybe it was just her, but glancing around, she saw several people muffling yawns. The guest speaker, Reverend Somebody, was on his way back east from someplace where supposedly he'd led a great revival. Lily decided people must have flocked to the front just to shut him up.

Finally, half an hour after the service normally ended, Reverend Brownfield took advantage of the man's difficulty finding a Scripture verse and jumped to his feet. He thanked him and offered a speedy benediction.

As soon as they were outside, Lily found Cade. She'd been late to church and sat in the back row by herself. "Ransom wants you to come over."

"Can it wait until after dinner?"

"I'm sure it can. He just ordered me to order you to come see him."

"Uh-oh. He sounds grumpy."

"That's putting it mildly. Snarling is more accurate." Lily hesitated, uncertain as to how much she wanted to share with Cade. Ransom was closing her out as surely as if he were building a brick wall between them. "He's different this morning."

Cade frowned, studying her. "How?"

She glanced around to make sure no one was close enough to hear them. "He's curt, even rude."

"Probably the pain. Ty said he was in a world of hurt last night."

"Yes, he was. But it wasn't quite as bad this morning." She sighed, wishing she'd paid more attention to her surroundings the day before instead of watching Ransom stop the cowboys from harassing the man from back east. If she had noticed the freighter sooner, she could have avoided the whole situation, and Ransom wouldn't have reinjured himself.

"He's pulling away from me," she said softly. "Away from all of us. He told Mrs. Franklin this morning that he'll be moving out as soon as he can rent a house. I think he's decided that he isn't going to get well."

Cade grimaced. "It's an understandable fear, Lily, and he's putting distance between you and him because of it. I'll take Jessie and the kids out for dinner, then be over when we're done. Why don't you come eat with us?"

She shook her head. "I'd better get back and fix him something to eat."

"He'll appreciate it, even if he doesn't say so. I don't know if he's admitted it yet, but he loves you."

She hoped with all her heart that he was right, though she hid her feelings with a shrug. "I don't know about that." But he had called her his woman. That had to count for something.

"He's also a proud man, used to being in control and handling problems with ease. This one isn't easy. Give him time to come to grips with it."

"I can't do much else, can I?" She waved at Matt when he noticed she was there. "I'll tell Ransom that you'll be over later."

Cade nodded and left to join Jessie and the kids.

Matt walked up, draping his arm around his sister's shoulders in a light hug. "I thought you weren't coming."

"Ransom changed my mind."

"He's still in a foul mood?" Matt moved his arm as they walked toward the boarding house.

"Rotten. He says he's moving out." She looked up at her brother—his height still amazed her sometimes. "He wants to see Cade this afternoon. I think he's given up and is going to resign his job."

"Maybe he should resign."

"How can you say that?" Lily frowned at him. "He's a lawman through and through. That's who he is."

"There's a lot more to him than that, Lil. But he's protected people for so long that he thinks that's all he's good for. Maybe God has something else in mind for him to do."

"What?"

Matt pulled a curl hanging along the back of her neck beneath her Sunday hat. "Probably dozens of things. Quit playing mother hen, Lily, and let the man do what he wants to do. Just pray for God to guide him."

Lily stopped and stared at her brother. "When did you get to be so smart?"

He grinned and playfully nudged her hat, though not hard enough to dislodge it. "When I got taller than you."

Laughing, Lily started walking again. "I don't think so, *little* brother."

He caught up with her. "Just remember what Granny used to say about keeping our noses out of other folks' business."

Ransom was asleep when they got home, so she made him a sandwich and tiptoed into his room, leaving the covered plate on the table by the bed. She stood there for a few minutes watching him, thankful that he appeared to be resting well. Finding her father's killers had faded as the priority in her life, though she still prayed daily—often many times a day—that they would be brought to justice.

During the night, her mind had accepted what her heart had known for weeks—she was in love with Ransom Starr. Was Cade right? Did Ransom love her, too? *Give me wisdom, Lord. Show me how to encourage him, to love him.*

As she took a step to leave, a floorboard squeaked, waking him. He turned his head and looked up at her. In that sleepy, unguarded moment, love glowed in his eyes and tenderness filled his countenance. Her heart sang. He stretched carefully, still groggy from sleep. "Church over already?"

"Yes, thankfully. We had a long-winded guest speaker, Reverend Whipple or Whippet, or something. He was trying to tie Jonah's whale to the fish where Jesus fed the five thousand with seven loaves and a few little fish. I couldn't make much sense of it."

"I can't think of a connection except they all swim." He winced as he sat up and let Lily stuff pillows behind him.

She wished he'd catch her hand and hold her there beside him as he had sometimes done in the past, but he seemed to remember that he was trying to put distance between them.

His voice and expression became cooler. "Did you see Cade?"

"Yes. He'll be over after they eat." She nodded to the plate on the table. "I made you a sandwich since you were asleep. But I can warm up some of the stew we had last night if you'd rather have it."

"Sandwich is fine." He yawned. "I'll probably go back to sleep after I eat."

Lily didn't need him spelling it out. She'd been dismissed. "I'll leave you to it then. I'm going to sit out on the back porch and read. Holler if you need anything."

"I'll be fine. Thanks."

She took a book outside, but she didn't read a word. Instead, she laid the open book on her lap and let her mind wander. No one else who lived in the boarding house was there at the moment. Even Matt had gone off to play baseball. He had joined the Willow Grove Rattlers and was practicing with them for the second time. He had played ball often in Iowa, though he'd never been on an official team.

Closing her eyes, she rested her head against the back of the rocking chair. It was more comfortable than the swing when she was alone. *If I ever get married,* she thought, *I want a porch swing.* Then again, maybe she wouldn't want one if Ransom wasn't her husband. Sitting in it would only remind her of the few evenings they had sat cozily side by side watching the sunset or the moon come up and the stars light up the heavens.

She couldn't imagine not having him in her life. How bleak and empty it would be. *Lord, I love him and want to be with him, even if he doesn't completely get well. I'd rather he did heal up, of course. I hate to see him in pain, but he's a fine man and one I'd be proud to have as my husband, no matter what.*

Praying silently for his health and for wisdom, both on his part and hers, Lily didn't hear Cade come through the front door. She realized he had arrived when she heard quiet conversation coming through the open windows from Ransom's room. It didn't stay quiet long. In less than five minutes, they were arguing.

"No, I won't," said Cade, his voice rising while it dropped even deeper. "You agreed to stay on and run things."

"That's the problem. I can't *run.* I can't even walk fast without falling on my face."

"You fell because the cane broke."

"The next one will, too, under that kind of pressure.

I can't do my job, Cade, and that puts people in danger. They can't depend on me. I can't protect them."

"Nobody can protect everybody all the time."

"I only had five blocks to cover, and I couldn't do it. Cade, I'm crippled. Maybe I won't always be, but right now I'm only half a man. I'm worthless as a sheriff."

Tears stung Lily's eyes, and she covered her mouth with her hand to stifle a cry of denial.

"Hogwash!" shouted Cade. "I won't listen to talk like that."

"What are you going to do? Beat me up? One punch would do it. On second thought, it wouldn't even take a punch. Just a shove would put me out of action."

Cade muttered something. Ransom's mumbled reply wasn't any clearer.

"Lily," roared Cade from the window. "Get in here and talk some sense into him."

She jumped, then stood and laid the book on the chair. *Please, Jesus, tell me what to say.* Buying time, she eased the screen door shut when she went inside. Another pause in the kitchen. Another deep breath. Another silent plea for guidance.

"What's the problem?" Slowly walking into Ransom's room, she spied his sheriff's badge on the floor. She didn't know whether Cade had dropped it or whether Ransom had thrown it.

"He says he can't be sheriff." Cade leaned against the window sill and crossed his arms, blocking three-fourths of the window. "That he's turning in his badge."

Lily took a deep breath, hoping with all her heart that what she was about to say was the right thing.

Watching Ransom, she stopped at the foot of the bed. "I think he should."

Hurt and disappointment flashed across Ransom's face, and Lily's heart sank. *Please God, don't let me be wrong.*

"What!" Cade sprang away from the window and took a step toward her, his hands at his side.

Lily barely noticed. "Not permanently, but until he's healed up and has his strength back." She kept her eyes on Ransom, holding his gaze. "I think he would heal better and quicker if he left protecting the town to Quint and Blake for now. My granny used to say that worrying about what they couldn't do—or what they thought people expected them to do—only made it harder for sick folks to get well."

Ransom raised an eyebrow, and Lily almost laughed. "Well, she didn't quite put it that way, but that's the gist of it." It was close to one of her sayings anyway. "It's not like you to sit around and wallow in self-pity." She hoped she was right, but if she wasn't, she would bully him out of it. "So you must have something else in mind, something new you'd like to try. Maybe it's even something God is leading you to do."

Surprise lit Ransom's eyes.

When she glanced at Cade, she saw he was surprised, too. Then he became thoughtful. "Is there something new you want to do?" he asked.

Ransom sat up a little straighter, excitement making his voice lighter. "I've been thinking about starting a detective agency. It might take a while to build up the business since I wouldn't be in a big city like Denver or Chicago, but I have a lot of contacts all over the country."

"Do you have some men in mind to work for you?" Cade motioned for Lily to take the rocking chair as he pulled up the straight back chair and turned it around, straddling it.

She picked up the badge and laid it on the table before she sat down.

"I do. I'd only start out with a couple. Maybe one lady who would be a valuable asset if I can get her."

That stirred Lily's curiosity and a bit of jealousy. "A female detective?"

"Sometimes a woman is best for the job. Georgia Nickson is a master at disguises. She's probably thirty but she can look twenty-five or fifty-five, act the part of a grand lady or a hillbilly, depending on what role is called for."

"So she's an actress?" asked Lily.

"When she's not working as an agent. She was with Del, my old boss, for a while, but the last I heard, she'd quit. In fact, she's part of the theatrical company that's coming for the opening of the Opera House. I saw her name in the *Gazette* advertisement last week."

"So you've been thinking about this since last week?" Cade rested his forearms on the back of the chair.

"Actually, I've toyed with the idea since the first of the year."

That was an interesting revelation. He had told her that he had decided to do something else before he got hurt, but he hadn't mentioned starting his own agency.

"What about a ranch? You mentioned that, too." Lily didn't want to throw cold water on his enthusiasm, but she didn't like the idea of some talented and probably pretty woman working for him.

"I've considered it, but I don't know much about running a ranch. I'd probably go belly-up the first year." He twisted his lips wryly. "Of course, an agency might fall flat, too, but I don't think it will take as much money to start and run. If it does fail, I'd probably still have some money left."

"You do know about being a investigator," said Cade. "You were good at it." He looked at Lily. "His boss raised a fuss when we asked Ransom to be sheriff. Said he didn't want to lose the best man he had. Do you know how to run an agency?"

"I filled in for Del several times when he was gone. I'll probably make some mistakes, but he taught me quite a bit. Unfortunately, he's passed on, so I won't be able to ask for more advice."

"Maybe Lily is right. It might be good if you weren't worrying about being sheriff right now and have something new and interesting to do." Cade glanced at Lily, then frowned at his old friend. "But don't think we'll let you go so easy. I'll count on you to give Quint advice when he asks for it, maybe even when he doesn't."

"I can do that, as long as it's all right with him."

"This is temporary. As soon as you're back on your feet, the job is yours if you want it."

Ransom grinned and visibly relaxed. "By then Quint might not want to give it up."

Cade groaned. "You tell Quint. It's going to be bad enough dealin' with Jessie."

"It's no different than what he's been doing," said Ransom. "In every way except the title, he's been sheriff for the last couple of months. He's the right man. People trust and respect him. He and Blake will do fine, better without having to worry about me gettin' in the way."

"You keep talking like that, and I'll dump that pitcher of water over your head." Cade stood and swung the chair back around, setting it next to the wall.

"And make Lily change the sheets? I don't think so. Thanks, Cade." Ransom pointed at the silver star. "You'll have to talk to Quint and pin that badge on him. I don't have the authority."

"I'll have to call an emergency meeting of the commissioners. I guess you're lucky. They're still in town. Quint's not going to like this." Cade scowled as he stomped toward the door. "You'd better pray hard that he doesn't quit. If he does, I'll have your hide."

Ransom looked at Lily as Cade went down the hall, muttering all the way. "Don't pay him any mind. He's not about to skin me."

"I didn't think he was." She pushed her foot against the floor, rocking the chair. "Don't move out."

"I need to, Lily."

"If it's because I'm here, Matt and I will move if there's an available house."

"It's not just you." Ransom looked away. "When I was working, boarding was fine because I wasn't here much. But I'm feeling closed in. I need some room to roam around, get up in the night and get out of this room if I want to."

"If you do that here, somebody will hear you and rush to see if you're all right."

He met her gaze. "Yep."

She wanted to tell him what was in her heart, but she was afraid he would think she was pushing him. "Well, don't think you're going to get away from me that easy," she said briskly. "I still intend to check up on you."

"You don't owe me anything."

She jumped to her feet, pacing across the room and back. She owed him more than he could ever know. "I care about you. Don't shut me out. I need your strength." And your love, her heart cried, but she bit back the words.

He snorted. "That's in short supply."

"Strength comes from the inside. You're no less a man to me because you couldn't stop that big galoot yesterday. You're a better man in my eyes because you tried." She returned to the rocking chair and sat down, leaning forward. "There were half a dozen men there and only one of them lifted a finger to come to my aid. The poor guy probably has a broken nose."

"The only thing that matters is that *I* couldn't help you," he said angrily. "*I* couldn't protect you."

"Even if you weren't hurt, you might not be able to. You can't always be there. No matter how hard you try." She leaned back in the chair and sighed, thinking of her father. "No matter how desperately you wish you could."

He sat quietly for a few minutes before looking back at her. "Give it up, Lily. You don't want a man like me."

She stood with a huff of exasperation. "Quit feeling sorry for yourself and don't tell me what I want. I'll make up my own mind about that, thank you very much."

As she stormed out of the room, she heard him mutter, "Contrary woman."

Reaching the hallway, Lily smiled. He had no idea just how contrary she could be.

Chapter Eighteen

A week later, Quint was still eatin' fire and spittin' smoke. Ransom had recovered quicker from the fall than anyone anticipated, but he obstinately refused to be sheriff. Cade and the commissioners were just as adamant that Quint was the only person they would hire to replace him. Despite his vehement and lengthy objections, Quint finally gave in just like he figured Cade and Ransom knew he would. He couldn't leave Blake to keep the peace alone. He cared too much for the people of Willow Grove and the county to leave them in the lurch.

Quint walked down to the train station to cool his temper and meet the westbound train. It paid to know who was arriving in town. On occasion, a few people had been escorted right back on again.

Halfway there, he met Prissy as she came around the

corner. He noticed the glint of sunlight in her golden hair, which irritated him even more. Why couldn't he simply ignore how pretty she was? He nodded, brusquely greeted her and kept walking. She quickly caught up with him. Sighing, he slowed his pace and shortened his stride.

"Is it true, Quint? Are you the sheriff?"

"Yes," he said curtly.

"You don't sound too happy about it."

"I'm not. Ransom is better suited to this job than I am."

"Not now, he isn't. Everybody is talking about how he fell on Saturday and then had to be taken home in a buggy."

Quint stopped abruptly. "Don't you have anything better to do than gossip?"

She frowned at him. "I'm not gossiping. Several people couldn't wait to tell me about it, whether or not I wanted to listen. I haven't mentioned it to anybody but you. I'm the brunt of enough talk not to do the same." She started walking, and he joined her. "I was trying to pay you a compliment."

"You have a backhanded way of doing it."

"Well, I hadn't gotten to the complimentary part yet." She smiled and playfully batted her eyelashes at him. He could get lost in those bright blue eyes. "I think you'll make an excellent sheriff. You've done a fine job the last few months."

Quint knew he was being silly, but her praise meant a lot to him. He slanted her a glance. "You really think so?"

"I do and so does everybody else."

"Thanks. Are you going to the train station?"

She nodded. "Millborn has been in Dallas for a few days. He said he'd be back today or tomorrow, so I thought I'd check the train and surprise him if he's on it."

So much for her brightening his rotten mood. "So are you goin' to marry him?"

"He hasn't asked yet, but he's talked about showing me England and about the lovely house he has in London. When he proposes, I'll say yes."

Quint nodded a greeting to another lady they met, pausing until there was no one else nearby. "Do you love him?"

"No, but I like him well enough."

He didn't want to think what she meant by that. Ransom had told him about seeing her and Millborn out at the ranch. "Has he ever hit you?"

"Of course not."

Quint noted the embarrassment coloring her cheeks. Interesting. Prissy wasn't a good liar. He'd figured she would be. "Ransom said he almost did at the ranch."

"Oh, he wouldn't have actually struck me. It was just a threat because he was angry."

Quint grabbed her elbow and drew her into an alley a street up from the train station. "Prissy, don't be stupid. When a man raises his hand to a woman, he's going to hit her. Maybe not every time, but eventually he will."

She didn't look at him. "I just have to be careful and not rile him, that's all."

"Then he has hit you." He gripped her shoulders. "Blast it, Prissy, tell me the truth." He felt like shaking some sense into her, but then he'd be just as bad as Millborn.

"Only once." When she looked up at him, the sorrow in her eyes made his heart ache. "I—I didn't obey him. I didn't do what he wanted."

"What—"

She put her fingers on his lips to silence him. Tears glistened in her eyes. "Don't ask, Quint. Please, leave it be."

Quint released her and stepped back, fighting to control his anger. "Where's your self-respect?"

"I lost it when I was fourteen," she whispered, a tear slipping down her cheek. "When Mama gave me to one of her gentleman friends."

Quint felt as if he'd been sucker punched in the stomach. "Lord have mercy."

"It could have been much worse. After that she decided I'd be more use to her if I caught a rich husband than I would be entertaining her customers. That's why she closed the Pink Petticoat in Raleigh and we moved here. Unfortunately, all her scheming hasn't quite worked out yet. But when I marry Millborn, she'll be satisfied."

"What about *your* happiness?"

She wiped the tear from her cheek and straightened regally. "I'll be fine. Being a baroness might be rather grand." The train whistle blew as it neared the station. "Come on, Sheriff Webb. We have a train to meet."

His head reeling, Quint followed her back to the sidewalk. "The hold your mother has over you…"

Her expression was resigned. "She'll tell everyone that I'm the daughter of a prostitute who doesn't know who her father is. And she'll say I've been following in her footsteps since I was fourteen. It isn't true, but some people here already don't think much of me. That's all it would take to convince the rest that I'm trash. It would be more than I could bear."

"But she'd be ruining her own reputation, too."

"She doesn't care about that. She's only playing the part of a respectable lady to help me find a rich husband. I think she misses her old life. If I don't marry soon, she'll have to do something to earn some money. What she'd saved and made from selling the parlor house is almost gone."

They reached the station a few minutes after the train pulled in. A few townspeople got off, along with another traveling salesman. Quint shook his head at this one. Dressed in a red plaid suit and top hat, he was asking for trouble if he didn't leave before the cowboys came back to town. The blacksmith's wife met her mother. The tailor met a cousin from the old country, Germany. A rancher and his family disembarked, followed by a finely dressed lady, probably in her late twenties.

When she reached the platform, she turned to the woman behind her carrying a baby. Her words weren't discernable but the accent was English. The nanny bobbed a shallow curtsey and stepped away from the train, waiting near the station. A man disembarked next, carrying an armload of small travel bags. He spoke to the lady, and she directed him toward the baby and nursemaid.

Quint had an uneasy feeling and sneaked a quick look at Prissy. She waited patiently, an expectant smile on her pretty face. Maybe he was borrowing trouble. Having English visitors in Willow Grove wasn't unusual.

A young boy about five years old hopped down the steps from the train and ran circles around the finely dressed lady. She said something to him, but he kept running.

At that moment, Millborn stepped off the train. "Edward, behave," he barked. The boy instantly obeyed, stopping beside the woman. "Stand still. Remain with your mother."

"Yes, Father."

Quint heard Prissy's gasp. He looked at her, watching the blood drain from her face. Millborn hadn't spotted them, which was just as well. Quint wanted to take him by surprise when he broke his nose. He took a step toward the baron, but Prissy laid a hand on his arm.

"I'm going to be sick. Get me out of here."

Quint put his arm around her waist, shielding her from Millborn's view and practically carried her around the end of the station. They hurried down the alley to the back of the smithy's where Prissy promptly lost her supper.

Quint was a believer, but he wasn't much for going to church or praying. He prayed now. *Please, God, don't let her be pregnant.* He hovered behind her. When she straightened, he handed her his handkerchief. "Are you carrying his baby?"

Prissy wiped her eyes and mouth and blew her nose. When she finally looked at him, he knew the answer from the bleakness in her eyes. "The ultimate disgrace. I'm really not any better than my mother."

"Have you told him?"

She shook her head. "No. And I'm not going to."

"He has a right to know. The least he can do is provide for you and the baby."

"What if he takes the baby away after it's born? I might not ever see my child again. He has a wife and family. I'm not going to hurt them or bring shame to them. Besides, he'll probably deny the baby is his."

"Not when I get through with him."

A tiny, sad smile touched her mouth. "I didn't know you had such a violent nature."

Neither did he.

"Don't worry about me. I'll figure something out." She was trying to put on a brave front. It might have almost been believable if her voice hadn't wobbled.

He put his arms around her, drawing her close. "I care about you, Priscilla."

"You care about everybody in this town, but this is going beyond your duty as sheriff." She tried to make her voice light as she rested her cheek against his chest.

"This has nothing to do with being sheriff, and you know it."

Prissy pulled away. "You're a good man, Quintin Webb, but you deserve somebody who hasn't been used and thrown away. I have a little money set aside. Running errands for my mother wasn't without some benefit. Keep a penny here, another there. Over the years, it's added up. I'll do what most women in my condition do. Move somewhere else and become newly widowed. I'm good with a needle. I'll go to work for a seamstress."

"And not make enough to raise a child on. Prissy, you don't have to do this."

"Yes, I do. I'll slip away on the train in the morning."

"I don't want you to leave." Quint had been attracted to Prissy for a couple of years, but he hadn't realized how much he cared for her until that moment. "Take a few days and think about it." Give him time to sort things out.

"There's nothing to think over. I need to get away from here."

"There are always options. You're surprised and hurt and scared right now. This is not the time to make a quick decision. People here are pretty forgiving, you know that. Look at how they decided not to hold Camille's past against her, and she'd been a professional gambler and even a man's mistress."

"What she did was a long time ago, before she came to Willow Grove, and she didn't have a baby." She briefly closed her eyes, then looked up at him. "You're right. I am hurt. He never said anything about marrying me, but the things he said and the way he treated me—most of the time anyway—made me think he wanted to." Her voice wobbled again. "And I am scared. Really scared. Mama is going to throw a fit. She knows about the baby. She wanted me to get pregnant so she could use it as leverage if he balked at marrying me."

"Will she try to hurt you?"

"She prefers theatrics over violence. She might dress up in sack cloth and ashes and go up and down the street crying that I've disgraced her."

"If she tries something like that, I'll throw her in jail for disturbing the peace. Was finding you a husband the only reason y'all left Raleigh?"

"I don't think so. She'd been talking about moving out west for a long time, but she always said we'd wait until I was eighteen. When I was sixteen, she came home one night in a big rush and said we were leaving right away. She was scared, and nothing much scares Mama. But she wouldn't talk about it. We packed everything up and left town the next morning."

"She was running from something. Is her real name Mabel Clark?"

"No. It's Daisy Beaumont."

"I'll wire the chief of police in Raleigh and see if I can find out something. Don't say anything to your mother until I tell you to. I'll send the telegram now, but I probably won't hear anything until in the morning. The trick will be to keep her from finding out about Millborn before then."

"She believes we'll be moving to England soon, so she's reading all the English novels she can get her hands on. She started *Vanity Fair* this afternoon. She'll stay up late reading and won't wake up until midmorning." Prissy gave him a quick hug. "Thank you for being my friend."

He wanted to keep holding her, to never let her go. But he didn't want to make a snap decision he might regret or push her into one she might regret. "We'll figure out a way through this, honey. Just don't panic and go runnin' off."

"I won't."

"Promise?"

She nodded. "I won't go anywhere without telling you, I promise. Now, go on and arrest somebody or something."

Quint gently kissed her on the forehead. Turning away, he walked purposefully back down the alley.

It was the hardest thing he'd ever done.

Chapter Nineteen

By nature, Quint was a private, somewhat shy man. He disliked the prominence that came with being a lawman, a distinction that only increased when word spread that he had become sheriff. People respected and admired Ransom, even held him a bit in awe. They shook their heads sadly over the state of his health and wished him well.

Then they turned around and treated Quint like a celebrity. It was almost as bad as it had been when he'd helped break up the rustlers two years earlier. He hated it when people made a fuss over him, exaggerating his deeds and trying to turn him into a legend.

But he hated injustice more. There had to be some way to make Millborn own up to his responsibilities, to get some recompense for Prissy. He mulled on it all evening and half the night. The few options that he came up with involving the baron would hurt or humiliate her even more.

Enough cowboys had stayed in town to keep him and Blake busy breaking up fights off and on all night. By the time he stopped an impromptu horse race down Main Street in the early morning, he was tired and threatening to throw all of them in jail.

He sent Blake home to eat breakfast with his wife and get some sleep. Quint grabbed a bite at the restaurant, sitting in the front window where he could keep an eye on things. When the last of the cowboys rode out of town, he breathed a sigh of relief.

Back in the office, he stretched out in an empty cell and took a nap. He was awakened by the telegraph operator bringing a reply from the police chief in Raleigh. Quint had worded his message carefully, only asking about Daisy Beaumont and not mentioning Prissy's mother by her assumed name. The telegraph operator was reasonably trustworthy, but it paid to be discreet.

Sure enough, Prissy's mother had been running from the law when she came west.

Quint did a quick survey of town, including the district, and decided things would likely be peaceful for a while. He walked up to the Clarks' house to see Prissy. When she answered the door, he asked her to come out onto the front porch. "Does she know?"

Prissy shook her head. "Not yet. She only got up about half an hour ago. Did you find out anything?"

"Your mother is wanted for questioning about a murder. He didn't come right out and say it, but I got the impression that they think she might have done it."

Prissy crossed her arms and walked to the end of the porch, away from the door. He went along, too. "I know my mother, Quint. She's not the best person in the world, but she wouldn't kill anybody unless it was in self-defense. She was very frightened that night, and like I said, nothing much scares her."

"People don't always act the way we expect them to. I'll listen to her side of it before I do anything."

"Are you going to arrest her?"

Judging from her expression, that would make him look real bad in her eyes. But he couldn't do his job based on what she thought.

"Not unless they have a warrant from a judge." He gave her a lopsided smile. "As annoyed as I am at your mama for the way she's treated you, I'm not planning to throw her in jail."

"But you still might." She turned away, looking across the street. He figured she was avoiding looking at him instead of admiring the neighbor's weedy yard.

"I've sworn to uphold the law, Prissy. If they give me a legal reason to hold her, then I'll have to do it. But the police chief didn't say anything about a warrant or that anyone would be coming out here to get her or talk to her. He didn't say whether she was a suspect or a possible witness. I'd have to know the specifics before I did anything. What about you? Have you decided what you'll do?"

Lowering her arms, she turned back around to look at him. "The only thing I can think of is to leave and start over somewhere else."

"You could marry me," he said quietly.

Her gaze flew to his. "Quint, no. I can't let you do this."

"I want to. I can't bear the thought of you going off by yourself somewhere and having that baby. I can't bear the thought of you leaving at all." He caught both her hands with his. "I want to be your husband and to raise that baby as my own."

"How could you look at him every day and not think about him being some other man's child? Some kid that you'd been saddled with?"

"Because the child is innocent. I'll be his father in every way that counts. He—or she—will carry my name. I'll be there when he's born and to see him grow up. I'll love this baby the way Cade loves Ellie and Brad. He doesn't love them any less than little Jacob."

"Jessie was married when she had them."

"You'll be married when this baby is born. I love you, Prissy."

Tears filled her eyes. "How can you?"

"I don't know how one person loves another, honey. I just know that I do. It's all right if you don't love me, as long as you care for me a little."

"You know I do." She leaned her forehead against his chin. "More than a little. But I don't want to ruin your life. Even if you didn't resent the baby, people will think you're crazy for marrying me. It will damage your reputation."

"No, it won't." Putting his finger beneath her chin, he tipped her head up so she would look at him. "You'd make me happy, Prissy. It's as plain and simple as that. I'm not a rich man, but I have a good job. Even if Ransom decides to be sheriff again, I'll make decent money as a deputy. I have two hundred head of cattle that Cade lets me run with his. Someday, maybe we can buy some land and have a little ranch to put them on. For now, we can buy us a house here in town and make it into a home." He smiled wistfully. "After I left my folks, I've lived on the range, in a bunkhouse and a boarding house. I've never had a home to call my own. I'd like that very much.

"Will you marry me, Priscilla Clark?" He frowned slightly. "Or is it Beaumont?"

"It's Clark, but I went by Beaumont when we were in Raleigh because that was the name Mama used. She was married to Mr. Beaumont for about a year when I was six. She ran him off because he was lazy and wouldn't work."

Prissy's mother came storming out onto the porch. "What's going on here? Take your hands off my daughter."

Quint turned toward the woman, slipping his arm around Prissy's shoulders, holding her against his side. "I've asked Priscilla to marry me, ma'am." *And you interrupted, so now I don't know if she will or not,* he thought irritably.

Her mother snorted. "She's going to marry Lord Millborn and become a baroness."

"No, I'm not, Mama. Millborn already has a wife and family."

"Who says?" Mrs. Clark, alias Beaumont, put her hands on her hips.

"I saw them get off the train yesterday afternoon. I'm positive she's his wife."

"Well, you've got yourself into a fine fix, now. If you think I'm going to keep supporting you and that brat, you'd better think again."

"Now is that the way for a loving mother to talk?" Quint pinned the woman with his gaze.

"Don't you be lecturing me on motherhood, Deputy Webb," she snapped.

"It's Sheriff Webb, Mrs. Beaumont."

"Since wh—" She stared at him. "What did you call me?"

"I believe the correct name is Daisy Beaumont. From Raleigh."

"You little idiot." Prissy's mother glared at her, then looked at Quint. "My real name is Clark. Never was officially married to that worthless Beaumont anyway."

"Prissy told me a few things about you." His voice hardened. "None of it flattering."

"If you think you're going to use that information somehow, you'd better think again. You slur my name, you slur your precious Prissy's name, too. I'll make sure everybody in town knows she's no better than me. She had her first man when she was fourteen. I bet she didn't tell you that, did she, Sheriff Webb?" she said with a sneer.

Quint's fingers tightened minutely on Prissy's shoulder. "Actually, she did."

Mrs. Clark's jaw went slack. She looked from Quint to Prissy. "Well, what do you know about that. You got more gumption than I'd figured, gal."

"I learned a few things about you on my own, Mrs. Clark. I had a very interesting telegram this morning from the police chief in Raleigh."

The color drained from Mrs. Clark's cheeks. She scanned the yard quickly, as if she expected someone to jump out from behind the large hydrangea. "Come in the house." She spun around and jerked the screen door open, rushing inside.

Quint grabbed the door before it slammed, opening it for Prissy and following her into the front parlor.

"I didn't kill Paul Downey." Mrs. Clark's bluster turned to panic.

"The chief seems to think otherwise."

"Oh, I'm sure he would." She looked around the room as if taking a mental inventory. "The rent's paid up for another two months, Prissy. There's money in the sugar bowl for food, but that's all I can spare. If you decide to leave, you can sell the furniture. It's decent stuff. You should get enough to buy a train ticket and keep you going for a few months." She hurried from the room.

Quint let her go, waiting to see what else she would say or do. Despite everything her mother had done to her, all her manipulation, Prissy believed the woman was innocent. He didn't know how she could, but she loved her mother. He owed it to Prissy to give her a chance to explain.

Pausing at the foot of the stairs, Mrs. Clark looked back when they stepped into the hall. "Did you say anything about Prissy? Or that I was going by Clark?"

"No." Quint walked toward her. She still appeared frightened, but the terror was gone from her eyes. "I only asked him for information about Daisy Beaumont."

"Good. Then he can't connect Prissy Clark to Daisy Beaumont. She'll be safe."

"I need you to tell me what happened, ma'am."

She sighed. "Yes, I suppose you do. A policeman

named Montgomery killed Paul." She gripped the stair rail, staring at a spot near Quint's boot with a frown. "They were mixed up in some scheme. I don't know what. Paul was my friend, and I was visiting him." She looked up, focusing on Quint. "I liked him. He was always good to me. When Montgomery knocked on the door, Paul told me to hide under the bed. There wasn't any other way out of the room. There was a window, but we were three floors up. They argued and Montgomery stabbed him. He left quick, shutting the door behind him. When I scrambled out from under the bed, Paul was already dead.

"Paul and I had met one of his neighbors when we were on the way to his room. Montgomery is high up on the force, and I expected he would be the one to investigate the murder. It wouldn't have taken him long to find out I'd been there. I went to my business partner and asked him to buy my share that night because I had to leave town. He paid me and didn't ask what kind of trouble I was in."

"What if someone saw Montgomery go up to the room?" asked Prissy.

"Either no one did or they didn't live long enough to tell. I can't go back to Raleigh. He won't take a chance on a trial. I'd be dead before they could arrest me. I can't stay here in case Montgomery comes looking for me."

Quint thought she was probably right. He wasn't quite sure why he believed her, but he did. Maybe he just wanted to, for Prissy's sake. Ransom had often told him that gut instinct was usually right. So he decided to go with it. "You'd better not head east. You might run into him."

Relief flooded Mrs. Clark's face. "You're not going to arrest me?"

"Well, ma'am, the chief only said they wanted to question you. He didn't ask me to hold you." Though in all likelihood, the policeman expected him to. "Either you're the best liar I've ever run into or you're telling the truth. Prissy doesn't believe you could kill anybody, so I think I'll trust her on this."

"Did my daughter say she'd marry you?"

"No." He looked at Prissy. "We were interrupted before she could answer."

"Then I'll leave you two alone while I go pack. I need to catch the afternoon train." She turned to her daughter. Quint was surprised to see the sheen of tears in her eyes. "He's not English nobility, Priscilla, but he's noble. He'll do right by you, child. Better than I have." Mrs. Clark went up the stairs, dabbing at her eyes with a delicate handkerchief.

When Quint opened his arms, Prissy stepped into them, resting her head against his shoulder, putting her arms around him and holding tight. "Thank you. I don't believe she killed that man. I can't believe it."

"Reckon we'll have to take her word for it. If they had any evidence against her, they'd have tried harder to find her. They knew when you left and what she looked like. You and your mother are both pretty women, the kind that stand out in a crowd. A good investigator wouldn't have had much trouble discovering what train you left on or tracking you all the way out here."

"What about now?" Prissy looked up at him with a worried frown. "Could they track her now?"

"Does she look like she did then? Other than being a little older?"

"No. She used Turkish henna to make her hair auburn, and she was thinner. She looks a lot different now with brown hair. Wears it different, too."

"She should be all right. I expect your mother is good at taking care of herself. What about you? Have you changed much since you were sixteen?"

"I've, uh, matured some. And Mama used Henna on my hair for years, too, because she thought red was prettier."

"I like it just the way it is." He couldn't imagine anything being prettier than her natural golden blond hair. He pulled her a little closer. "Now, Priscilla, you were about to agree to marry me."

"I was?" She slid her arms up around his neck, tilting her face toward his.

"Yes, ma'am." Quint kissed her tenderly. Her response was just as tender. She was no novice, but he wasn't going to let that bother him. He loved her no matter what she had done before. It was the future that mattered, not her past. He deepened the kiss ever so slightly to show her he wasn't totally green himself. When he raised his head and looked down into her pretty, beloved face, she smiled up at him dreamily.

"Yes." Her expression sobered, and she searched his eyes. "I'd be honored to be your wife, Quintin Webb. I promise that I will be faithful and true to you. I won't give you any reason to doubt me, and I'll do my best not to do anything to make you ashamed of me." She lowered her gaze. "At least not anything else."

"Honey, if I was ashamed of you, I wouldn't be gettin' hitched, now would I?"

She laughed softly. "I guess not." Her smile faded. "But we'd better have the wedding soon. I'm two months along."

"How about Sunday after church? I expect we could get Reverend Brownfield to perform the ceremony."

"Not at church. Whenever I go to church I feel like everybody there knows how big a sinner I am."

"We're all sinners, honey." He dropped a kiss on her forehead.

"Yes, but most people don't flaunt it like I did. It would be better to have a small wedding, maybe here at the house with just your family."

"And Ransom. Can't leave him out. What about your friends?"

She shrugged. "The only real friend I had was Millie Brown, and she's up in Montana somewhere with her new husband. What will your sister say? Will Jessie be mad?"

"Maybe, but she'll come around when I explain how things are."

Prissy looked at him in alarm. "You're going to tell her about the baby?"

"No. I'll leave that up to you if you decide you want to. I was talking about loving you."

Prissy laid her cheek against his shoulder. "You're too good for me, Quint. I don't deserve you."

"I won't hear talk like that, Priscilla Clark, soon-to-be-Webb. But I will be good to you. That I promise." He released her and stepped back. "I have to get back to work. Do you want to meet for supper?"

"Not tonight. I'll fix something for Mama and then see her off on the train. It's strange. I've wanted to be out from under her thumb for so long, but now that it's happening, I feel sad. I think I'm going to miss her."

"You love her." Which told him a great deal about Prissy's heart. Although he could hear Mrs. Clark slamming drawers and doors upstairs, he dropped his voice to almost a whisper. "I don't know how you can, but you do. I think she loves you, too, in her own way."

"We've had some good times along with the bad. I'm going to ask her to keep in touch. Do you mind?"

"As long as she doesn't try to take you away from me."

"Don't worry. I'm not any use to her now. Even if she did come up with some plan, I won't be a part of it. I can do that now, thanks to you."

"I'll tell Jessie and Cade tonight. Do you want to come with me?"

"No, thanks. I'm not a coward, but I'd rather you handle that alone. Jessie's liable to be mad as a hornet, and she's too nice to show it in front of me."

Quint smiled and walked toward the door. "All the more reason for you to come with me."

"I'm worn out. After I see Mother off, I'm going to bed."

"Sleep as late as you want to, but come to the office tomorrow around noon, and I'll buy you dinner. We can go to the courthouse and get the wedding license. After that, we can stop by the parsonage and talk to Reverend Brownfield."

"Quint, are you certain about this?" Her face wrinkled in a worried frown.

Chapter Twenty

When Ransom stopped by the sheriff's office Wednesday morning, Quint was sitting behind the desk. He had seen him there hundreds of times when he was a deputy. A twinge of regret that he wasn't the one occupying that chair and wearing the sheriff's badge both surprised and annoyed him. "How's it going?"

"It's been quiet since the cowboys left yesterday morning."

"They had plenty of celebrating to do after that long cattle drive." When Ransom sat down in the extra chair, Quint started to get up. "Stay put. That's your chair now."

"Doesn't feel like it," said Quint with a frown. "None of this feels right."

"Give it a few more weeks." Ransom reached backward over his shoulder, hooking the cane on the top of the high backed chair. "I saw Millborn going into the hotel with his wife and kids yesterday."

"I wanted to punch him in the nose, but Prissy stopped me." Quint leaned back in the chair, tapping his fingertips against the chair arm. "What I really want to do is thrash him within an inch of his life."

"Can't do it as long as you're wearin' that badge."

"Another reason to take it off."

"It wouldn't do any good except work off some of your anger. He toyed with her, but he can't marry two women."

"No, he can't." Quint grinned, his expression filled with mischief. "Which is good since I'm going to marry Prissy."

"You're what?" Ransom barely kept from shouting. He wanted his friend to be happy, but he was afraid Quint was asking for a lot of heartache.

"We're picking up the license and talking to Reverend Brownfield today. We're gettin' married Saturday at Cade and Jessie's. You're invited."

"This is awful sudden, isn't it?" Ransom had a good idea why, too, but he'd be hanged before he mentioned—again—how familiar Prissy was with his lordship.

"No reason to wait." Quint's expression sobered. "Like we figured, her mother was pushing her to go after Millborn—and all the others. I was talking to Prissy at the station when Millborn and his family came in from Dallas. She was so humiliated to discover that he was married that she was going to leave town.

"She was determined to get away from her mother

and run her own life. The more I thought about her leaving, the more I realized how much I love her. I know it sounds *loco*, but I do."

"What does Jessie think about it?"

"She was a bit put out at first. She likes Prissy well enough but thought she was just marrying me to show Millborn she didn't need him."

Ransom agreed with Jessie, but he didn't say so.

"It took some talking, but I convinced her that it wasn't a snap decision. I've considered courtin' Prissy for over a year now. So Jessie and Cade came around and decided they'd be happy for us."

"Which you knew they would. I suppose Prissy jumped at the chance to marry you," Ransom said dryly.

"No. She appreciated the offer, but she said she couldn't let me do it." Quint frowned at Ransom's skeptical expression. "She was afraid she would damage my reputation."

"I don't know as people will think any less of you, though they might think you've gone plum crazy."

"Prissy said the same thing." Quint got up for some coffee. "Want a cup?"

"No thanks."

"She's mindful of what people think of her, but I don't give a hoot what they think. I love her and want her for my wife. I didn't convince her until yesterday. I don't believe I'll have to worry about her chasing other men. I know you have doubts, but at heart she's a good woman. Her mother's something else, but she's left. Decided since Prissy wasn't going to marry a wealthy man, she'd get on with her life. She'll probably look for a wealthy man of her own."

Quint poured the coffee and returned to his chair behind the desk. "Are you still planning to move?"

Ransom nodded. "I need a place of my own where I can think without interruption and work on the plans for the business whenever I want to."

"And where you won't run into Lily every evening and morning. I thought you were gettin' serious about her." Quint blew on the coffee to cool it.

"I am, but I don't think that's very smart. Don't you tell a soul I said anything about it."

Quint laughed. "I won't have to say a word. Everybody in town can see the sparks fly when you two are together."

"I don't want her tied to me by guilt, because she thinks she's responsible for this." He lifted the cane from the back of the chair.

"She *is* responsible for it," Quint said quietly. "I expect she'll always feel some guilt about it. But that's not what's tying her to you. She's as much in love with you as you are with her."

Ransom grabbed hold of the edge of the desk and hoisted himself to his feet, leaning on the cane. "Since when did you become an authority on love?"

"Since I've watched my three best friends get hit with Cupid's arrows." He grinned again, looking happier than Ransom had ever seen him. "Since he hit me with one, too."

"He has been busy the last few years." Or God had. Ransom didn't believe in Cupid any more than Quint did. "I have to know that I can provide for her." He also had to get past feeling inferior because he had trouble walking. During the night, God had prodded him about conceit and prejudice. Ransom didn't believe he looked down on people who were crippled. Given his feelings about being in that situation, however, he was trying to sort out whether or not he looked at other people the same way.

He'd had to admit to a fair amount of pride, too. Not being able to help Lily had torn him apart, but it had little to do with pride. He feared for her safety and that of everybody else in town if they were dependent upon him.

Falling on his face on Main Street was another matter. He had been humiliated and that didn't sit well. He was still working through that one.

"If I do decide to court her, it will look better if we aren't living in the same house, even if it is a boarding house."

"*If* you decide to court her? What have you been doing for the last couple of months?"

"A bunch of things, including gettin' all tangled up with her. I need to stay away from her for a while, see how I feel when I'm not around her so much."

"I can tell you how you'll feel—lousy." Quint picked up his hat. "You rented an office yet?"

"In the next building, where Pilgrim's insurance was. You want to help me set it up?"

"Nope. I'm going to stroll around town and look important. If I'm lucky, I'll run into Millborn and bully him a little. Then I'm going to meet my lady for dinner and go buy a marriage license."

Ransom held out his hand, shaking Quint's. "I wish you well, my friend. May God bless you both."

He was mighty afraid they'd need all the blessings they could get.

* * *

Quint checked his pocket watch for the third time. One o'clock. Prissy was an hour late. He hadn't thought much about it when the watch said half-past twelve. Some women were always a little late. But an hour was pushing it, especially when he hadn't seen her since yesterday. "That's it, woman. If you aren't awake and spiffed up by now, that's just too bad."

Walking outside, he smiled at the thought of her coming to the door disheveled and sleepy. She might as well get accustomed to him seeing her like that. His stomach rumbled and he considered stopping by the restaurant and picking up some chicken for dinner. If he took it up to Prissy's house—soon to be their house—they could have a picnic on the back porch. He wouldn't go inside since she didn't have a chaperon. Even though they would be married at the end of the week, he was determined to observe propriety.

Ransom stepped out of his new office as Quint shut the sheriff's office door. "Been stood up?"

"Don't think so." Quint adjusted his hat against the early afternoon glare. "She's probably primping." Or she might not feel like eating dinner, thought Quint, remembering how she'd been sick when she saw Millborn. Maybe nerves made morning sickness worse, so that it happened anytime during the day.

Ransom smiled as he joined Quint. "You need to tell her that she's pretty enough without primping."

"I will, but I'm not going to tell her you said so." A movement down the street drew Quint's attention. Ransom turned almost at the same time.

One of the men from the McKinnon Ranch came

racing into town, ignoring the ordinance that horses were to be kept to a walk downtown. He and a couple of other ranch hands had left earlier with a loaded supply wagon.

"Looks like there's trouble." Quint hit the dirt at a run, meeting the cowboy as he drew his horse to a stop in the middle of the street. Ransom wasn't far behind him. "What's wrong, Wylie?"

"We found Prissy Clark about four miles out of town." The horse pranced nervously, and he brought her under control. "She's been beat up real bad."

Quint sucked in a breath, his head spinning. Ransom stepped up and put a steadying hand on his shoulder.

"Did she say who did it?" asked Ransom.

"No." Wylie dismounted. "She roused for a minute and asked for Quint, then she passed out again." He handed the reins to Quint. "Take my horse. Clancy and Silas are unloading the wagon so we can bring her into town. I'll go get the doc."

Quint swung into the saddle and looked at Ransom. "Go pin that deputy badge on. If Millborn tries to leave town, shoot him."

"He won't leave. But remember we have to prove he did it."

"Or hired somebody." Before Quint had gone a block, he spotted the doctor rushing out of his office toward the livery where he kept his buggy. Quint urged the horse to a run as soon as it was safe. Even with the little mustang mare putting her heart into it, it seemed as if it took forever to reach Prissy.

Silas Westwood stood at the end of the wagon, dragging out a fifty-pound bag of salt and setting it next to a pile of boxes and sacks at the side of the road. When Quint stopped and dismounted, the young cowboy pointed toward a shallow gully about thirty feet away.

"She's over there. We thought we'd better not move her until the doc looks at her. Wouldn't have seen her at all if Wylie hadn't noticed the sunlight shining off something. It was a buckle on her shoe. Must have gotten knocked off when they threw her in the gully." He nodded to two short pieces of rope lying on the wagon seat. "Her hands and feet were tied when we found her."

Quint silently cursed Millborn and whoever helped him, then nodded and handed Silas the reins. He had such a big lump in his throat, he couldn't talk. Walking toward the gully, he tried to prepare for the first look. At least she was alive. *Please, God, don't let her be hurt bad.*

Clancy Smith stood up when Quint approached the gully. Before he became deputy sheriff, Quint had worked with Clancy for years at Cade's ranch. He held women in high regard. All the men did.

Fear knotted Quint's stomach, and he thought his heart might pound right out of his chest. When he got closer, he realized Clancy was shielding her face from the sun. They had covered her with a blanket, but her arms were free, her hands resting on her stomach as if to protect her child.

Her wrists were bruised and raw. One was badly swollen, maybe broken. There were bruises on the other arm, too. Her knuckles were scraped and a couple of fingernails broken. His brave, sweet love had put up a fight. When he looked at her face, his eyes misted with tears.

"Aw, sweetheart," he said softly, blinking back the moisture. Both her eyes were swollen shut, though only one was badly bruised. Her nose was swollen and purple, but it looked straight. He didn't think it was broken. Her lip was cut and puffy, but her jaws appeared all right. At least he hadn't smashed in her face. Someone had put a folded blanket beneath her head for a pillow.

Clancy met his gaze, his expression grim. "I can't tell if her wrist is broken or sprained. I think she may have some cracked ribs. She's not breathing real good. There's a big knot on the back of her head. Several bruises on her legs." When Quint frowned at him, he hurriedly explained. "There's blood on her dress. I was looking for cuts."

"Were there any?"

"No." Clancy's voice dropped to barely more than a whisper, even though Silas stayed at the road. "She's lost a lot of blood, Quint."

Quint closed his eyes. *Please, God, no. Not the baby. Please, don't let Prissy die, too.* When he looked at Clancy, he saw understanding and sympathy in the old cowboy's eyes.

"Best I could tell, the bleeding has stopped," Clancy said quietly. "She's come to a couple of times. The first time she asked for you. The second she didn't say anything. I gave her a little water and told her Wylie had gone after you and a doctor."

"Thanks." As Clancy walked toward the road, Quint climbed down the gully and kneeled beside her, between her and the sun. He lifted the blanket and almost wept. Her skirt and the ground beneath her were soaked with blood, most of it dried. Her ankles were raw and bruised, where they'd been tied. She'd been out here hours, maybe even all night. Hurt and tied up. Left to die.

Rage swept through him, a blinding, murderous need to punish the man who did this to her, whether it was Millborn or somebody else.

He gently smoothed the hair back from her forehead. "He won't get away with this. You're going to be all right." *Please, God!* "You rest. The doctor will be here soon." He carefully took hold of her hand and kept talking quietly. *Where's that blasted doctor?*

She stirred and moaned. Her eyelids twitched but her eyes were too swollen to open.

Quint leaned closer, holding her hand and lightly caressing her forehead. "It's all right, Prissy."

"Quint?" she whispered.

"I'm here, sweetheart."

"You came." Her voice was weak, her breathing shallow.

Dread curled around Quint's heart. *Please, God, don't let her die.* "You knew I would."

"Yes."

"Let me give you some water." Opening a canteen that lay nearby, he carefully lifted her head and gave her a small drink. He eased her head back down on the blanket. Quickly putting the lid on the canteen, he tossed it aside and took her hand again.

"You rest, honey. The doctor will be here soon." She coughed and cried out in pain, grabbing her side. "Hold on, Prissy. Don't you go and die on me," he said sternly. "I'm planning to grow old with you."

She squeezed his hand. The pressure was faint, but he felt it. "Stay," she whispered before she drifted back into unconsciousness.

He didn't know whether she was telling him to stay with her or promising that she'd stay with him. He prayed it was both.

The doctor and Wylie arrived a short time later. Doctor Wilson examined her while Quint stood nearby, his back to them. "Quint, could you come help me?"

"Yes, sir." He jumped into the gully a couple of steps away.

"Let's put her wrist in a splint. Wylie told me they thought it might be broken, so I brought some with me. I think it's sprained, but I want to keep it stabilized until I can examine it better." He laid one of the long, flat boards beneath her arm, extending beyond her fingertips. "If you'll lift that just enough for me to slide my hand underneath, I'll wrap this bandage around it."

Quint complied and the doctor quickly had the bottom splint in place. He laid the second piece of wood along the top of her arm, and Quint held it while the doctor wrapped it, too. Doc Wilson tied a sling around her neck and very carefully slid her arm into it.

"Now, I need you to lift her head and shoulders so I can bind her ribs. If any are cracked, it should make the trip to town easier and help her breathing, too."

Quint carefully lifted her, holding his body out of the way so the doctor could wrap the sturdy bandage around her. Once that was accomplished, he gently laid her back down. "Is she going to be all right, Doc?"

"Can't say for certain until I do a better examination, but my best guess right now is that she will."

Relief swept through him.

"If she doesn't take pneumonia. Always a risk of that with a beating like this and the way she's breathing. She lost a lot of blood," he added, frowning as he packed his equipment back in his bag. The doctor looked at Quint. "Did you know she was pregnant?"

"Yes. Two months along." Quint glanced at the men hovering by the wagon. "Did she lose the baby?"

"I'm afraid so."

"They didn't…" He couldn't bring himself to ask if she'd been raped.

"No. The beating probably caused the miscarriage. Hard to say. Sometimes a woman loses a baby for no apparent reason. But I suspect that's what the assailant was hoping for. He hit her in the face, obviously, but the bulk of the blows were in her midsection. I don't know if whoever did this wanted her killed, but they didn't want that baby to live."

"How can anybody be that cruel?" Quint couldn't understand it. If Millborn was bedding her he had to know the risk. Was he so callous that he could kill his own child?

"Some people are just mean through and through." The doctor stood and brushed the dirt off the knees of his trousers. "If you'll carry her to the wagon, we'll try to make her comfortable."

Kneeling on one knee, Quint carefully picked her up, trying to keep the blanket around her. It was difficult to get up the side of the gully, but the doctor gave him a hand. Clancy ran to help, then picked up the blanket they'd been using for a pillow and handed it to the doctor.

Quint gently laid her in the wagon bed, making sure the sling held her arm in place. The doctor added the folded blanket beneath her head. As Quint tucked the other blanket around her, she moaned again.

"You're in the wagon now, honey. We're taking you back to town, and Doc Wilson's going to fix you up."

She tried to lick her lips.

Silas handed him a canteen. Murmuring his thanks, Quint leaned over the side of the wagon and carefully lifted her head. "Here's some more water." He dribbled a little into her mouth. She drank and opened her mouth for more. He gave her another small drink and eased her head back onto the blanket.

"Prissy?"

"Um?"

"Did Millborn do this to you?"

"No. Stranger." She struggled with the word and lapsed into unconsciousness.

"You'll have to question her later, Sheriff. Be thankful she's unconscious, son. Why don't you ride back here and hold her on your lap? She might breathe better if she's not lying flat, and you could keep her from bouncing around so much."

Quint climbed into the back of the wagon and sat down, lifting her carefully, praying that she would stay out cold until they reached town. He didn't know if people were aware of pain when they were unconscious, but he thought maybe it was God's gift to help them cope with it.

Clancy climbed onto the wagon seat and released the brake, snapping the reins. The wagon lurched.

Quint cradled Prissy against him, absorbing the

movement. Realizing that Silas and Wylie were staying behind to guard the supplies, Quint called his
thanks. He knew they would have done the same for
anyone, but that didn't lessen his appreciation. They
had saved Prissy's life.

He looked down at Prissy's battered face and
pledged retribution on the one who had tried to ruin it.

Chapter Twenty-One

Jessie, Lily and Ransom were waiting when they pulled up in front of Doctor Wilson's. Jessie hurried down the steps to the wagon, exclaiming when she saw Prissy's face. "Oh, Quint!"

"Doc thinks she'll be all right." Quint laid Prissy carefully on the wagon bed as close to the tail gate as he could get. Climbing out of the wagon, he let his sister hug him, while he thanked Clancy and waited for the doctor to park the buggy.

Lily turned to Doctor Wilson when he joined them. "I got your message. I'm glad to help you any way I can."

"Good," said the doctor. "She'll need someone watching over her for a while."

"I'll help, too, Doctor Wilson," said Jessie. "Lily and I have already talked about a schedule."

The doctor nodded and opened his office door. "Put her in the back room, Quint."

Quint awkwardly lifted Prissy, settling her against him once he had cleared the side of the wagon. He glanced at Ransom, noting that he was wearing the deputy's badge. "Millborn still here?"

"Spending a quiet afternoon at home. Blake is keeping an eye on their house."

"We'll be going there directly." Quint carried her inside and laid her on the bed. Lily followed them into the bedroom, but Jessie waited in the doctor's office. Probably to make sure he didn't intend to shoot Millborn on sight.

Prissy moaned and reached blindly for him. "I'm right here, honey." He closed his hand around hers. "I'm going to leave you with Doctor Wilson and Lily. They'll take good care of you."

"The baby?" Her voice was soft, barely more than a whisper.

Quint caught Lily's startled expression when he looked at the doctor, silently asking if the physician wanted him to tell her.

The gentleman nodded sadly and ushered Lily out of the room.

Quint had prayed on the way back to town, asking God how to handle it. Saying "You lost the baby" seemed cruel, like it was her fault.

"Your baby is in Heaven with Jesus, honey."

She sobbed and clung to his hand. A tear squeezed past one swollen eye and slid down her cheek. "I wanted it."

"I know you did. You would have been a good mother to that little one."

He let her cry for a few minutes, murmuring sooth-
ing words, stroking her forehead with his fingertips,
hating that he couldn't take away her pain. "Don't cry,
honey. You're too weak. You need to conserve your
strength so you can get well. Shush, sweetheart. Rest."

She slowly calmed down, but Quint thought it was
more because she was exhausted, rather than his comfort.

"Why did he...do this?"

"I guess Millborn wanted to make sure you didn't
bother him anymore, didn't want to deal with a baby."

"He doesn't know. Was a cowboy."

"Only one man?"

"Yes."

"Do you know him?"

"No. Big." Her voice broke. "Mean."

Quint smoothed her hair again. "Would you recognize him if you saw him again?"

"Yes."

Quint almost stopped questioning her because she
was so tired. But he needed to know what happened.
"Were you on the way back from the train station?"

She shook her head slightly. "House. Around eight."
She took a deeper breath, grimacing with pain. "Put the
cat out. Man was on the back porch. Hit my head." At
least she seemed to be breathing better.

"And knocked you out?"

"Yes. Woke up on the road."

"Were you in a buggy?"

"Yes."

"Were your hands and feet tied then?"

"Yes. I tried to fight. He hit my face. Shoved me...out

of buggy. Don't remember anything else...until morning."

"That's a blessing. Was he still there when you woke up?"

"No. Stomach hurt, sick. I was...afraid for baby."

"I'm so sorry this happened, Prissy. But we'll find him, and he'll go to prison. You rest and let the doctor and Lily take care of you. I'll come back later."

Her fingers tightened on his hand. "Need you."

Quint smiled, wishing she could see it. Bittersweet pain touched his heart. "I need you, too, Prissy."

Her fingers relaxed as she fell asleep. Quint left the room quietly.

Lily followed the doctor back into the bedroom, pausing to touch Quint's arm as she passed. She didn't say anything when he looked at her. She didn't have to. Sympathy was written all over her face.

After Lily closed the bedroom door, Jessie wrapped her arms around him, holding him fiercely.

He stood there for a few minutes, letting her love try to soothe his aching heart. "I guess Doc told you she had a miscarriage."

"Yes." She looked up at him. "Only because we'll be taking care of her. I assume the baby was Millborn's?"

"Yes."

"Were you going to marry her because she was pregnant?"

"I'm going to marry her because I love her." Seeing his sister's concerned frown, he sighed. "But that's why we hurried things up."

"We'll still have the wedding at the house, whenever she's well enough." Jessie released him.

"Thanks, Sis."

She touched the star on his chest. "Remember this when you go after Millborn. You're hurt and angry and probably want to kill him with your bare hands, but you're the law in the county now. If you want others to uphold it, you have to do the same."

"I could leave the badge with you." He was half-serious.

"You could, but you won't. You'll do what's right, Quint, because you always do. Besides, Ransom's going with you. He's waiting outside in a buggy so he won't slow you down. If you get too nasty, he'll whack you with his cane."

Quint forced a tiny smile for her benefit. "Ask the Lord to keep me from wringing Millborn's neck."

"I can do that. Better yet, I'll ask Him to give you wisdom and patience so you make certain you have the right man."

"Who else would have done it?"

"I expect he's probably behind it, but don't let your anger cloud your judgment."

"Yes, bossy."

She smiled at him and motioned for him to go. "Be careful, big brother."

He nodded and went out the door. After he climbed in the buggy, he told Ransom the little bit that Prissy had been able to share. He also told him about her condition and the baby, not wanting to surprise him when he questioned Millborn. After Ransom expressed his sympathy, Quint waited for him to offer some advice on confronting Millborn. But Ransom kept his counsel to himself, his way of showing Quint the confidence he had in him.

When they pulled up in front of the house owned by the English ranching syndicate, Quint jumped out of the buggy. Under the pretense of waiting for Ransom, he walked slowly around the horses, took a deep breath and forced down a surge of rage. *Father, help me to stay calm and think clearly.*

Ransom climbed slowly out of the vehicle and joined him. "Ready?"

"Yeah. I might break his nose, but I won't shoot him."

"That's a start. Hold off on the nose until you question him, then if he doesn't cooperate, you'll have some leverage."

Blake came across the street from where he'd been watching the house. "How is she?"

"Probably a couple of cracked ribs. Maybe a broken wrist and a concussion. Black eye. Doc thinks she'll recover." Quint didn't see any need to mention the baby to Blake since he would be staying outside.

"Sorry she's hurt so bad, but glad to hear she'll be all right. Where do you want me?"

"Guard the back in case he decides to run." Not that he'd get very far unless he had a horse hidden nearby.

Quint and Ransom waited a few more minutes to give Blake time to get in position. They moved onto the porch, and Quint rapped sharply on the door.

A butler opened the door, his nose in the air. It lowered slightly when he noticed their badges. "May I help you, gentlemen?"

"I need to speak with Millborn." Quint tried very hard to be polite. It wasn't easy when he was seething with anger.

"I'll see if his lordship is receiving guests." The snooty butler started to shut the door.

Quint stuck his boot in the opening, blocking it. He shoved on the door, and the butler stumbled aside as he walked in. "I'll see Millborn now."

The immaculately dressed servant sniffed in disdain and rushed down the hall in a huff. Quint and Ransom followed him right into Millborn's office.

"You can't just walk in here," cried the butler.

"We already did." Quint focused on his prey. He walked around the desk. Reaching down, he grabbed a handful of Millborn's white silk shirt and fancy blue jacket and hauled the astonished nobleman right out of the chair. "Baron Millborn, you're under arrest for the kidnapping and attempted murder of Priscilla Clark."

Millborn sputtered for a second until Quint released him. "I have no idea what you're taking about." He straightened his suit coat, glaring at Quint, then turned to Ransom, his expression becoming arrogant. "Sheriff Starr, you need to tie up your bulldog."

"He's the sheriff, now. You deal with him."

Millborn blinked and looked back at Quint, his gaze narrowing on the sheriff's badge. "I haven't seen Prissy since before I went to Dallas."

"Who did you hire to kill her?" Quint moved a step closer.

Millborn moved back, running into his chair. "No one! Why on earth do you think I'd harm Prissy?"

"You've hit her before." When Quint clenched his fists, a hint of fear crept into the man's eyes. "Your wife showed up and suddenly Prissy and the baby were an inconvenience."

To Quint's surprise, Millborn's expression softened slightly, but he stood his ground. "Baby? She never said anything about a child."

"So you beat her up simply because you wanted her to stay away from you."

"No! I haven't been near her. Nor did I have someone beat her. I wouldn't do such a thing." He held up his hand as if to stop Quint's next comment. "Yes, I hit her, but only one blow."

"Maybe I should hit you—just once, so you'll see how it feels."

"T-that isn't necessary." Millborn sat down and fumbled with the handle on a desk drawer.

Quint tensed, his hand dropping to his pistol.

Millborn pulled out the drawer and removed a fancy black box. "I bought this for her in Dallas." He opened it, revealing a gold and diamond necklace.

Quint drew a quick breath. It was worth a small fortune.

"It is customary to give a mistress a parting gift. If one is fond of her, one gives something of great value. Something not only beautiful, but which she could sell if she ever needed money." Millborn closed the box and laid it on the top of the desk. "As you can see, I am fond of her. I would never have done her any great harm. Now that I know she is with child, I shall do the honorable thing, of course, and make a substantial provision for them."

"Honorable?" shouted Quint. "You seduce a young woman and get her pregnant when you're a married man. She didn't know that. She thought you were going to marry her and take her to England. Now you say you'll do the honorable thing by providing for her and the baby?"

Quint paused, regaining control, lowering his voice to a normal level, vibrating with cold fury. "You can't provide for your child, Millborn. The beating caused a miscarriage. The doctor believes that was the purpose · of the attack. He hit her in the face until she couldn't see, broke a couple of ribs and maybe her wrist and tied her hands and feet. Then he tossed her in a gully four miles out of town and left her to die."

Quint watched the baron's eyes widen, then close as he absorbed the news. He had not believed Millborn's protests of innocence until that moment. Seeing the pain on the man's face made him reconsider.

"Will she live?" The Englishman's eyes were still closed, his face contorted with grief.

"The doctor thinks so. If she doesn't come down with pneumonia or some other problem doesn't set in."

"Her lovely face? Will it heal?"

"I think so. Nothing seemed broken. I don't think he hit her hard enough to damage her eyes, but we won't know for a while." Quint straightened, watching the baron closely.

When Millborn looked at him, the bleakness in his eyes told Quint that the Englishman was not responsible for what happened to Prissy.

"I'll put up a reward for the assailant's apprehension." Millborn cleared his throat. "It's the least I can do." He glanced toward the door behind Quint and Ransom, and his face filled with regret. "Elizabeth…"

Quint turned so he could see the doorway. Lady Millborn stood there, tears streaming down her face.

Millborn rose from the chair, and Quint stepped aside so he could go to his wife. She wasn't much older than Prissy. He felt sorry for her. The way she was crying, she must have not have known about his infidelity until then. Tough way to learn of it. He glanced at Ransom, who watched them with a thoughtful frown.

"Lady Millborn, you should come sit down," said Ransom in a kind voice. He motioned toward a chair in front of the desk. "This must be a great shock."

Quint was surprised when the baroness let her husband help her across the room. He'd expected her to slap *him* or at least scream at him. Millborn deserved that and more.

Lady Millborn sat down, twisting a lace trimmed handkerchief into a long spiral. "She wasn't supposed to be hurt."

Quint stared at her. Surely he had misunderstood her. "Excuse me, ma'am. What did you say?"

She swallowed and cleared her throat, glanced at her husband, then met Quint's gaze. "He was only supposed to frighten her into leaving town."

"Elizabeth?" Millborn dropped into a chair next to her, his expression stunned. "What have you done?"

Lady Millborn appeared fragile and dazed.

Quint gentled his voice. "Tell us how all this came about, ma'am."

"Mrs. Clark came to see me yesterday afternoon."

I should have known, thought Quint, stifling a groan.

"She told me about my husband's affair and that her daughter was carrying his child. She said no one else knew, and that if I paid her five hundred dollars, she and Miss Clark would go away and never bother us again.

She said they would leave on the evening train. I gave her the money. I sent my maid to the train station to make certain they left, but only Mrs. Clark got on the train. Priscilla stayed."

Trembling, the baroness wiped her eyes with the wadded handkerchief. "I was angry and afraid she would try to force Millborn to take her to England with us, to set her and the baby up in a home nearby and provide for them the rest of their days." She glanced at her husband. "I could not have born the shame of such a thing." Looking back at Quint, she continued. "I asked Giles to find someone who would threaten her, frighten her into leaving."

"Who is Giles?" asked Quint.

"Our footman." Millborn glanced at his wife. "He escorted my family to Dallas from New York. It would appear he was overzealous in following my command to protect my wife."

Lady Millborn looked up at Quint, her expression pleading. "I never meant for her to be hurt. Giles understood that. The man he hired was only supposed to threaten to harm her if she didn't leave."

"Where is Giles?" asked Quint, turning to the baron.

"I don't know." Millborn picked up a bell on his desk and rang it.

The butler appeared in the doorway instantly. Quint figured he'd been hovering in the hall. "Yes, milord?"

"Fetch Giles and be quick about it."

The butler bowed, then disappeared. A few minutes later, he returned with the man Quint had seen get off the train with Millborn and his family.

Giles glanced first at Lady Millborn, then at Quint

before focusing on the baron. He bowed slightly. "Yes, milord?"

"You will answer Sheriff Webb's questions, Giles. Truthfully and thoroughly."

"Yes, sir." The footman turned to Quint, his expression wary.

"Who did you hire to attack Priscilla Clark?"

"No one! I paid a ruffian to threaten her, but I gave him explicit instructions that she was not to be harmed in any way."

"His name," snapped Quint.

"John Dillard. Quite an unsavory looking character, but his appearance seemed appropriate for the task."

Quint knew Dillard. He doubted there was anyone meaner within a hundred miles of Willow Grove. He'd worked for Millborn's ranch until a few weeks earlier. He turned to Millborn. "Didn't you fire Dillard for fighting?"

"Yes. He was constantly stirring up trouble."

"What did you tell him, Giles?"

"That Lady Millborn wanted Miss Clark to leave town and never come back." The servant's gaze skittered to the baron and back to Quint. "He was to tell her never to try to contact Lord Millborn about the baby. If she did, there would be dire consequences." Giles frowned and rubbed the back of his neck. "He didn't understand what I meant by that, so I told him to threaten her, to tell her she would be hurt if she didn't do exactly as Lady Millborn said. Then I paid him the fifty dollars her ladyship had given me and left that disreputable saloon."

"So he knew about the baby." Quint looked over at

Ransom, noting that he was leaning against the wall. "Lord Millborn's baby."

Ransom nodded. "He saw killing Prissy and the baby as a way to get back at Millborn for firing him."

Quint started for the door. "He's probably still in the district spending his blood money."

"Sheriff, what about my wife?" asked Millborn. "And Giles? Will there be charges against them?"

"That's up to the district attorney. But don't leave town. If nothing else, they're witnesses against Dillard."

"Sheriff Webb…" At Lady Millborn's plaintive voice, Quint stopped and looked back at her. "Please ask Miss Clark to forgive me."

"That's something you'll have to do yourself, ma'am."

"You and Blake can take care of Dillard." Ransom pulled the buggy up in front of the livery and unhooked the deputy badge, handing it to Quint. "Now you know the who and the why, so all you have to do is arrest him."

"Don't you need to go along and corral me?"

"You handled Millborn with a reasonable amount of control. I expect you'll do the same with Dillard. But watch him. He won't just mosey on into the jail."

"If he's heard that we found Prissy, he may be gone already."

Ransom scanned the street. People were grouped together in twos and threes. "Folks are talkin' all right. You'd better hustle on over there as soon as Blake catches up with us."

"He's coming around the corner now." Quint

climbed out of the buggy, trying not to let his impatience show as Blake approached. The deputy must have run part of the way to get there so quickly.

"That didn't take long," said Quint when Blake walked up.

"I cut through some yards. Stirred up a few yappy dogs and one cat, but Mrs. Peabody was the only one who yelled at me."

"That's 'cause she couldn't tell it was you. We should buy her some eyeglasses in the interest of protecting the town."

When they got to the red-light district, Quint took one side of the street and Blake the other. They moved down the sidewalk, looking through the saloon windows to see who was inside. When Quint spotted Dillard, he motioned to Blake and stepped back so no one would see him.

The deputy trotted across the street, joining him. "You want me to go in the back door?"

"Yes." Quint waited a couple of minutes, then drew his pistol from the holster. When he walked through the swinging doors of the saloon, everyone in the room froze. Dillard sat in the center of the room, playing cards with three other men.

Quint walked slowly toward him. He stopped about ten feet away where he could keep him in sight when the other men moved. "John Dillard, you're under arrest for kidnapping and attempted murder."

The men at the table jumped to their feet and scrambled out of the way.

"I ain't kidnapped nobody. I been here playin' cards all day. Ain't that right, Al?"

"Been here since about five this morning," said the bartender, glancing at Blake as he took up his position between the assailant and the back door.

"It happened last night." Quint watched Dillard closely, his mouth going dry. The man had both hands under the table. "Put your hands up in the air, palms forward, where I can see them."

"Glad to oblige, Sheriff." Dillard put his left hand up in the air, but the coldness in his eyes warned Quint as his right arm moved minutely.

Heart pounding, Quint fired at his chest, his aim true. The shot knocked Dillard and the chair over backward, a pistol tumbling from his hand. Quint moved around the table, kicking the gun away, but there was no need. Dillard stared glassy-eyed at the ceiling.

Quint drew a deep breath and holstered his gun.

Blake did the same. "That was close."

"He won't be trying to murder any more women." Had he killed him because he hurt Prissy? If any other woman had been involved, Quint wouldn't have thought twice about it.

"Or you and me. You'd probably be dead if you hadn't pulled the trigger when you did. Wish we had a better way of collecting all the weapons instead of only the obvious ones."

"Can't search every man, horse and wagon."

"Can't say as I've ever seen a horse packing a pistol," drawled Blake.

Quint knew he was trying to lighten the tension, but he could only give his deputy a hint of a smile. "A wagon, either." He looked around the room. "Some of you boys haul him over to the undertaker's."

"I'll take care of it," said Blake. "You go see Miss Priscilla."

As Quint walked toward the door, the bartender called, "It was you or him, Sheriff Webb. If anybody questions it, you got a dozen witnesses." Murmurs of affirmation hummed around the room.

"Thanks." He looked back at the man behind the bar. "Keep track of who's here in case anybody has questions."

"Sure thing."

Quint walked back downtown, taking it a bit slower than when he'd rushed to the district. He needed time to calm down before he saw Prissy. He went over the shooting and decided he couldn't have done anything different. If he hadn't shot when he did, Dillard might have shot right through the table. When Quint had pulled the trigger, he wasn't thinking about Dillard hurting Prissy. He'd been trying to save his hide, plain and simple.

Chapter Twenty-Two

The doctor kept Prissy at his office for a couple of days. Either Lily or Jessie stayed with her the whole time, then Lily went with her when the doctor sent her home. Ty said that her job at the store would be waiting whenever she was ready to go back to work.

Lily supposed they could find someone else to stay with Prissy, but she wanted to do it. She enjoyed working at the store but taking care of someone who was ill was more rewarding. Lily also felt a kinship with Prissy in having lost a loved one.

When the swelling in Prissy's face went down, they were all greatly relieved that her vision hadn't been damaged. She was weak from the blood loss and the sprained wrist was very painful. Thankfully, the pain in her ribs eased quicker than expected, and the doctor decided they'd only been bruised, not cracked. She'd had a concussion, too, and dealt with occasional head-aches and dizziness.

Back in her own home, she had more freedom to get up and move about. She was good to lie down when she needed to, so Lily didn't fuss at her to rest. Quint came to see her every day, often more than once. Lily was touched by his tenderness toward Prissy. She couldn't help but think that most men would not have been so kind and forgiving of the woman's indiscretion.

The district attorney decided against prosecuting Lady Millborn and Giles on the condition that they leave Willow Grove as soon as possible.

To Prissy and Lily's surprise, Lady Millborn paid them a call a week after Prissy had been hurt.

Lily almost didn't let the woman in when she answered the door. "Prissy is resting."

"We're departing this evening. It is very important that I speak with her. I will only take a few minutes. Please, Miss Chastain."

Lily hesitated, then relented. "All right, but if you start scolding her, I'll shove you right back out this door."

"If I start scolding her, you'd have every right to throw me out."

Lily led the baroness into the parlor where Prissy was resting on a chaise lounge. The window and front door were open, so Prissy had heard their exchange. "Lady Millborn."

"Miss Clark."

"Please sit down." Prissy motioned toward a chair across from her.

Lady Millborn sat down and glanced at Lily as she

started toward the doorway. "There is no need to leave on my account, Miss Chastain."

"Nor mine," said Prissy. "Please stay."

Lily sat down, the tense silence getting on her nerves. She watched as Lady Millborn glanced at the faded bruises on Prissy's face and sling around her arm.

The baroness cleared her throat. "Miss Clark, I've come to ask your forgiveness. My intention was only to frighten you into leaving as your mother had said you would. I never meant for that horrid man to hurt you. My servant specifically told him he was not to harm you, but Giles did not know the man held a grudge against my husband."

"I understand, Lady Millborn, and you are forgiven. I don't know you, but you don't strike me as a person who would try to have someone killed. I also owe you an apology. If I had known Millborn was married, I never would have gotten involved with him. I foolishly thought he was courting me."

"You are not accustomed to the ways of English aristocracy, where it is common for a man to have a mistress. In England, it is generally known that the baron is married." She sighed heavily, and Lily was struck by the realization that her ladyship was not much older than she was. "However, even there, Millborn had an alliance with a young woman who was innocently beguiled into believing he was courting her. In that instance, I found out and introduced myself before any great harm was done."

"No harm other than humiliation and maybe a broken heart," said Prissy.

"Yes. Bad enough, certainly, but not so grave as if there had been a child involved." Her fingers tightened on the handle of her purse. "I deeply regret what happened to your baby. I have lost two children of my own, and I would never wish that pain on another woman." She seemed to realize how tightly she was gripping her purse and relaxed her fingers. "I hear that Sheriff Webb has been most attentive to you."

"We are going to be married after I get well."

"I'm glad. He will be a strong champion for you. I thought he was going to rip Millborn apart the day they found you."

"Perhaps it would have been better for you if he had," Prissy said with a hint of smile.

"If he had only been defending your honor, then yes, perhaps it would have. Oh, dear, I suppose that makes me seem bloodthirsty. As tragic as this has been, I hope Millborn will learn from it. He does not know that I *always* hear of his dalliances."

Lily decided that since they both had asked her to stay, she wasn't going to sit there like a bump on a log. "Why do you put up with it?"

Surprise darted across Lady Millborn's face. "It is common in our society."

"That doesn't make it right. Does he know how much it hurts you?" Lily glanced at Prissy to see if her new friend thought she was way out of line.

"I believe he has an inkling of it now."

"You should tell him," said Prissy. "Just come right out with it. Underneath all that arrogance, a bit of kindness comes through now and then. Even if it doesn't change him, it will do you good to let off a little steam."

Lady Millborn smiled as she stood. "It might at that. I wish you and Sheriff Webb much happiness."

"I wish the same for you and your husband, Baroness. I truly do."

"Thank you. We are leaving on the evening train for California, so neither of us should trouble you again." When Lily started to get up, Lady Millborn shook her head. "You don't need to see me out, Miss Chastain. Goodbye."

Lily bade her goodbye and stayed where she was. When the baroness disappeared down the street, she looked at Prissy. "I don't think anybody would believe us if we told them about that conversation."

Prissy laughed. "It was odd, wasn't it? But I feel better. I needed to apologize to her. I wronged her as much as she wronged me."

"I don't think it was quite the same. She's not walking around with bruises and a sprained wrist."

"She's worse off than me. She's married to the clod."

That evening, when Quint stopped by, he hung his hat on the hall tree and walked into the parlor, bending down to kiss Prissy. "How's my woman?"

"Better every day. How's my man?"

"Doin' just fine. I watched Millborn and his family leave on the westbound train this evening."

"That's a relief for all of us." Lily sat in the rocker by the window, planning to visit for a few minutes before she left them alone.

"Lady Millborn said they were going to California," said Prissy. "She came by this afternoon for a mutual apology."

Quint sat down on the couch by Prissy. "I reckon both of you owed one and deserved one." He handed her a fat envelope. "I found this on my desk this afternoon. It's addressed to you."

Frowning, Prissy opened the envelope and several one hundred dollar bills fell into her lap. "What on earth?" She looked in the envelope again. "There's a note, too." Unfolding the note, her eyes grew wide as she read. "It's from Lord Millborn. He asks me to please accept the money as restitution and also as a wedding present."

Quint whistled and picked up the money. "There's a thousand dollars here."

Prissy stared at the money, her expression bewildered. "I feel like he's paying me for my services."

"No, he's trying to make amends for you being hurt in the only way he knows how." Lily shook her finger at her. "He said it himself. This is restitution. You were a victim. He and his wife caused you harm. You deserve every penny." She grinned and winked at Quint. "And if you don't like looking at it that way, choose the other angle. It's a wedding present."

Quint smiled and handed Prissy the money. "You'd better put this in the bank instead of the sugar bowl. If anything, he's trying to buy me off. Make sure I don't get riled up again and come after him. We can use it and they owe us, so take it."

"All right." Prissy tucked it inside her sling. "But let's wait a while. Maybe that way, the folks at the bank will think it came from Mama. If we deposit it now, they'll figure it came from Millborn. They're supposed to be discrete, but you know as well as I do that they gossip just like everybody else."

Lily chuckled and left them playfully bickering about what to do with the money. Personally, she thought Millborn should have coughed up ten times that amount.

On Thursday morning, when Prissy suggested that they invite Quint and Ransom to supper, Lily jumped at the chance. She had only seen Ransom a few times in the two weeks since the assault. She missed him terribly and was annoyed that he was keeping his distance.

"Ransom might not come," she warned. "He has the crazy idea that I shouldn't want a man like him."

"Every single woman in the county—well, except me," Prissy said with a smile, "would give their eyeteeth to be courted by him." She paused thoughtfully. "He means because he has to depend on the cane?"

"To him, it's a symbol of all the things he can't do right now. He worries about earning a living and being able to protect me."

"The incident with that freighter. Poor Ransom, it must have upset him terribly not to be able to help you. And to fall in the street..." Prissy shook her head. "He's a proud man. He must have been so humiliated."

"He only fell because the cane broke." Lily worked hard to keep the irritation out of her voice. She and Prissy had become friends, but she wouldn't let anybody deride Ransom.

"I know, but I doubt that made much difference to him."

"No, it didn't. But it should have."

"I wish you could have seen him when he first came to town and confronted that outlaw in the courtroom," said Prissy. "Wyman had grabbed the pistol he had hidden under the table and was threatening everyone. Cade was on one side of the room and Sheriff Procter on the other, but neither of them had their guns drawn. Sheriff Procter was a highly respected lawman, and Cade had been with the Texas Rangers. Though he hadn't been a Ranger for years, he'd helped the sheriff capture the gang that Wyman led.

"I was sitting in the middle of the courtroom. Half the people hit the floor when Wyman pulled the gun. The other half, me included, froze in our seats. When the sheriff took a step toward him, Wyman pointed his gun at the judge and said he'd kill him if anybody tried to stop him. He ordered the judge to come down the steps and said they were going for a little ride. Ransom, a stranger to most of us then, came walking down the aisle, incredibly handsome and calm as could be."

"With his pistol drawn, I assume." Lily had been thumbing through a cookbook before Prissy started her story. Now, it lay on her lap, forgotten.

"No, they were still in his holsters. He had pushed his jacket back out of the way, but he held his hands out to his sides. He looked the way I'd always expected a gunslinger to look—black suit, white shirt, gun belt slung low on his hips. Except he wore a deputy badge.

"Ransom asked Wyman about some people in Denver that he had killed. I don't remember exactly what he said, but it rattled Wyman. Then Ransom stopped, maybe twenty feet from him and asked Wyman if he thought he could kill him before Ransom shot him."

"He challenged him? A known killer holding a

gun?" Lily knew Ransom was brave, but that seemed to border on being foolhardy.

"That's right. Wyman thought he'd be charged with murder, but Ransom said it would be self-defense since he challenged him. Even got the sheriff to agree." Prissy frowned and pursed her lips. "Though I've always wondered if that was really true."

"I've heard that Ransom killed him."

"That he did. He had Wyman distracted, so the sheriff took another step toward him. That spooked Wyman and he swung around, pointing the gun toward the audience."

"You must have ducked then."

"I should have, but I was so fascinated by what was happening that I just sat there. I was watching Ransom, but I could see Cade and the sheriff, too, kind of in the background. When Wyman moved his gun toward the audience, Cade and the sheriff reached for their pistols. They both had reputations for being fast with a gun. But Ransom drew his pistol and fired before they even got theirs out of the holsters. His bullet hit Wyman, and he fell to the floor, dropping the gun."

"Was he still alive?"

"Barely. He died maybe a minute later. Ransom walked over to him. The last words that outlaw heard were Ransom's. His voice was hard as steel and filled with loathing. He wasn't loud, but it was so quiet in the courtroom that everyone must have heard him. He leaned over Wyman and said, 'That's for three-year-old Nellie O'Malley. One shot. Right through the heart. Just the way you killed her.'"

Lily gasped. "How horrible! Wyman had killed a little girl?"

"He killed the whole family."

Lily remembered Ransom's comment a few days after she and Matt had moved into Mrs. Franklin's boarding house. He'd been trying to convince her that killing her father's murderers wouldn't ease her pain. He'd talked about having momentary satisfaction from the revenge but that it wouldn't last. That the men he killed haunted his dreams. *Surely not Wyman,* she thought.

Prissy shifted in the chair, a sign she was growing weary. "You should have seen him that day. He was like a gallant hero you read about in history books, standing tall and strong for justice. Half the women in town fell in love with him right then."

The enormity of what she and Matt had done hit her anew. "Now he can't even walk without a cane." Lily's pain and regret thickened her voice. *Lord, how can he not blame me?*

A stricken look settled on Prissy's face. "Oh, dear, I didn't tell you that story to make you feel bad. I just wanted you to understand how proud we are of him. I'm sorry, Lily. I shouldn't have prattled on so."

"It's all right." Lily set the cookbook on the table beside her chair. "I wish I could have seen him then. He must have been quite grand." *Please God, let him get completely well. Let him be that strong, confident man again.*

Lily smiled, hoping it masked the ache in her heart. "You need to rest, and I need to go to the grocers as well as invite the gentlemen to supper."

"I am tired." Prissy wrinkled her face and winced. "Talking too much. I'll go lie down and you go flirt a little with Ransom."

Lily laughed as she helped Prissy from the chair. "I think that's a very good idea. He's probably decided I've forgotten all about him."

"As if you could." Prissy's smile held a hint of wistfulness. "I envy you and Ransom. It's plain to see that you're both in love."

"Quint loves you."

"I know. I don't see how he can, but I'm convinced that he does. I care very much for him, too."

"But you don't love him?" Lily suspected Prissy didn't realize the depth of her feelings.

"I think I do, but my emotions and feelings are all topsy-turvy these days. I don't quite trust them. I want to love him. I desperately want to be a good wife to him. He's such a good and kind man. Brave, too."

"He's all of that and more. He fights for justice, too."

"Yes, he does. How can I not love him?"

Lily watched Prissy make her way slowly down the hall. Her new friend had refused her help walking the last couple of days, but she always kept an eye on her anyway. She decided that she and Ransom should spend a little time on the back porch tonight so Prissy and Quint could be alone. She had a feeling that Prissy might want to say some things to Quint in private.

So she would drag Ransom outside. It would be a sacrifice, but she would gladly do it to promote the romance between Quint and Prissy. Sacrifice, my foot, she thought with a giggle. She could hardly wait to spend some time alone with him.

Chapter Twenty-Three

When Ransom looked up from the paperwork on his desk and saw Lily coming through the doorway, happiness rushed through him. He hadn't seen much of her lately. It seemed as if it had been a year. He stood, and resting one hand on the desktop to bear a bit of his weight, he walked around to meet her. Stopping, he settled one hip on the corner of the desk, half sitting, half leaning against it.

Lily stared, her smile growing even more beautiful. "Look at you!" She walked right up and surprised him by sliding her arms around him in a hug.

He hugged her back. "Hi, sugar."

She tried to press her cheek against the side of his neck, but the curled brim of her hat got in the way and a feather tickled his nose. Pulling back, she made a face. "I wore the wrong hat."

Ransom chuckled and rubbed his nose to keep from sneezing. He looked into her eyes and melted at the love shining there. "Wrong for hugging." Tipping his head and leaning toward her, he whispered, "But not for kissing."

She closed her eyes and lifted her face, welcoming his gentle touch. Tenderness spiraled through him, making his heart ache with longing. How had he ever thought that if he stayed away from her, he'd forget her? Mindful of where they were and the windows overlooking the street, he kept the kiss short.

He raised his head, resting his hands at her waist. "What brings you downtown this morning?"

"Grocery shopping so Prissy and I can invite two handsome gentlemen to supper this evening."

Ransom grinned lazily. "Safe to assume I'm one of the invitees?"

"Yes. Quint has already accepted."

"Then I'd better come and keep you company."

"Thank you kindly. We'll eat about six-thirty." She moved back a step, glancing at the cane propped up against a file cabinet. "You're walking better."

"Some. I can move around the office pretty much. My leg is getting stronger, but most of the time I still need to lean on something. I've managed a few steps without holding onto something, but not many."

"You'll get there. Just give it time."

"I'm more encouraged about it this week. Though it seems to be a little better every day, I have to keep the cane handy around the house. Don't have enough furniture yet to fill in all the gaps."

"Matt told me that you'd moved out of the boarding

house." She sounded disappointed, even though she'd known his plan.

"Yep. I'm in Ty's rental house on Third Street. The jeweler who was living there moved into his new house a couple of weeks ago. Mine is practically straight down the alley from here, so I can walk the two blocks without a problem. I like having the elbow room, but I miss Mrs. Franklin's cooking. Yours, too."

"All the more reason to come eat with us tonight. Are you staying there by yourself?"

"Yes. So far I'm managing all right. I hired a housekeeper to come in once a week and tidy up. I usually cook my own breakfast, then eat dinner and supper at one of the restaurants." Carrying hot water to the bathtub was a royal pain, but he accomplished it, even if it was barely enough to bathe in.

She walked around the office, skimming her fingers over the desk and file cabinets. "And your business? Is it coming together?"

"My first agent, Karl Lloyd, signed on two days ago. He worked for a different company than I did, but he has a good reputation. Camille is printing up a stack of announcements for the Starr Detective Agency." He grinned at her smile. "Has a nice ring to it, doesn't it?

"I've been addressing envelopes and writing some personal notes to send along with some of them. They'll be going out by the end of the week. There will be an ad in the *Gazette* starting this week. Probably won't get too much business from it, but you never know. We'll be running ads in all the major newspapers in the state for a while, starting this week, too."

"You have been busy."

"Yep." It didn't stop the loneliness. He liked having a place of his own where he could relax uninterrupted and not hear the noise of the other boarders. But at times, it had been too quiet, too empty. He'd missed Lily and Matt, too, for that matter, though he'd seen her brother almost every day. "Matt's been coming by here pretty often. He misses having you around, but I think he feels all grown up fending for himself."

"He hasn't needed anyone telling him what to do for a year or two."

"He's a very reliable young man." Ransom caught a flitting expression of sadness on her face. "But he'll always need his sister. Maybe not to boss him around, but he still needs you." So do I, he thought. "Prissy must be feeling better if y'all are having company."

"She hasn't regained her strength yet, and her ribs are still a bit sore. The doctor has decided she must not have cracked them, though, because she's improving so quickly. Her wrist hurts, but not as much as a few days ago. The swelling has gone down in her face and most of the bruising is gone. She cries over the baby sometimes, but Quint visits her every day. It's amazing how much he lifts her spirits."

"So no regrets that she didn't catch a rich husband?"

"No. She treasures Quint's love far more than she would a fancy home and wealthy husband."

"That's good." Ransom grinned as she walked back toward him. "Quint won't ever get rich being sheriff."

"Do you miss it?"

He considered her question. "More than I thought I would. The job is eighty percent boredom and twenty percent excitement. I miss making the rounds every day, visiting with folks along the way."

"You don't have to stay cooped up in here."

"I don't, but I can't go too far. Somebody might come in wanting to hire us."

"I'll hire you to look for the men who killed my father."

"Sugar, if I thought we could find them, that would have been Karl's first case—at my expense." When he saw her expression soften and tears mist her eyes, he opened his arms.

She stepped into his embrace, resting her head against his shoulder, keeping the wayward feather well away from his nose. "You wouldn't make any money that way."

"I wouldn't be doing it for the money." But for love. He left the words unspoken, but as her arms tightened around him, he figured she understood. "We haven't gotten a single lead from all those wanted posters we sent out. They've either gone into hiding or changed their looks so much that nobody recognizes them."

A motion across the street drew his gaze, and he quickly released her. "Ty's running down the sidewalk. Go see if you can find out what's wrong."

Lily ran to the door and threw it open, taking a few steps onto the boardwalk. "Ty, is it Camille?" she called.

"She's having the baby!" He didn't miss a step.

Ransom worked his way around the desk to get to his cane.

"Do you need me?" Lily ran down the boardwalk, keeping abreast of Ty.

"Jessie's with her. Doc Wilson, too. Pray!"

"We will," called Lily. She came back through the office door when Ransom was halfway across the room. "Camille's having the baby."

"I heard. Along with everyone else on Main Street," he added with a smile.

"He looked terrified. He needs you with him."

"Me?" Ransom suddenly realized he was a coward when it came to women having babies.

"Yes, you. Unless Cade is in town."

He breathed a sigh of relief. "He is. He had some business at the bank this morning."

"Brad must be going after him. He was behind Ty, then cut across the street."

"Cade will be a lot better support than me. He's been through this with Jessie."

Lily tipped her head, her eyes narrowing. "You're scared to go over there."

"I'd be in the way."

Her lips twitched. "Uh-huh."

"But I can pray. You told him we would."

"Yes, I did." She shut the door and held out her hand.

Ransom took it in his, blessing the Lord for the bond they shared. Lowering his head, he prayed quietly, "Heavenly Father, be with Camille and the baby. Please keep them safe and give her a quick delivery. Be with Ty and help him not to be afraid." But how could he not be, given his tragic past?

"Guide the doctor, Lord. Give him the wisdom and ability that he needs at this time." Lily's hand tightened around his. "Give Camille strength. Let this baby be healthy. Please don't let anything go wrong. Fill them with Your love and Your peace. In Jesus's name, amen."

"Amen." Ransom brought her hand to his lips, kissing the back of it. "I suppose I should wander up there in a little while and keep him company."

Her smile lit her face and warmed his heart. "I'm sure he'll appreciate it. You'll let me know when the baby is born?"

"I expect the whole town will hear Ty shouting hallelujah, but, yes, I'll let you know."

"Now, I'd better go do my shopping and get back and check on Prissy." She reluctantly pulled her hand from his. "I'm so thankful that God hears us whether we pray out loud or silently as we go about our business, and that He hears the prayers of our hearts when our minds can't form the words. Even when I couldn't bring myself to pray, He heard my heart's cry."

"To ease your pain." He traced her jaw with his fingertip.

"Yes, and to heal you."

Ransom's throat tightened. "He's done a lot, for which I'm mighty grateful, but I'm not all the way back yet."

Standing on tiptoe, she brushed a feather-light kiss across his mouth. "You're a fine man, Ransom Starr." She laid her hand over his on the handle of the cane. "Good enough for me whether you need this thing or not."

When she walked out the door, Ransom returned to his chair behind the desk. This time, his weak knees had nothing to do with his injury.

Sarah Elizabeth McKinnon was born at five-thirty that afternoon. When Jessie stuck her head out the bedroom door to tell Ty that he had a baby girl and that both she and Camille were doing fine, Ransom expected him to at least let loose with a rebel yell. Instead, Ty nodded and quickly walked out the back door.

Since Ransom was in the kitchen swiping a cookie from the cookie jar at the time, he peeked out the window to make sure his friend was all right. Ty leaned against the porch railing, his back to the house, his head hanging down. Judging by the way his shoulders shook, Ransom figured he was sobbing in relief and thanksgiving.

Cade walked into the kitchen and looked out the window. "I'll give him a couple more minutes before I go out. He's tried so hard not to be afraid, but I don't see how he could help it."

"Not after what happened to Amanda and their son," said Ransom. "How does a man get over a loss like that?"

"I don't think he could have if he hadn't had the Lord to comfort him. He'd go out on the range by himself for days, sometimes weeks at a time. I figured he needed the solitude, but I always wondered if he'd come back."

Ransom pulled out a chair at the kitchen table and sat down. "As close as you two are, I'm surprised you could stand it."

"I had to, though there were several times the first year after Amanda and Will died, that I insisted he go camp somewhere on the ranch or in our territory. At least that way, I'd have a better chance of finding him if he didn't show up after a few weeks. I'm so thankful God sent Camille to be a part of his life."

Ransom agreed, though he might have courted her himself if Ty hadn't been in the picture. He'd thought about it again when Ty and Camille had a falling out—before Ty proposed—but he could see she loved his friend. He hadn't wanted to play second fiddle. Now he knew why he'd waited—God had other plans for him.

Jessie came into the kitchen. "Where's Ty?"

"Out on the porch." Cade looked at her.

Ransom noted that she understood what he left unspoken. He and Lily sometimes did that, too, an indication of how close they were. This was such an emotional time, if he didn't watch it, he'd be proposing to her before the evening was over.

"Well, when you think he's ready, tell him it's time to meet his new daughter." Jessie smiled at Cade, her face filled with love. "She's a beautiful little girl. Healthy and strong." A baby's wail came from the bedroom. "Good pair of lungs, too."

"And they're both all right?" asked Cade, a trace of worry in his expression.

"Doing fine. Doc says he's never seen as easy a birth with a first child."

"God is good." Cade's voice was thick with emotion.

"Yes, He is." Jessie returned to the bedroom.

A minute later, Brad and Ellie burst through the back door. "We heard a baby crying," said Brad.

"You have a new cousin." Cade scooped Ellie up in his arms. "Sarah Elizabeth has arrived."

"A girl. Hurray!" Ellie hugged her daddy's neck. "Can we go tell everybody?"

Cade winked at Brad. "Do you want to or is this just Ellie's idea?"

"I'd like to. All the neighbors are sitting on their front porches anyway, waiting for news."

"All right. But if you go beyond our block, stay together."

"Yes, sir."

"Will you tell Lily?" asked Ransom. "She's still at Miss Prissy's. They were anxious to hear the news."

"Be glad to. Then we'll run downtown and tell everybody." Brad's grin quickly faded. "Aunt Camille and Sarah are all right, aren't they?" He glanced toward the back porch. "Uncle Ty looked like he'd been crying."

"If he has, it's because he's so relieved and so thankful that they're both just fine." Cade kissed Ellie on the cheek and set her down on the floor. "It would be best if you don't say anything about the crying part. To him or anybody else."

Ellie nodded. "'Cause grown men aren't supposed to cry. Women can bawl all they want, but men can't. Seems real silly to me, but that's the way it is."

"Yep. That's the way it is." Ransom held out his hand. "Come give Uncle Ransom a hug before you go act as the town crier."

"I'm too happy to cry." Ellie skipped over and hugged his neck when he bent down.

"You don't need to. Town criers go around and tell people what's happening. Kinda like Aunt Camille's newspaper, but they holler it out instead of writing it." Ransom planted a kiss on her forehead. Not for the first time, he wished he had a little girl like Ellie of his own.

"Or what's not happening." Cade rested his hand on Brad's shoulder. "Remember reading about them in your history book?"

"They're the ones who walk around the city and if everything is okay, they holler things like, 'Twelve o'clock and all is well.'"

"So we need to take a watch." Ellie looked up at her father and held out her hand.

Cade laughed. "I don't think you need to tell everybody the time on this trip. Just go tell them about the baby. But don't be too long. Your mama has a pot of stew simmering on the stove."

"Yum." Ellie rubbed her stomach. "We'll be home when my tummy tells us to."

"Fair enough." Cade chuckled as the kids raced to the front door. "I think it's time to go congratulate my little brother."

"I'll catch him on the way by." Ransom stood as Cade went out on the porch. When he and Ty came back in a few minutes later, Ransom held out his hand. "Congratulations, Papa."

Ty beamed and vigorously shook his hand. "Has a nice ring to it, doesn't it? You and Lily better get hitched or you'll be left behind."

"Quit giving me orders and go kiss your wife." Ransom pulled his watch out of his pocket. "You've got fifteen minutes to show off that baby before I have to head over to supper with Lily and Prissy."

"You'll get a quick look before you leave, but it might be right down to the wire on the time."

Ransom smiled and slapped him on the back. "Good enough."

Ten minutes later, Ty slipped out the bedroom door with a tiny bundle in his arms. "She's still a little red."

Cade and Ransom immediately hovered around him.

Ransom was awestruck. The closest he'd come to seeing a newborn was Cade's little Jacob, and he'd been several hours old at the time. "She's so tiny. A lot smaller than Jacob was."

"That's because her daddy isn't as big as her uncle." Ty grinned at Cade and pulled the soft yellow blanket back so they could see her strawberry blonde hair.

"Look at that," said Cade. "She has Camille's hair."

"She's the spittin' image of Camille," said Ransom, lightly touching the downy curls on her head. He smiled at Ty, feeling more emotional than he'd expected or cared to admit. "You got yourself a little princess."

Ty gave him a silly grin. "Now I have two princesses. Sarah and her mama."

Quint came in, easing the screen door closed behind him. "Brad and Ellie are running up and down Main Street, shouting 'It's a girl and all is well.'"

Cade and Ransom laughed. Ty smiled and got misty-eyed. "Yes, sir, all is well. Thanks be to God."

Ransom figured the other two men added a silent amen just as he did.

Chapter Twenty-Four

After supper, Ransom and Quint helped clear the table. Ransom followed Lily into the kitchen on the last trip, carrying the dish with about four bites of chicken and dumplings left in the bottom. "I think I should clean this up for you."

Lily laughed and nodded toward a drawer. "The spoons are in there."

Ransom leaned against the cabinet and finished off the main course. "You know," he said, pointing the spoon at Lily, "you make better dumplings than Mrs. Franklin."

"Why, thank you. That's a high compliment." Lily scraped the remnants of food on the plates into a bowl for the cat.

"Yes, it is. Everything was excellent." He smiled at her. "But then I already knew you were a good cook.

When you were taking care of me, sometimes you'd smell like cinnamon or vanilla. I used to try to guess what you'd been baking."

"Were you right?"

"Every once in a while. Do you want some help washing these up?" He'd noticed that Quint made a hasty retreat after they carried everything into the kitchen.

"No, thanks. I'll do them later. I don't want to waste my time with you doing dishes." She put some soap in the dishpan and added hot water from the teakettle. After putting the plates and silverware in the water to soak, she sidled up next to him. "We should go sit on the back porch for a while and give Quint and Prissy some time alone."

He grinned mischievously. "Which conveniently gives *us* time alone, too."

"Just coincidence." She flicked her finger beneath his chin. "Though her mother had the foresight to put a comfortable two-person wicker settee on the porch."

Illumination from the kitchen window gave them enough light to see each other clearly, but the porch was dark enough to shelter them from any neighbor's curious eyes. They sat down on the settee, and Ransom laid the cane beside it.

At times he hated that piece of wood. Other times, it seemed almost a part of him. He still prayed that he'd be rid of it someday, but he was learning that needing a cane to get around wasn't such a terrible thing. By God's grace, he had improved far more than either of the doctors had expected. He was very thankful for that. "You were right."

She looked at him, then shifted slightly so she could see his face better. "About what?"

"Turning the sheriff's job over to Quint took a heavy load off my shoulders. Since I quit worrying about not being able to do the job and not meeting the expectations I thought people had of me, I'm much more relaxed. I've been sleeping better." When he wasn't thinking about her and missing her. "Which it seems, led to healing quicker. Even Doc Wilson is amazed at the improvement."

"I'm thrilled that you're so much better." She sighed contentedly and moved again, resting her side against his.

Ransom put his arm around her shoulders, holding her comfortably. He wondered how she was dealing with her grief. Though she had made her peace with God and gained solace and strength from church and reading her Bible, he knew her heart still ached over her father's death. When his parents died, moments of loss and grief had hit him unexpectedly for months. Had she needed his comfort? Needed him to hold her? "How are you doing?"

"All right most of the time. Taking care of Prissy has been good for me."

"You have a gift for taking care of sick folks."

"I just do the best I can. I like being in the store and meeting different people during the day, but it's more rewarding to help someone who is sick. With Prissy, I could sympathize about the baby because of losing my parents. It's been very hard on her."

"Lord willing, she'll have other children."

"She wants to, and Quint has assured her he likes children. I can vouch for that because I've seen how much he loves Cade and Jessie's kids." She was quiet for a minute. Ransom waited, letting her get her thoughts in order. "I miss Papa so much. Sometimes, it just hits out of the blue. Or something will remind me of him, and my heart aches. I want justice for him. I've tried to pray for the men who killed him, but I can't. All I can do is ask God to keep them from hurting any-one else."

"Do you still want to kill them?"

"Sometimes, though I don't think I could do it. I've asked God to take the hatred from my heart and replace it with forgiveness, but maybe it's something I have to do myself."

"I'd have a tough time doing that. The fact that you're trying has to be a good thing in God's eyes."

"I hope so." She took a deep breath and smiled. "It's been an eventful day."

"Yes, it has." He wasn't only thinking of Camille and the baby, but also of Lily's parting words when she left his office that morning. In fact, he'd spent a great deal of time during the day thinking about what she said, even while he was keeping Ty company.

"I appreciated you sending Brad and Ellie over to tell us before they ran downtown," said Lily. "I'm so happy for Ty and Camille and especially thankful that everything went well."

"I expect everybody in town shares those senti-ments. They're both well-liked around here. How are things at the boarding house?"

"Matt says that Perry Edwards, who took your room, snores terribly. Everyone is cranky. I dread going back. Matt and I are looking for a house to rent."

It was on the tip of his tongue to tell her that she could move in with him, but that would mean asking her to marry him. He wasn't ready to do that. Not yet. He hadn't even told her how he felt about her. He should. Lost in thought, his heart pounding, he missed part of what she said.

"—told her we didn't need anything fancy. It's not, but it would suit us. I'll only be staying at Prissy's another couple of weeks. Maybe only one." She leaned a little closer. "I think Prissy has realized that she's in love with Quint and is going to tell him tonight."

"That's why we're out here?"

She rested her head against his arm and looked up at him with an impish smile. "It's one reason."

She didn't have to spell it out for him. He lowered his head toward hers. "Here's another." He touched her lips gently at first, then turning more fully toward her, slid his other arm around her waist and deepened the kiss. One kiss led to another…and another, until they were both breathless.

Ransom held her close, resting his cheek against the top of her head. When he could talk he said softly, "I love you, Lily."

She wiggled a little, and he eased his hold so she could look up at him. "I love you, too. Just the way you are. I hope and pray that you get completely well. But I'll never think any less of you if you have to use that cane."

"I hope I reach the point where I don't, but I'm gettin' used to it. Most of the time it doesn't bother me as much as it did. Sugar, I love you, but I can't ask you to marry me."

Her crestfallen face made him mentally kick himself. He shouldn't have said anything. But it wouldn't be fair for her to expect a proposal and not get one. "Not yet. I want to marry you, Lily. I want to spend the rest of my life with you, but I have to know I can provide for you and our family. Maybe it's pride, but I'd like to think I'm just being practical. I have to make certain my business succeeds."

She frowned, pursed her lips, tapped her foot, then frowned again. He was in trouble. Then she looked up at him, her eyes shining with love, and he knew he was a goner. "You could still ask. We wouldn't have to get married until your business was up and running."

"What if I don't get a single client?"

"Then we'll think of something else. I've barely touched the money Papa left us." She laughed self-consciously and shook her head. "I can't believe I'm sitting here badgering you to propose. I can wait until you're ready—for a while anyway. But not if you put it off for years."

"I wouldn't expect you to. In the meantime, Miss Lily Chastain, I'd like to court you right and proper." Show every man around there that she belonged to him so they wouldn't try to weasel into his territory. And hope it worked. A ring on her finger would be a better deterrent, but he refused to make her a promise that he wasn't certain he could keep. "Would you attend the opening of the Opera House with me on Saturday evening?"

"Why thank you, kind sir. I'd be delighted." She batted her eyelashes at him.

Ransom laughed and squeezed her shoulder. Maybe he was doing things right after all.

* * *

On Saturday afternoon, Red Mulhany opened the Opera House door so Ransom could go inside. He locked it again and grinned at Ransom. "I don't let just anybody in here, you know."

"I appreciate it. Are they finished with the rehearsal?"

"Almost. You say you know Miss Nickson?"

Ransom nodded as they walked across the ornate lobby to the double doors of the theatre. He figured he might as well explain to Red. If Georgia went to work for him, everybody in town would know it anyway. "She worked for the same detective agency that I did in Denver."

"A lady detective. Don't that beat all. Is she going to work for you?"

"I'm going to ask. She might not be interested." Ransom scanned the room, admiring the fine mahogany woodwork and large paintings depicting scenes from around the world. A red Brussels carpet covering the floor added to the elegance. "I have to hand it to you and the McKinnons. This is one of the nicest theatres I've ever been in."

"My missus and Camille helped us figure out how to decorate the place. They had some good suggestions for the design of the building, too." Red looked around, pride shining on his face. "It's a long way from the Tripoli."

"A great improvement. I expect the entertainment will be better, too." Ransom grimaced at the memory of a theatrical troupe Mulhany had brought in for a week at his saloon. Mulhany had been told it was high-class entertainment, but it turned out to be so bawdy and obnoxious that the city council passed an ordinance that would have fined Mulhany for every performance.

"I know it's better. We saw it in Fort Worth before we contracted with them to come out here." Red shook his head. "Learned my lesson at the Tripoli. Did I ever thank you for the way you read that ordinance? Made those actors—if you can call them that—think you were going to fine them, too. When they hightailed it out of town, it saved me a bunch of money, not to mention more embarrassment."

"That was my intention. It appears you like running this place better than the saloon."

"That I do. I'd wanted to sell it and open an opera house for years. I couldn't have done it without the McKinnons' money and hard work. We have entertainment lined up for most of the summer and fall, plus some local folks who want to show off their talents." Red listened at the door. "They have only a few more lines, if you want to slip on in."

"Thanks." Ransom opened the door, went inside the large auditorium and waited by the back wall. Georgia stood with her hands clasped at her heart, watching in apparent adoration as her hero stood over the prone body of the vanquished villain and proclaimed his victory and undying love for the heroine. When he finished his lines, everyone relaxed. The villain yawned and stretched, then turned his head and spotted Ransom.

"Could you hear us, sir?" He got to his feet.

"As well as if I was in the front row. The theatre has

excellent acoustics." Ransom started down the sloped aisle.

"Ransom!" Georgia squealed and dashed for the stairs. She raced up the aisle but slowed when she saw the cane. When she reached him, she threw her arms around him in a quick hug and planted a big kiss on his cheek. "Uh-oh. Now you have big red lips on your face."

Grinning, Ransom pulled his handkerchief from his pocket and rubbed his cheek. "You haven't changed a bit."

"Ah, well, what good is life if I can't live it exuberantly?" Her gaze skimmed over him, landing briefly on the cane. "I heard about you becoming the sheriff here, but I don't see a badge."

"I turned the job over to someone else."

She took a seat and motioned for him to sit beside her, next to the aisle. "What happened?"

"Got knocked off the hotel balcony and hurt my back. It's gettin' better, but I couldn't handle being sheriff."

"Did you catch the hombre?"

"He came clean a few days later. A sixteen-year-old kid trying to protect his sister." At her questioning expression, he smiled. "The sister had crawled through a window into a hotel room to retrieve some money that had been stolen from them."

"You spotted them and went to see what was going on." Georgia leaned against the arm of the seat watching his face. Even in all the theatrical paint, she was pretty.

"That's basically it, except they didn't know I was

the law. To make a long story short—he tried to knock me down but hit too hard and I went flying. They felt so bad about it that they confessed. They wound up helping take care of me while I healed."

Her face lit up, and she clasped her hands together. "Oh, do tell me a romance bloomed."

Ransom laughed at her antics. "As a matter of fact, it did. I'm hoping to marry her one of these days."

"What's wrong with right now?"

"I'm unemployed. Though I've started an agency. Want to work for me?"

Her eyes narrowed, her expression thoughtful. "Who else do you have?"

"Karl Lloyd. He signed on this week."

"He's good. I haven't done anything for about six months. I also found romance." She shrugged, but he saw the pain in her eyes. "Unfortunately, he wasn't the settling down type. Maybe I'm not, either. But I'm already bored traveling with the group. Edward is running the Denver agency. He took over when his father got so sick."

"Del was a good man." There was a long history of animosity between Edward and Georgia. "But Eddie is another story. You're no longer connected to them?"

"Nope. I resigned the day Del said he was leaving. Edward has a whole new crop of agents working for him. From what I hear, they're amateurs, botching cases left and right."

"Then I won't feel bad soliciting some of their old customers. You want in? I can't pay much until I get some clients."

"The money isn't a problem. I know you'll be fair."

She thought for a second. "Sure, I'll do it. If we don't have any business within a few months, I'll find something else to keep busy."

"Agreed." Ransom held out his hand, and they shook on the deal.

"When do I get to meet your sweetheart?"

"Ty said they're having a little party at Talbot's for you folks after the first performance. He invited Lily and me. So you can meet her tonight after the show."

"You can't get married unless I approve of her," she said with a mischievous grin.

Ransom stood and stepped out into the aisle. "You will."

Chapter Twenty-Five

Standing in the lobby of the Willow Grove Opera House that evening, Lily glanced around, noting the speculative expressions when folks looked at her and Ransom. Outwardly, her smile was appropriate for a comment Cade made, but secretly she was smiling about the subtle way Ransom declared that he was courting her. He stood a little closer than usual, often with his arm lightly around her, resting his hand at her waist. At times when he looked down at her, his love was reflected in his face. She saw it easily and suspected other people did, too. When Matt caught her eye, glanced at Ransom, then back at her and winked, she knew it.

She had worn one of her favorite gowns, a short-sleeved, light peach silk trimmed with an inset of cream-colored lace. A single strand of pearls and a pearl comb in her pinned up curls dressed it up. She carried a light-weight cream shawl to use later when they left the theatre.

All of the ladies had on their finest dresses, ranging from fancy to Sunday best. Ransom and the McKinnons wore dark suits and white shirts, more or less standard fare for Ty and Ransom, while Cade was more comfortable in a colored shirt and denim. She hid a smile as she looked around—even the cowboys had cleaned up extra special for the evening.

"It's about ten minutes until they start," said Ty. "Shall we go up to our box?" He looked at Camille, clearly torn between being pleased as punch that she was there but also worrying that she should be home resting. "Can you make it up the stairs, sweetheart?"

"I'll be fine. I'm so thrilled that it's finally opened." She looped her arm through his. "And that Sarah settled down to sleep right away. I should have enough time to enjoy the performance and stop by the party for a few minutes before going home to feed her. Mrs. Endicott is such a dear to watch both Sarah and Jacob this evening. I promise, if I start getting too tired earlier, I'll tell you and you can take me home."

"Good enough." Ty and Camille slowly walked up the wide staircase, along with Cade and his family to the second level box seats, a benefit for being the owners. Ransom and Lily followed them. Matt had opted to sit with his friends on the main floor near the front. Ty opened the door to the first box. "Here we are. Best seats in the house."

"We didn't even have to buy a ticket," said Cade with a chuckle.

"But they didn't come cheap." Ty grinned over his shoulder as he escorted Camille inside.

There were two rows of wide, comfortably padded seats in the box. The McKinnons took up the first row. As Ransom and Lily moved to their places, they were joined by Mr. Hill, Camille's partner at the paper, and his wife. A couple of minutes later, Asa Noble, who was Cade's right-hand man at the ranch, and his wife, Lydia, slipped into the other seats. They were all the McKinnons' guests for the evening. Quint and Prissy had opted to come to a performance later in the week to give her a little more time to heal.

Red Mulhany walked out in front of the heavy red velvet curtain to the center of the stage. "Ladies and gentlemen, boys and girls, welcome to the grand opening of the Willow Grove Opera House." He smiled as the audience applauded loudly. "We have some fine entertainment for you tonight. There will be a matinee performance tomorrow afternoon, then afternoon and evening performances every day through next Saturday to give everyone an opportunity to see them.

"We appreciate the good turnout tonight." There wasn't an empty seat in the whole building. "Please thank my associates, Ty and Camille McKinnon, and Cade and Jessie McKinnon, for the huge part they played in making the Opera House a reality." There was another boisterous round of applause and cheers as the McKinnons smiled at their friends and neighbors.

"Please welcome the Dazzling DeVilles." As Mulhany swept out his arm, the curtains opened and were quickly drawn to the sides.

Three men dressed elegantly in black suits and white

shirts with ruffled lace jabots came dashing across the stage in a series of back flips. Somersaults followed with one man going the opposite direction of the other two, sailing over them as they rolled beneath him. A pretty woman, dressed in a fancy evening gown, walked out onto the stage as they ended that segment.

She smiled at the audience and held out her arm to focus attention on the men as one lifted another up on his shoulders. The second man stood—shakily for a few seconds—then found a secure stance. The third man ran from one side of the stage, hit a springboard and flew through the air, doing a somersault and landed on the second man's shoulders.

The crowd roared their approval. Ellie hopped out of her seat and jumped up and down in excitement until Cade corralled her and settled her on his lap.

As the performers carried a table and two chairs onto the stage, Lily looked around. Her friends back in Iowa would never believe that a wild western town could have such a luxurious theatre. But they didn't know the quality of the people who inhabited West Texas, the ranchers, the businessmen and women, the cowboys, freighters and railroad workers. All were represented in the audience, and she expected that each and every one of them took pride in the building.

Balancing tricks followed the gymnastics, culminating in a gentleman doing a horizontal handstand on a board balanced on the backs of two chairs. Lily didn't know how he could hold himself straight out, parallel to the floor, all his weight on his hands. The woman gracefully walked up some portable steps to the table, then onto a chair and finally stepped on the man's back and stood. The crowd loved it.

Next came the Bluebird Minstrels. Lily was surprised to see that the singers were actually black men, not white men with black faces as she had seen in Des Moines. They had a banjo, tambourine and fiddle. The group sang a series of southern songs, some sad and some funny.

As she listened, Lily noticed that many in the audience, including the friends in the box with her, reacted far differently than most in Iowa had. In Des Moines, the songs had merely been interesting or fun to sing when a group got together.

Here, where many were from the South, hearts were touched. As they sang about the Swanee River, longing for the old plantation and the old folks at home, many a wizened cowboy wiped a tear from his eye.

Lily had been born the last year of the Civil War. Her father had been an only son, so he'd been exempt from conscription. Her mother's brother fought for the North and died at Gettysburg. Many of their neighbors had lost loved ones. Still, it had little effect on her. By the time she was old enough to understand what happened, her parents had tucked away their grief and life went on.

Camille had told her that her parents owned a plantation in Louisiana but had lost it during the war, their beautiful home burned to the ground. Cade and Ty had lost their father in battle, then their home, and lastly their mother to a broken heart. The young boys had headed west, barefoot and penniless, but with a will to find a new life.

As the song continued, Ty put his arm around Camille and she wiped her eyes. Jessie reached for Cade's hand and held it tight.

Lily glanced at Ransom. Seeing his misty eyes reminded her that she knew nothing about his childhood. He'd been grown when he lost his parents, but he would have been ten when the war started, fifteen when it ended. She didn't even know where he had lived during that time. She curled her fingers around his hand, searching his eyes when he glanced at her. Reading her thoughts, he leaned over and murmured, "Texas."

The next song was a lively rendition of "Camp Town Races" and lifted spirits that had been momentarily melancholy. For the most part, the rest of the minstrels' performance consisted of lively or silly tunes, shuffling dances and a few jokes. There were none of the songs about freedom for slaves that she had heard in the show in Iowa.

The next-to-last one, called "Susan Jane" had them all laughing on the second verse.

"Her mouth was like a cellar,
Her foot was like a ham,
Her eyes were like an owl's at night,
Her voice was never calm;
Her hair was long and curly,
She looked just like a crane,
I've bid farewell to all my love,
'Goodbye, Susan Jane.'"

The final song was "Dixie." Lily recognized the melody when the musicians began to play, but she was

unprepared as the majority of people in the audience—
her friends among them—stood and began to sing
along with the minstrels. Lily quickly stood, but the
swell of emotion flowing through the theatre—and the
sense of being an outsider—kept her from joining in.

"I wish I was in the land of cotton,
Old times there are not forgotten;
Look away! Look away!
Look away! Dixie land.
In Dixie land where I was born in,
Early on one frosty mornin',
Look away! Look away!
Look away! Dixie land."

She had heard the Union version a few times, a song
of disdain regarding the Confederacy and all it stood
for. Among her friends in Iowa, the version they sang
around the parlor piano was the one that filled the
Opera House.

She learned in school that it had originally been written for a minstrel show in New York a few years before
the war. When it was performed at a theatre in New Orleans shortly after Louisiana seceded from the Union,
its popularity spread like wild fire. After it was played
at Confederate President Jefferson Davis's inaugura-
tion, it quickly became the unofficial war anthem of the
South.

It was more than a war song. She and her Iowa
friends had sung the tune for amusement. Here it was
an anthem of the heart, stirring souls twenty years after

the war had ended. By the time they were through the first verse and reached the chorus, her eyes stung with tears.

> "I wish I was in Dixie,
> Hooray! Hooray!
> In Dixie Land I'll take my stand,
> To live and die in Dixie,
> Away, away,
> Away down south in Dixie,
> Away, away,
> Away down south in Dixie."

She noticed Camille wipe her eyes again, and even Ransom rubbed his cheek.

The other verses were about a foolish marriage, buckwheat cakes and 'Injun' batter that made you fat or a little fatter. They were sung with enthusiasm and a bit of humor, but each time they sang the chorus, it was a cry of hearts torn asunder by tragedy and loss.

She was ashamed to realize that she had given little thought to what the war had done to the South and the people who had lived there. While she truly believed slavery was wrong, she now understood that not only those who owned slaves had lost their homes and way of life.

When the song ended and folks resumed their seats, Mulhany stepped onto the edge of the stage. "Let's hear a big round of applause for the Bluebird Minstrels." The audience complied, though Lily thought they were slightly more subdued than when they had clapped for various individual songs.

The minstrels departed and the heavy curtain was drawn.

Mulhany walked to the side of the stage and made a grand sweep with his arm, a top hat upside down in his hand. "Please welcome the Paramount Players."

As the curtains parted, Lily clapped along with everybody else and sat up straighter for a better view, particularly one of Miss Georgia Nickson, star of the show.

When an attractive, curvaceous blonde walked out onto the stage twirling a pink parasol, Ransom leaned over and whispered, "That's Georgia."

"She's very pretty." Lily tried hard not to let her jealousy show.

"Not as pretty as you." Ransom threaded his fingers through hers.

Lily laughed softly. "You do know how to charm the ladies."

His expression was pure innocence. "Just speakin' the truth, sugar."

She didn't believe him—she saw her reflection in the mirror every morning—but she appreciated the compliment. It helped her to relax and enjoy the production of *Miss Southwick's Refusal.*

Georgia strolled through the city park represented by a few fake trees and street lamps. Each gentleman that she passed attempted to start up a conversation and walk with her, but she rebuffed them with one witty comment after another.

When she reached the right side of the stage, a dapper gentleman entered on the left, whistling a merry tune. Georgia stopped and looked behind her, then turned to the audience. Leaning forward and putting her hand to the side of her face as if she were sharing a secret, she declared, "Here comes my future husband, Poindexter Calloway." She straightened and slanted a coy look in Dex's direction, then smiled at the audience. "Of course, he doesn't know it yet."

As the first act continued, Dex became enamored with the lovely Miss Southwick, with the action pausing a few times while she shared secrets with the audience.

But alas, Randall Snodgrass, the corrupt politician, had his eye on Miss Southwick, too. In the second act he pressed his suit and she refused—several times, each with more humorous exaggeration than the last. Snodgrass mulled her rebuffs for a few minutes, then kidnapped her, plucking her from the green velvet settee in her parlor. With Georgia thrown over his shoulder kicking and screaming, he headed for the side of the stage—pausing so she could look out at the audience and beg someone to tell her dear Dex what had happened.

Act three opened with Dex explaining to the audience that they didn't have to tell him. Wiggling a finger in his ear, he proclaimed, "Even a deaf man could hear her shrieks."

In typical hero form, Dex bested the evil politician and saved the lovely Miss Southwick. Standing over Snodgrass, his foot planted on the villain's chest, Dex declared his undying love while Georgia gazed up at him in rapt adoration.

As the performers took their bows, the crowd

clapped and cheered. Ransom looked at Lily with a rueful smile. "Not the greatest play I've ever seen."

"It was fun. Georgia is quite talented."

"She's even better when she's not on a stage. She can charm information out of men without them even realizing they've revealed it."

Lily looked down at the lovely blonde once more and tightened her hand on Ransom's arm. Why couldn't the woman have buck teeth, and the personality of a turnip?

Chapter Twenty-Six

At Talbot's Restaurant after the show, Ransom propped his leg up on a spare chair and watched Georgia and Lily across the table as they conversed politely. Georgia had been a good friend when they worked together, but their relationship never went beyond that. He hoped that she and Lily could be friends, too.

"I have to tell you that he saved my bacon more than once," said Georgia. "Ransom, do you remember that time in Chicago when Sam the Snake dragged me up on the roof and threatened to throw me off?"

Ransom laughed and winked at Lily. "If you thought she was screaming tonight, you should have heard her then."

"Well, I was scared. He didn't earn that nickname by going to church on Sundays." Georgia turned back to Lily with a cynical smile. "We knew he and his friend, Larry, had stolen a safe full of expensive diamond necklaces and bracelets, but we didn't know what they'd done with it. The jeweler who hired us was more interested in getting his gems back than putting the thieves behind bars. I was pretending to be Larry's new sweetheart—in his absence."

"Only she did too good a job of convincing Sam. We didn't know that he and Larry had had a falling out and Larry made off with the loot. Sam figured she knew where Larry was and he was determined to find out."

Georgia laughed and shook her head. "I didn't have a clue. We'd lost him, too. Sam dragged me out the back door of his club and up the back stairs to the roof. Ransom was playing billiards and supposedly keeping an eye on me—"

"I was keeping an eye on you until some guy took a swing at me." Shrugging, Ransom shifted his gaze to Lily. "He took exception to a difficult shot I made. It took me a few minutes to convince him that you can't cheat at billiards unless you sneak a ball in a pocket or something. By the time I'd knocked him out, Georgia had disappeared.

"I ran to the front sidewalk to look for her. That's when I heard her shrieks from up on the roof. So I had to go back through the club and find the back stairs."

"Obviously, he reached you in time," said Lily with a smile. "Did you throw Sam off the roof?"

Ransom narrowed his gaze. Lily's smile was a little too bright, and he detected fleeting sadness in her eyes. "No, a pistol pointed at his head did the trick."

"Ransom claimed I was his sister and chewed him

up one side and down the other for trying to hurt me. Then he scolded me for keeping bad company."

"His sister?" This time Lily's laugh was genuine. "That's a stretch."

"It was pretty dark. I hustled Georgia out of there before Sam could think much about it."

"Did you ever recover the jewelry?"

"Yes, a few weeks later. We kept Sam under surveillance with Georgia in one of her prime disguises." He grinned at her. "As an elderly street beggar."

"Amazing what a dirty—and itchy—gray wig and some stage paint will do. Ransom did his part, too."

"More billiards?" asked Lily.

"Nope. I helped out at the newspaper stand across the street. I could have set up my own stand for what it cost me to hang out there. Eventually, Sam found Larry and we nabbed them both. They went off to jail and the diamonds went back to their owner."

"Good for you." Lily picked up her purse. "Well, it's getting late. I'd better get back to Prissy's. It's nice to meet you, Georgia."

"You, too, Lily. I'm sure we'll have more chances to chat. My contract with the troupe ends in two weeks, then I'll come back here and go to work for Ransom."

Ransom stood, smiling at Georgia. "Drop by the office if you have time. I'd like for you to look over my list of potential clients. Maybe you can think of some others."

"I'll come by Monday morning." She glanced at Lily, then looked back at him and winked. "You were right."

"Knew I would be." He pulled out Lily's chair as she

stood and followed her out the front door. They walked across the street to the buggy he had parked in front of his office.

"What were you right about?"

"You." He assisted her into the buggy and walked around to the other side. "Georgia said I couldn't marry you unless she approved. I told her she would, and she does."

"Oh."

"What did you think we were talking about?"

"I don't know." She fussed with her skirt, rearranging it. "Maybe that she misses working with you. Misses you."

Ransom flicked the reins, driving away from the office and downtown. He waved to a couple of people who called to them, then turned up the street in the general direction of Prissy's house. Instead of turning down Prissy's street, he kept going. "I think we have time for a little drive in the moonlight, don't you?"

"I suppose it's all right if we aren't gone too long. Quint is probably still with Prissy."

"He should be. I didn't hear of any problems after the performance. Though I'm surprised there weren't any. I was afraid 'Dixie' might cause a brawl considerin' we had some Union boys in the audience, too. I suppose they kept their mouths shut in honor of the grand opening."

"Or because they were greatly outnumbered. We sang that song in Iowa, but certainly not with the same feelings. I'm ashamed to admit that I never thought much about how people in the South suffered."

"Did your daddy fight in the war?"

"No, but my mother's brother was killed at Gettysburg. They never talked about it much. How about your father?"

"He was a cotton broker in Galveston. We lived in town, didn't have a place out in the country. We didn't own any slaves. It was something my parents never would have done. In the years before the war, like many Texans, he was very attached to the Union. But he deeply believed in states' rights. He didn't like the Northerners telling us how to live.

"It was a hard decision, but he went along with secession when it was put to a vote. I had two older brothers who volunteered as soon as Texas was officially part of the Confederacy. Ned fought under Rip Ford in South Texas along the Rio Grande." He sighed, the memory still painful. "He was only nineteen when he died in a fight with Union soldiers trying to invade from Mexico."

"I'm so sorry." Lily laid her hand on his forearm.

He was surprised at how comforting that simple touch was, even through his suit jacket. "I was the baby of the family, eleven when he died. Ned was my hero, even before he went off to war. After he died I was determined to run off and fight the Yankees. Mama finally convinced me that I had to stay home to protect her. My father had joined up six months earlier, even though he was forty-four years old. He'd fought in the Texas Revolution and was still fit. I think he couldn't resist a good fight. He and Tom were in the same company.

"I was glad I stayed with Mother. On October fourth, a small Union fleet sailed into Galveston harbor and captured the city."

"My goodness! Did anything happen to you and your mother?"

"No, thank the Lord. We were scared out of our wits, though, and couldn't get word to Daddy and Tom that we were all right. We didn't stay occupied long. On New Year's Day, General Magruder sent troops across the railroad bridge that connected Galveston to the mainland. They crossed at one in the morning, so the Union boys were asleep. At the same time, two river steamers that had been converted to gunboats sailed into the harbor and attacked the Union ships.

"Mama and I watched the battle from the second story of our house. One of the Confederate ships took a hit and sank, but the other one moved alongside a federal ship and the Horse Marines stormed aboard and captured it. The Union flagship ran aground and blew up. The rest of their navy fled the harbor and the federal infantry eventually surrendered."

"Your father and Tom, how did they fare?"

"They both made it. They were stationed together at Fort Griffin, guarding Sabine Pass. They saved us from another invasion later that year. There were only forty-seven of them in the fort, commanded by Lieutenant Richard Dowling, an Irish barkeeper from Houston. When four Union gunboats came up the channel, the men at Fort Griffin opened fire with their six cannons." He chuckled and turned off the road about a mile out of town, driving across the flat prairie. "Those Texans knew how to shoot. Didn't matter to them that they were using cannons instead of pistols or rifles. They got off one hundred seven rounds in thirty-five minutes."

"That's amazing," Lily muttered softly, making him

smile as she did the math in her head. "That's almost eighteen shots per cannon in barely more than half an hour."

"They were pretty accurate, too. Put two boats out of commission, so the other two hightailed it back down the channel. The Union general who was in charge of the invasion thought there must have been a large force at Fort Griffin, so they withdrew all the way back to New Orleans. My father and brother, along with all of Dowling's men, received medals."

Ransom pulled the buggy to a halt when they were far enough from the road not to be seen. He guided the horse around until the full moon was right in front of them.

She knew his mother had been dead five years, his father, four. "Where is Tom now?"

"He's out in the Oregon territory. He left right after the South surrendered. Said he wanted to live someplace fresh and clean, that hadn't been tainted by the war. I've been out there a few times. He has a wife and four kids. Has a big farm in the Willamette Valley."

He looped the reins over the rail in front of them and turned toward her. "Can you get rid of that hat? You have a propensity for feathers, Miss Chastain."

Lily pulled the hatpin from the hat and eased the fancy concoction away from her hair. "I like feathers."

"They're fine on birds, even on hats, as long as they don't get in my way when I'm kissing you."

She set the hat on the floorboard by her feet and smiled up at him. "We don't want to interfere with that."

Ransom cupped her face in his hands and kissed her

gently. "Georgia is an old friend, sugar. I like her, admire her abilities, and enjoy her conversations but she's not your rival. I've never had a romantic interest in her—or her in me. There never will be. There's no spark. Now, it's a different story between you and me." He kissed her again, putting his arms around her and drawing her close, giving her a good idea what he meant.

Before long, he drew back, knowing that if he didn't they might do more than they should. He cleared his throat and faced forward, resting his arm across her shoulders. "We'd better concentrate on admiring the scenery."

Lily laughed softly and rested her head against his shoulder. "I'm not sure I can concentrate on anything right now."

"Can you see the man in the moon?"

She tipped her head. "Yep. Got a big face."

Ransom chuckled. "That he does."

They sat there for about a half an hour, comfortable with each other, enjoying the beautiful night sky, cheering at a shooting star, and laughing when Lily got spooked by a coyote's howl.

Ransom wondered why he was so all-fired set on waiting to get married. Could this be one of those times his father had warned him about—when stubbornness was just stupidity in disguise?

Chapter Twenty-Seven

Prissy and Quint were married the following Saturday afternoon at Cade and Jessie's house in town, ignoring the old saying that Saturday was an unlucky day for a wedding. They also went against the tradition of having the wedding in the morning, because the minister had to perform a funeral then.

Besides Ransom, Lily and Matt, only the family and Reverend Brownfield and his wife attended. After the ceremony, they enjoyed a generous supper that Jessie had prepared.

Full of his sister's good cooking, Quint wandered outside for a breath of air. Jessie stood at the end of the porch, looking out across the neighborhood, her hand curled around a post. When he stepped out, she glanced over her shoulder, and he noticed the sheen of moisture on her cheeks.

"I hope those are happy tears," he said quietly as he joined her.

"I'm not sure what they are." Jessie wiped her face with the corner of her apron. "I want so much for you to be happy."

"I am." He settled his arm across her shoulders. "It will work out, Jess."

"I hope so. I don't want to see you hurt."

"There's never a guarantee of that, is there? I'm not going into this marriage blind. Prissy and I have spent a lot of hours talking about the past, about our feelings, about our hopes and dreams. I believe she's been honest with me, painfully honest at times. I've tried to do the same. I know you think I'm perfect, but I'm not."

Jessie laughed and slid her arm around his waist. "Maybe I should talk to Prissy. Fill in some of the things you left out."

"Such as?"

"Skipping school every chance you got to go fishing."

"Told her all about it."

"What about when you were thirteen and stole that bottle of moonshine from Alby's still? And then you got Gus drunk. Poor kid, he was only ten years old."

"He drank me under the table. It's a wonder we ever sobered up. That stuff was rank."

"Well, did you tell her about it?"

"No, but if that's the worst you can do, I reckon I don't have to worry."

The screen door opened and Prissy stepped out, pausing in the doorway. "Oh, excuse me. I didn't mean to interrupt."

"You didn't." Jessie beat him to it. "I'm trying to think of tales of his youth that he might not have told you."

Prissy laughed and walked to the end of the porch. "He's told me a lot. He was a scamp, wasn't he?"

"That pretty well describes him. He was a good big brother, though. Always coming to my rescue if somebody picked on me."

Not always, thought Quint. He hadn't been sure that her first husband was cheating on her, so he hadn't done anything. He'd let her down on that one. "It was an easy job. Jessie got along with about everybody."

"Prissy, do you need to go rest a while?" asked Jessie.

"No, I'm okay for now. I'm just sad that Mama couldn't be here. She drove me up the wall with her crazy ideas and the way she pushed me to do things I didn't want to do. It's silly, but I miss her."

"I don't think it's silly at all." Jessie smiled and looped her arm through Prissy's. "She might not have been the best mother in the world, but she is your mother. Let's take a walk. I'll show you my little garden, and you can tell me something nice about her."

Quint bit back a snort. Prissy would have to think hard to come up with something.

Then he heard her say, "She used to sing me to sleep when I was little. And last year when I had a bad cold and cough, she made me chicken soup. I didn't even know she could cook, but it was very good."

They went around the corner of the house, and Quint shook his head, wondering if he would ever understand the workings of the female mind. He hoped Mrs. Clark would let them know where she wound up. He wouldn't give two cents to see her again, but if Prissy wanted to, he'd make certain it happened.

"All by your lonesome already?" Ransom walked out the back door, carrying a large piece of Jessie's chocolate cake. He took a bite and sat down on a wrought-iron and wooden bench.

Quint wandered over and sat down, too. "Jessie and Prissy are looking at Jessie's pea patch."

"Looking at vegetables on her wedding day? Isn't that a mite odd?"

"They're talking. She's missing her mama. Don't know why, but that's the way of it."

"Prissy is more forgiving than I'd be." Ransom licked some icing off a finger. "Weddings make people sentimental."

"Even you?" Quint tried to relax, but he was getting wound up tighter by the minute. It had never occurred to him that Prissy might be upset on her wedding day. Maybe she really didn't love him—though she said she did—and was regretting it already. Had he made a big mistake?

"Yeah, even me. I think I'll miss my folks on my wedding day."

"So there's going to be one?"

"I haven't exactly proposed, but Lily knows I want to marry her."

Quint glanced toward the house and lowered his voice. "What are you waiting for?"

"To make certain I can provide for her and a family."

"Of course you can. You might not feel up to being

sheriff—which I still think is a mistake—but you're plenty smart. You won't have any trouble running a business, whether it's the detective agency or something else. I know of at least three men in town who are chompin' at the bit to try to court her. You'd better get your brand on that pretty little filly or somebody else will cut her out of the herd and have her roped before you can holler."

"What three men?" asked Ransom with a scowl.

"The butcher, the baker and the cabinet maker."

"Are you joshin' me?"

Quint smiled and shook his head. "I know it sounds like it, but I'm not. All three of them have asked me if you were serious about her. Along with two ranchers and a handful of cowboys. You need to get an engagement ring on her finger pronto."

"I've got the ring," Ransom whispered.

"Then quit acting like a 'fraidy cat and give it to her."

Ransom started to say something, but Jessie and Prissy came around the corner.

"What's this? Y'all come back empty-handed? I was all ready for a mess of blackeyed peas." Quint searched Prissy's face, smiling to hide his concern as he stood.

"They aren't ready yet, and you know it." Prissy came over and put her arm around his waist, sidling close. When she smiled up at him, her eyes shining with happiness, his doubts and worries evaporated.

"What I know, Mrs. Webb," he murmured in her ear, "is that I love you."

"I love you, too." She tipped her face up for a kiss. He gladly obliged.

Ransom got up and opened the door for Jessie. "Come on, Jessie, we're in the way."

"Now, whatever gave you that idea?" Laughing, she went inside with him.

Quint kissed his bride again, then held her close. "Feel better since you and Jessie talked?"

"Yes. I know she must have plenty of doubts about me, but she's being very sweet. She said she hopes we'll become close, like sisters."

"That sounds like Jess. She's always wanted a sister."

"I think it would be nice, too."

Quint nodded. "You know what else would be nice?"

"What?" She looked up at him, a tiny smile playing about her mouth.

"For us to go home. I'm mighty fond of my family and friends, but I'd like to be alone with my bride."

"We need to thank them."

"Can't just sneak off the back porch and go up the street?"

"No." She tucked her arm through his. "We need to be polite. Besides, I think Ty and Cade decorated our buggy while we weren't looking."

"That doesn't surprise me."

When they walked inside and announced they were leaving, Cade held up his hand. "Before you go, we have one more wedding present to give you."

Quint looked over at the stack of fancy dishes, linens and a pair of silver candlesticks on the bureau. "Y'all have already given us plenty."

"Those things will wear out eventually." Cade

cleared his throat. "This won't." He handed Quint a folded piece of paper.

Opening it, Quint gasped. It was the deed to two sections of land, almost thirteen hundred acres. As he showed it to Prissy, he met his brother-in-law's gaze. "Y'all shouldn't have done this."

"Well, we can always take it back," said Cade with a grin. "But I don't think you want us to. It's about a mile north of the ranch house, so we figured when you build a house we'll practically be within shoutin' distance. It's where those cows of yours always wind up anyway, so you might as well own the land."

"I don't know how to thank you." Quint shook hands with Ty and Cade and gave Jessie and Camille a hug. He noticed that all four of them hugged Prissy, and that made him smile.

"Just be happy," said Jessie. "We all know you're a cowboy at heart, so even if you keep working as a lawman, now you'll have a place to go when you want to corral cows instead of cowboys."

Quint laughed and hugged Prissy to his side. "I can do that now out at your place."

"It's not the same as having a ranch of your own," said Ty.

"No, it's not. And y'all know I've always dreamed of having one. Thank you." Feeling sentimental—Ransom was right about that—and afraid he was going to get all misty-eyed and embarrass himself, Quint grabbed Prissy's hand and pulled her toward the door. "Come on, wife, let's go home. The in-town one."

They raced outside, leaving the gifts to be retrieved in a day or two and ran to the waiting buggy. His family and friends, even the minister and his wife, all charged after them, laughing and cheering.

Sure enough, someone had tied tin cans and old shoes to the back of the buggy. Almost seemed a waste for a trip of a whole five blocks, but he didn't mention it. Picking Prissy up with a grand swoop, he lifted his laughing bride into the buggy, then ran around the back, almost tripping over a boot, and jumped in beside her.

"I'll be along in a few minutes and take the horse and buggy back to the livery," called Matt.

"Thanks!" Quint clucked to the horse and shook the reins. Off they went down the street, calls of blessings and good wishes mingling with cans clanking and boots thumping along the dirt road.

He tethered the horse in front of Prissy's house, now his house, too, and walked slowly around to her side of the buggy. Holding out his hand, he helped her from the vehicle. They strolled up the walkway arm in arm, but he stopped her when they reached the front door.

Opening the door, he blocked her way. "Welcome home, Mrs. Webb." He picked her up, grinning when she wrapped her arms around his neck. He carried her inside, kicking the door closed behind them.

"Welcome home, Mr. Webb." She kissed him tenderly, then laid her hand on his heart. "This is my home, in your heart. I don't care whether we live in this house or another, or a tent out on our new ranch."

He gave a quick, hard kiss. "You'd live in a tent?"

She pursed her lips, then grinned. "Not for long."

"That's what I figured." Laughing, he carried her upstairs.

Chapter Twenty-Eight

Ransom lay in bed Saturday night contemplating Quint's admonition. His friend was right. If he wanted to marry Lily, he'd better make sure everybody else knew it by putting a ring on her finger. A nice Sunday picnic after church would be a romantic way to propose. They could get away from town and prying eyes. As he was sorting through possible destinations, he heard the patter of rain on the roof.

Groaning, he rolled over and pounded the pillow. The picnic was out. Sitting on the muddy ground didn't come close to being romantic. They could still go for a drive. He could always take her to a picturesque site and give her the diamond ring he had tucked away in his sock drawer. Yawning, he decided that would have to do. He didn't think she'd complain.

It rained all day Sunday.

Ransom sat with Lily at church, then took her and Matt out to dinner. He went back to the boarding house with them and sat in the parlor visiting for a couple of hours. Lily informed him that she and Matt weren't moving after all. Mrs. Franklin had given her newest tenant the boot because of his snoring.

Ransom was disappointed to hear that, though he didn't say so. He'd decided that if they rented a house, Matt would make a good chaperon. He figured her brother probably would have given them a little time alone if he dropped by in the evenings. That wouldn't happen at the boarding house.

When he got ready to leave, she walked out onto the front porch with him. He noted that the rain had slacked off, now that it was too late to go anywhere. "What days will you be at the store this week?"

"The only day I have off is Thursday. Ty has a new shipment of dresses and fabrics coming in so we'll be busy."

"If the weather clears up, would you like to go for a drive and a picnic on Thursday?"

"I'd love to."

He was tempted to kiss her right there in cloudy daylight in front of all the folks who were probably peeking out their windows. But he didn't want to embarrass her or cause talk. Instead, he ran his fingertip along her jaw. "Come by the office tomorrow if you have a few minutes."

"All right."

Whistling, he walked home with a lighter step.

On Wednesday, the Starr Detective Agency acquired its first customer. A banker in Austin thought someone was embezzling, but he hadn't been able to prove it. If Ransom hadn't been afraid of doing himself damage, he would have danced a jig. This was right up Karl's alley. He sent him off to do the job and wrote to a couple of other agents who had expressed interest in working for him. He couldn't hire them yet, but would as soon as he needed them.

His back and leg had been so much better the last few days that he could move around the house and the office without holding onto anything. He'd almost taken a couple of tumbles, though, so he wasn't ready to venture around town without the cane.

"And tomorrow, we'll get engaged," he whispered to himself. "Yes, sir, things are looking up." Which was exactly what he should be doing. "Thank You for Your blessings, Lord. Please help Karl solve this case. Please let Lily say *yes* tomorrow." He didn't have much doubt that she would, but he'd learned long ago not to count on anything until it was signed, sealed and delivered.

Standing in front of his office window, he watched Quint go down the street, glancing in the saloons and businesses as he made his rounds. It still surprised Ransom that he missed being sheriff. For all the griping he'd done to himself over the past year, the job and the folks he'd served had found their way into his heart.

The understanding with Cade and Quint still stood—he could ask for his job back at anytime. It didn't seem fair to Quint, though, especially now that he had a wife to support. He'd wait a while and see how the agency did. Could be he was just bored, and that would pass when he got more clients.

He stood there for a few minutes, sipping his coffee, smiling now and then as people walked by and saw him in the window. He was about to go back to his desk when he noticed two strangers riding into town. They rode slowly, scanning the street and businesses. Unease crawled along the back of his neck. Without thinking, he set the cup down and reached for his gun belt hanging on the wall. He buckled on the gun belt, letting it rest comfortably along the top of his hips, his gaze never leaving the men. They stopped at a hitching rail one store down from the bank.

Dismounting, they looped the reins around the rail and glanced up and down the street before stepping up onto the boardwalk. They were wearing pistols, but that wasn't uncommon when strangers first came to town. The storekeepers were good to mention that they were supposed to check their guns at the sheriff's office. If they didn't comply with law on their own, the sheriff or deputy would soon enforce it.

They paused, looking in the window of the drugstore. To Ransom's surprise they went inside, coming out a few minutes later with a couple of pieces of stick candy. Instead of going into the bank, they wandered down the street a block and into Rhode's Mercantile, one of Ty's smaller competitors.

Ransom put on his hat and suit jacket, which covered his holsters. He grabbed the cane and headed across the street to the mercantile. Walking into the store, he saw the strangers in the shirt department. He stopped and pretended to look at some gloves before wandering in their direction. Another warning went off in his mind as he surreptitiously studied them. They looked familiar, but he couldn't place them. Both wore beards, which probably served as enough of a disguise to keep their identities from jumping out at him.

One of them picked up a shirt and they both headed for the register. Ransom held up a folded shirt as if inspecting it, hiding the buckle on his gun belt. They walked right past him, noting his cane and instantly dismissing him. A month earlier that would have made him mad and hurt his pride. Now, he was thankful they ignored him.

"You fellers new in town?" asked the clerk as he rang up the purchase.

"Just passin' through. We're on our way to San Angelo."

"Well, if you don't plan on riding out right away, you'd best stop by the sheriff's office and check your guns. There's a law against wearing firearms in town. Wouldn't want to see you gentlemen waste your money on a fine."

"Thanks, we'll keep that in mind. Got better things to spend it on."

"Yeah, like whiskey and women," the other one said with a chuckle.

Ransom kept thumbing through the stack of shirts until the men went out the door.

"Can I help you, Sher—I mean, Mr. Starr?" The clerk smiled sheepishly.

Ransom nodded toward the stock boy who was filling a thread display with colorful spools. "No, but Jimmy can."

The young man looked up, meeting Ransom's gaze. "What do you need, sir?"

"Go down the alley and find Sheriff Webb. He was headed toward the east end of town a few minutes ago. When you go out onto Main Street, be sure and walk. Act like there's nothing wrong. When you find Quint, tell him I think we may have trouble brewing at the bank."

"You mean like a robbery?"

"Maybe. Now git. And don't let those hombres see you."

"Yes, sir." Jimmy ran out the back as Ransom went to the front.

"Should I go get the deputy?" Sweat beaded on the clerk's bald head and his hands shook.

Ransom figured he'd make a scene the minute he set foot out the door. "No, we'll be all right. I'm probably borrowing trouble anyway. You stay in here for now. I don't want to risk tipping them off."

As he stepped out of the store, Ransom caught a glimpse of Lily going into the bank. *Lord, no! Get her out of there!* Keeping his eye on the men, he hurried down the sidewalk, the cane tapping rapidly. One stuffed the shirt in his saddlebag. Ransom desperately hoped his instinct was wrong, that they would mount up and ride out of town.

Elton White staggered out of the Senate Saloon, and Ransom barely avoided colliding with him. "Elton, get out of the way," he ordered quietly, craning his neck to see around the big man.

"Sure, sheriff." Slurring his words, Elton smiled and sidestepped, moving in the wrong direction, bumping into him.

But he held his ground. Ransom moved the other way, trying to go past him.

"Sorry." Elton hiccupped and shifted, again blocking his path. The rancher laughed and shook his head, almost falling down. "I jes' can't get it right."

Ransom grabbed his arms, holding him still. "Stay right there. Don't move."

He worked his way around Elton, his heart leaping to his throat when the men pulled their guns and walked into the bank. They didn't even try to hide their faces. They were out to make names for themselves.

Please, God, protect her. And everybody else in there, he added as an afterthought.

The cane slowed him down. He was leaning on it too much; it would break any second. *Don't let me fall, Lord. Please, don't let me fail her.*

Ransom threw the cane aside. Somewhere in the back of his mind, it registered that he was running—not particularly fast and with a limp—but he was covering the distance a lot faster than when he had the cane. *I trust You, Lord. I trust You.*

He saw Quint running from the opposite direction, and relief swept through him. They arrived at each end of the bank building at about the same time.

He squelched the impulse to rush into the bank. That would only get somebody—maybe his precious Lily—killed. Ransom drew to a halt and caught his breath. So did Quint. Nodding to him, Ransom took a few steps until he could see through the bank window. Quint edged along the wall and peered through the other window. Conveniently, the men had left the door open for a quick getaway.

Lily stood at the end of the counter. One outlaw was only a few yards from her, his gun trained on the teller as he filled a cloth bag with money. The other outlaw had the barber and the shoemaker pinned in the corner. Everyone was mostly ignoring Lily.

Ransom moved a step closer. At this angle he could see her clearly. Her eyes were wide with fright, but another emotion mingled with the fear. Wrath. He glanced at the outlaws and realized where he had seen them— on the wanted posters of the men who killed Lily's father.

She slipped her hand into her purse, and Ransom's heartbeat quadrupled. *No, sugar, no. Don't go for your gun.* He weighed their chances of taking them. Not good. *Lily Chastain, don't you dare pull that gun!*

She didn't, but he knew good and well she had her finger on the trigger. With a cloth purse, it would be easy to shoot right through it. Sure enough, she shifted every so slightly, pointing the end of the purse directly at the outlaw closest to her.

"Excuse me, sir?" Lily's voice trembled a little.

What are you doing? Don't call attention to yourself! Ransom inched closer to the door.

"What?" The outlaw darted a glance toward her before turning his attention back to the teller.

"Your beautiful watch is dangling from your pocket."

The outlaw looked down to check it.

Ransom and Quint rushed through the door. "Drop your guns!" ordered Ransom. He covered the man closest to Lily. "Now!"

The outlaw dropped his pistol onto the floor and put up his hands.

"Kick the gun over this way." Ransom didn't take his gaze off him until he did as ordered. Relaxing minutely, Ransom looked at Lily and bit back a groan. She had her pistol out of the bag and was pointing it at the bank robber.

Quint focused on the other one. "Drop it. Nice and easy."

The man hesitated, then sighed heavily and obeyed.

"Kick it over this way."

"Come get it."

"Do what I tell you or I'll shoot you where you stand," snapped Quint.

The barber nodded vigorously. "He'll do it. Won't miss, either."

Frowning at the barber, the outlaw kicked the gun in Quint's general direction.

"Lily, you can put your pistol down now," Ransom said gently.

"No. This man killed my father."

"I ain't killed nobody." The robber stared at her gun and swallowed visibly. "You got me mixed up with somebody else."

"No, I don't. You have my papa's watch. You're the man who was at the hotel. You registered as Smith, but I doubt that's your real name. You killed my father, and I'm going to kill you."

Ransom frowned. Lily told them that Smith had stolen the watch, but she was positive Price had killed him. "Lily, you'd be committing murder."

"An eye for an eye."

"Sugar, put the gun down."

"No." She glanced at Ransom, then frowned at Smith. "I have six bullets. One for each limb, one for his heart and one for his head."

She'd tried to tell him something with that quick look. Ransom decided to play along. He didn't think she meant to kill the man, but if he had to, hopefully he could grab the gun before she actually started shooting. "Well, I reckon you have a right to revenge."

"No," choked Smith.

"That's right," said Lily. "Revenge is sweet." She raised the gun, taking careful aim. "Maybe I should start with your ears. Take off your hat."

"No," cried Smith, jerking his hat down tighter on his head, then sticking his hands up in the air again. "I stole the watch, but Price shot him." He pointed at this partner. "He killed your father, not me."

"Shut up," yelled Price.

"No, I'm not going to hang for something you did." Smith turned toward Lily. "We was just goin' to rob him. I didn't have no part in the killing. Price did that out of pure meanness. I was scared to say anything 'cause he would have killed me, too."

"There you have it, Quint." She motioned to the other outlaw. "Price is the man who murdered my father. Now you have two witnesses, Smith and me." Lily's voice was steady and calm, but when she lowered the gun and put it back in her purse, Ransom noticed her hands were shaking.

"Come here, sugar," he said softly. Keeping his gun on Smith, he put one arm around her and held her close. He kissed her temple. "It's over, Lily. We have them." She merely nodded.

"You boys ran all out of luck," said Quint. "The district court meets tomorrow. You'll know your fate by tomorrow evenin'."

Lily stared at Price when Quint spun him around toward the door. "My father was a kind, decent man. You didn't have to kill him."

The outlaw's face twisted into a sneer. "You were there?" When she nodded, he said, "I should've waited 'til you came out of hiding." His gaze raked over her. "I didn't know what I was missing."

"Get him out of here before I shoot him myself." Ransom tightened his hold on Lily until Quint shoved Price out the door. He released her and motioned for Smith to follow them. "Walk across with me, sugar, so I know you're okay."

Halfway across the street, she stopped. Ransom glanced over his shoulder and saw she was staring at his legs. "Come on, Lily."

She raced to catch up, her eyes sparkling with excitement.

"What's the matter?" he said with a grin. "You've seen me walk without a cane before."

"Only in your office." She ran ahead of him, then walked backward to watch him. "I could hug you right now."

"Give me a few minutes, and I'll take you up on it." When he reached the steps to the sidewalk, Ransom held his breath. He used the same method he'd used with the cane, put his weight on his right leg, step up with the left one. He felt a tiny twinge in his back, but his legs felt solid as he brought the right one up, too. He repeated the maneuver for the other two steps, breathing a sigh of relief when he was safely on the sidewalk.

Quint came out of the sheriff's office. "I'll take him.

You got other things to attend to." His gaze flicked to Ransom's empty hand and he grinned. "Come see me later. I've got something to give you."

Quint herded Smith through the office into the jail.

Ransom holstered his pistol and turned to the gathering crowd. "Everything is fine, now, folks. There was an attempted holdup at the bank, but Sheriff Webb arrested the robbers and your money is safe." He nodded toward the bank. The barber and shoemaker were standing in front of it already giving their version of the events. "They can tell you all about it."

"Looked to me like Quint had some good help." Nate Flynn, the saloon owner, stood nearby, his shotgun in his hand. "You handled it fine."

"You dropped this, Ransom," called someone from the back of the crowd. "Though it doesn't look like you need it." The cane was passed up and handed to him.

"Thanks. I'll tuck it away just in case I get another hitch in my get-along." Years from now, it would help him remember the past months and God's faithfulness. *God is our refuge and strength, a very present help in trouble.* He hoped he never needed such a strong reminder of that truth again.

Chapter Twenty-Nine

Ransom closed the door to his office and unbuckled his gun belt, hanging it on the hook by the window. Grabbing Lily's hand, he led her to the corner and into a small store room. He had to leave the door partially open for light, but nobody could see them unless they came looking for them.

"I've never been so scared in my life." He pulled her into his arms and held her tight, crushing her straw hat and not caring a bit. It didn't seem to bother her.

"I was scared, too. But when I realized who they were, I got mad."

"I noticed." He released her and searched for the pin holding the hat in place.

"I almost shot them before you came in." She stood still as he took off her hat and tossed it aside.

"I know. I saw you put your hand in your purse. You

almost gave me a heart attack." He put his arms around her again, smiling when she slid hers around his neck.

"No, before that. My first thought was to pull that gun out of there and kill them on the spot." Shuddering, she looked up at him. "For a minute I didn't care if anybody else got shot or not. All I could think of was making them pay for how they hurt us. Then God reminded me to seek justice, not vengeance. So I waited, hoping He would guide me to do that. When I caught a glimpse of you outside the window, I knew you would take care of it."

"It wouldn't have gone so well if you hadn't distracted them. Getting Smith to confess Price's sins was a stroke of genius."

"You said it would be good if we could get Smith to turn against Price."

"I did?"

"Yes. A few days after Matt and I moved into the boarding house. You were trying to talk me out of killing them."

"Ah. I remember now."

"He'll be convicted, won't he?"

"I can't think of any reason he wouldn't be. Smith might try to deny what he said, but we had a whole roomful of witnesses who heard him. Heard Price basically confess, too, for that matter." Ransom lowered his head, kissing her with all the love and relief that was in his heart. He sensed the same emotions in her as she returned his kiss. He held her tightly against him, never wanting to let her go.

"Marry me, Lily," he whispered, then kissed her again before she could answer. When he raised his head, he smiled sheepishly. "I planned to propose tomorrow on the picnic, not in a storage closet. But since I've started this, I'll finish it." She opened her mouth to speak, but he laid his finger across it to stop her. "Wait here. I'll be right back."

With a bemused smile, she nodded and leaned back against the wooden shelves that held stacks of paper and empty files waiting for cases. "Shall I tidy up?"

Ransom laughed. "I haven't been here long enough for things to get dusty. This will only take a minute." He pulled the door the rest of the way open and peeked around the corner. No one was hovering outside. They were probably still over at the bank. He walked to the desk and took the engagement ring and box out of the middle drawer, then hurried back to Lily.

Leaving the door ajar, he opened the box and removed the ring, glancing up to see her smile. "I don't know why I've been bringing this with me all week. Guess I was afraid somebody would try to steal my socks and find this instead."

Taking her hand, he kissed the back of it, then met her gaze. "My precious Lily, will you marry me?"

"I'd be honored to." Her smile grew even brighter as he slid the solitary diamond ring onto her finger. "It's beautiful."

Amazingly, it fit. He'd been worried about that. Cradling her face in his hands, he kissed her gently. "I don't want a long engagement."

She blinked. "I thought you wanted to wait until your business was thriving."

"I got my first customer this morning."

Grinning, she looped her arms around his neck and toyed with his hair. "Sounds like it's thriving to me."

"How about two weeks from today? I've heard that Wednesday is the best day of all for a wedding."

"You know the old saying?"

"Can't recite it, but I've heard it. Jessie insisted on going by it when she and Cade got married." Thinking about it made him smile. "Funny, she doesn't seem like the superstitious type. I remember that Wednesday is best because that's the day she and Cade got married. If Quint has to take Smith and Price to Huntsville or Rusk, that will give him plenty of time to make the arrangements and get there and back."

Her smiled faded, the sparkle dying out in her eyes. "That's where the prisons are?"

"Yes. Rusk is a new one in East Texas. Huntsville is farther south, but it's crowded, so most new prisoners go to Rusk. Both can be reached by train, so it will take days, not weeks." He searched her face, frowning at her troubled countenance. "I don't know what the sentence will be. Judge Meadows has never sentenced a man to hang, but this might be the first one."

"I thought I wanted them to die, to pay the ultimate price for their sins, but now I don't know. I can't bear to think about a hanging and my wedding at the same time."

"Then we'll only think about the wedding and let the judge and jury handle Price and Smith."

"I'll have to testify."

"All you have to do is tell them what happened. Tell them what you told me and Quint. Put it in God's hands." He could see that the reality of capturing her father's killers and of what would happen the next day was starting to sink in. "So, are we set on the date for the wedding?"

She shook her head, her thoughts obviously coming back to the present. "Yes, two weeks from today. That should give us time to take care of everything. We need to get a license."

"That'll take ten minutes. We can take care of it sometime next week."

"I have to go back to work."

"I think you should go tell Matt that we've caught the killers, then go get some rest."

"I couldn't rest. I'm too jittery. Besides, I want to pick out a new dress. We need to invite our friends. You know Mrs. Franklin will be brokenhearted if we don't have the wedding at the boarding house."

"Which means y'all will want to cook up a feast. Do you want to invite friends or family from Iowa?" He made a face. "Then we'd probably have to wait longer."

"No, it's not necessary. I'd rather wait and have a few people visit later."

They heard the office door open. "Ransom, are you in here?" called Ty.

"Uh-oh. We've been caught." Ransom opened the door, following Lily out of the storeroom. "We're here."

"Hiding out?" Ty shut the outside door and came farther into the office. "I won't ask what you were doing in the store room."

Ransom put his arm around Lily, anchoring her to his side. "For your information, we were getting engaged."

"Congratulations." Ty grinned at Lily. "It's about

time he got smart." His expression sobered as his gaze settled on Ransom. "I missed all the excitement at the bank. Quint said they're the men who killed your father, Lily. I'm thankful they're in the calaboose now."

"So am I."

He looked back at Ransom. "Thanks for helping Quint."

"Nothing could have stopped me after I saw Lily go in there."

"From what I heard, you were already working on it before you saw Lily." Ty glanced around the office.

"That's right." Ransom had a good idea what was coming next.

"Quint's going to offer you the sheriff job back. Take it. You know you won't get an argument from the commissioners. You could keep your agency going, too. You're meant to be a lawman, Ransom. We need you."

"I'll think about it." Ransom pressed Lily closer. "I need to talk to Lily, too."

"Then I'll leave you to it." Ty stopped before he opened the door and looked over his shoulder. "When's the wedding?"

"Two weeks from today if we can pull everything together," said Lily.

"Even if we can't."

"I'm about ready to open those crates." Ty smiled, his eyes sparkling with mischief. "I ordered two or three dresses that would be mighty pretty for a wedding. If you don't dawdle too long, you can have first choice, Lily."

"I'll be along directly."

Ransom chuckled at her priorities. "Women."

"Better get used to it." Laughing, Ty left them alone.

Ransom turned to face his love. He wanted to see her eyes. "Is it all right with you if I become sheriff again? I won't do it if you don't want me to."

"You might as well. You'd be right in the middle of things anytime something happened anyway." She caressed his cheek, her expression soft with love. "I've been praying for the day when you would be able to be sheriff again. Yes, I'll worry. Every time you're in danger I'll be scared, but you're in God's hands. Even when you could barely walk, you stood up for justice. There is no one that I trust more to keep this town safe. Do you want to do it?"

"Yes. Today I felt like I was coming home after a long journey."

"You were. A long, difficult one." She kissed him. "Take the job with my blessing and my prayers."

"Only if I'm sure Quint doesn't want it. He'd offer even if he did."

"You could always be deputy."

"I could try, but I'd probably be too bossy. Run and see Matt, and tell him what happened. Then pick out a new dress. I'll go talk to Quint and come by and check on you in about an hour."

"Yes, sir."

"Told you I was bossy."

She laughed and smoothed her hair. "You're getting even for all the times I ordered you around. Is my hair mussed?"

"Nope. But you'll have to go hatless. I think I broke the brim on the one you were wearing."

She wiggled her fingers, the light sparkling off her diamond. "I'll trade hats for diamonds any day."

Lily went to find Matt, and Ransom went to see Quint.

"How is she?" Quint set his pen on the desk beside a notepad.

"Relieved that Smith and Price are in jail, anxious about the trial. It won't be easy for her. But she has a wedding to plan. That should distract her."

"You did it?" When Ransom nodded, Quint stood and held out his hand. "Congratulations. Ty and Cade were right. Gettin' hitched is a good thing. When's the wedding?"

"Two weeks from today. I figure if you go to Huntsville, that will give you time to get back."

"It should. I don't think the judge will hang Smith, but he might Price. It was cold blooded murder."

"I hope he doesn't. I think it would bother Lily more than she realizes." Ransom glanced at the paper on the desk. "Making notes?"

"Figured I'd better jot down a few things while they were fresh in my mind." Quint smiled and sat down, leaning back in the chair. "The previous sheriff taught me to do that. Said it would be helpful in court. You were right."

"Easy for things to get jumbled up when everybody's talking about it."

"You were back to your old self today. In control, assessing the situation, making the right decisions, walkin' normal."

"Almost normal." Ransom sat down. "I may always have a bit of a limp, but it didn't hurt enough to be bothersome."

"Do you want your job back?"

"Do you want to keep it?"

"Nope. I'd be happier as deputy. I can get more time off that way. I've got a ranch to set up."

When Quint started to unpin his badge, Ransom held up his hand. "You'd better keep that until the commissioners approve the switch. It wouldn't be official otherwise."

"They'll approve it. But you're right. Cade will be mighty happy to hand this back to you."

Ransom glanced around the office, mentally adding a file cabinet or two. "I'll be glad to take it. Reckon they'd get miffed if I ran my detective agency out of here?"

"Don't see why they'd care. At least until you become so famous that customers are lined up on the sidewalk."

"That'll be the day." One he didn't expect to happen. "If I can keep Karl and Georgia busy and maybe a few additional agents, I'll be happy."

No, that wasn't right. He thought of Lily and looked around the office once more, knowing that tomorrow it would be his again. *I'm happier right now than I've ever been.*

"The jury is coming back." Quint leaned out the courthouse door, motioning to Ransom and Lily as they sat on a bench on the courthouse grounds.

Matt squatted nearby, trying to coax a squirrel to take a peanut. He straightened quickly and tossed the nut, sending the squirrel scampering away.

"They've been gone less than an hour." Matt looked

toward the building with a frown. "Doesn't seem like very long."

"They didn't have much to deliberate." Ransom stood and held out his hand to Lily. "Even though Price denied it, Lily and Smith's testimony is enough to convict him."

He put his arm around her as they walked toward the courtroom, and she wondered if he could feel her trembling. Reliving the nightmare of her father's murder had been difficult, but she'd made it through her testimony without too many tears. She'd glanced at the jurors' faces as she went back to her seat and had known that justice would be served.

They reached their chairs in the front row as the judge came in.

"Court is now in session. The right honorable Judge Meadows presiding," intoned the bailiff.

As the judge sat down, the jurors filed in, their expressions somber. Smith swallowed hard, but Price stared at them as if, even now, he could intimidate them.

"Mr. Foreman, have you reached a verdict?" asked the judge.

"We have, your honor." The jury foreman, a rancher that Lily hadn't met, opened a folded sheet of paper.

"Wait just a minute, Henry, before you read that." The judge motioned to Price and Smith and their court appointed attorney. "The defendants will stand."

Amid shuffling of chairs and feet, they rose.

Lily wondered if their hearts were pounding as hard as hers. She reached for Matt's hand, and felt Ransom's arm tighten around her shoulders.

"Mr. Foreman, how do you find?"

"Regarding the charge of robbery against Jasper Price—guilty. Regarding the charge of murder against Jasper Price—guilty. For Milo Smith, on the charge of robbery—guilty. On the charge of accomplice to murder—guilty."

Lily closed her eyes, weakness washing over her. Ransom pulled her close and somehow leaned around to put a hand on Matt's shoulder, too. A loud hum of comments and a few cheers from the full courtroom echoed in her ears. She didn't think any of the commotion came from their friends, then changed her mind as she heard Alvah's voice above the din. They had all come to support them—the McKinnons, Quint and Prissy, everyone from the boarding house, along with others from town that she knew and some she didn't. She supposed a murder trial was quite a novelty in Willow Grove.

The pounding of the gavel hushed the noise. "That's enough! I'll have order in my courtroom or you'll be escorted out." Judge Meadows focused on Lily. "Miss Chastain, the bailiff informs me that you have something to say to the court. Is that correct?"

She caught Ransom's startled expression out of the corner of her eye. She stood. "It is, your honor."

"Very well. Go ahead."

Lily looked down at Matt for confirmation of their agreement. Long after everyone else at the boarding house was asleep the previous night, they sat up talking and praying. When her brother nodded, she cleared her throat. Price, Smith and their attorney turned to look at her, along with everyone else in the courtroom.

"We understand that it is up to you to pass judgment on these men, your honor, but my brother and I request that you do *not* sentence either of them to death." A soft gasp whispered through the room. She gripped the back of the chair in front of her and met Price's surprised gaze.

"It is our hope that they will discover the redeeming grace and forgiveness of Jesus, that they might find salvation through Him. We don't know if that could happen in the few days between now and a hanging. We ask that you give God time to soften their hearts." She looked at Smith, then back to Price.

"I wish I could tell you that I forgive you for killing my father. I can't. But my brother and I have asked God to forgive you and to show you the way to Jesus. Perhaps as we continue to pray for you, we will find our hearts softened as well, and we can forgive."

She looked back at the judge. "Thank you, your honor."

He nodded and turned his attention to Price and Smith, who were still standing. "Jasper Price, during my tenure in this court, I have not yet sent a man to the gallows. Given the nature of this murder, I had decided to make you the first." The color drained from Price's face. "However, in light of Miss Chastain's hope for your redemption, I've changed my mind. You'll have a long time to dwell on your sins. May God change your heart. I sentence you to life in Rusk Penitentiary."

Price swayed and sat down.

"Milo Smith, I sentence you to two years at Rusk Penitentiary for robbery with an additional ten years as an accomplice to murder. The sentences will be served consecutively."

"Your honor, my client fears for his life if he is placed in the same prison as Price," said their attorney. "We request that you send him to Huntsville, instead."

"Very well. Huntsville it is. Sheriff Starr, see to your prisoners. Court dismissed."

"Do you have to go?" asked Lily, suddenly feeling exhausted, both physically and emotionally.

"No. Quint and Blake will take care of it. They'll transport them to prison, too." Ransom nodded to Quint and Blake as they escorted the handcuffed and shackled prisoners out a side door. "They know I need to be with you."

"Yes, you do." Lily looped her arm through Matt's. "I think we need to go over to your house for a while. Matt can play chaperon."

Matt grinned and leaned close to her. "I won't make a very good chaperon. I'll fall asleep as soon as I hit a comfortable chair."

Ransom rested his hand on her brother's shoulder and smiled. "That'll do just fine."

Chapter Thirty

Ransom scanned the faces of the dozen or so guests waiting with him in Mrs. Franklin's parlor. Their excited chatter and laughter hummed in his ears. He'd thought he would be nervous on his wedding day, but so far, it hadn't hit. As he'd expected, he missed his parents and his brother Ned. He hoped that somehow they and Lily's parents were looking down from Heaven to view the wedding.

He'd write his brother Tom in a week or two. The whole brood might show up one of these days for a long visit, and he wanted some peace and quiet with his new bride before that happened.

Now that Ransom was sheriff again, if the detective agency didn't become a rip-roaring business, he made enough to provide a decent home for Lily and any family the Lord blessed them with. The agency was get-

ting off to a good start, though. Georgia's laughter drew
his gaze. She had arrived just in time for the wedding
and would be going off on a case the next day.

Price and Smith were where they wouldn't be a threat
to Lily and Matt. Given Price's statement to Quint as he
delivered him to the state pen—that hanging would have
been better than being locked up in that place—God
might be waiting a long time for the man's change of
heart.

While Quint was gone, a Lieutenant Montgomery
from the Raleigh police department came to town looking for a woman named Daisy Beaumont. Ransom had
never heard of her, nor did he recognize her from the
description. But when the man described her daughter,
he suspected the policeman was talking about Prissy
and her mother. Montgomery didn't have a warrant for
an arrest, and he was a little too hazy about why he
wanted to talk to her for Ransom's comfort. Since he
didn't have any idea where Prissy's mother had gone,
and knew Prissy didn't, either, he sent the officer back
to Raleigh empty-handed.

The commissioners had surprised him by deciding
to keep Blake on a permanent basis. He didn't know
how long their good will would last, but for now, it
made it real easy to take his bride off on a honeymoon
to New Orleans.

*Lord, thank You for all the blessings You've given
me—my health, my job, Lily. How can I ever thank You
for Lily? I'm not sure I'd be up and walking if it hadn't
been for her. Help me to be a good husband, to love her
the way she deserves to be loved.*

A hush fell over the group, and Ransom turned toward the hallway. Lily and Matt paused as the others moved aside, making an aisle for them.

Everyone else faded from Ransom's sight as he gazed upon his bride. His love. His heart. She was lovely every day, but today beyond compare. Her soft white silk gown was richly adorned in lace, including a lace drapery across the skirt front. The big bustle was all the fashion, larger than what she usually wore, and almost made him chuckle.

She carried a bouquet of yellow roses, a tribute to her adopted state. Tiny yellow rosebuds were entwined in her hair like a coronet. She told him that her necklace had belonged to her mother, thus the sapphire pendant met the requirements of something old and something blue. The dress was new and the scrap of handkerchief peeking out of her long sleeve was borrowed from Prissy. Matt told him earlier that he planned to put a penny in her shoe.

Ransom's eyes misted as she walked toward him, his heart overflowing with love and thanksgiving.

For Lily, the moment was both joyful and bittersweet. She would have given anything for her parents to be there. Walking across Mrs. Franklin's parlor to Ransom's side, she hoped that God in His goodness somehow let them share in her joy. She knew they would approve of the man she had chosen.

She would not have thought him any less a man if he still needed the cane. But her heart filled with praise to God that he stood tall and strong, his health and confidence restored. In his black suit and tie, crisp white shirt and gray silk vest embroidered with silver, he had never looked more handsome.

She remembered the Scripture he shared with her the first time he held her and tried to comfort her broken heart. *And we know that all things work together for good to them that love God....*

She'd been so filled with grief, so full of hate. She couldn't believe that God could bring good out of their sorrow and pain. But Ransom had believed, even then he had seen a glimpse of what God planned for them. *I met you.* How many times had his words kept her from giving in to despair?

As he took her hand in his, she looked into his deep blue eyes and saw her love reflected there, her future and God's blessing.

And in her heart of hearts, no truer prayer was ever whispered.

Thank You, Jesus.

Take 2 inspirational love stories FREE!

PLUS get a FREE surprise gift!

Mail to Steeple Hill Reader Service™

In U.S.
3010 Walden Ave.
P.O. Box 1867
Buffalo, NY 14240-1867

In Canada
P.O. Box 609
Fort Erie, Ontario
L2A 5X3

YES! Please send me 2 free Love Inspired® novels and my free surprise gift. After receiving them, if I don't wish to receive anymore, I can return the shipping statement marked cancel. If I don't cancel, I will receive 4 brand-new novels every month, before they're available in stores! Bill me at the low price of $4.24 each in the U.S. and $4.74 each in Canada, plus 25¢ shipping and handling and applicable sales tax, if any*. That's the complete price and a savings of over 10% off the cover prices—quite a bargain! I understand that accepting the books and gift places me under no obligation ever to buy any books. I can always return a shipment and cancel at any time. Even if I never buy another book from Steeple Hill, the 2 free books and the surprise gift are mine to keep forever.

113 IDN DZ9M
313 IDN DZ9N

Name _____ (PLEASE PRINT)

Address _____ Apt. No. ____

City _____ State/Prov. _____ Zip/Postal Code ____

Not valid to current Love Inspired® subscribers.

Want to try two free books from another series?
Call 1-800-873-8635 or visit www.morefreebooks.com.